THE
JUSTI
PLAN

THE
JUSTI
PLAN

JON MAGUIRE

A CIP catalogue record for this book is available from the British Library

ISBN 978-0-9556011-0-1

Printed and bound in Great Britain by Cox & Wymans Ltd, Reading, Berkshire

Printed on paper from a sustainable source

First published 1998

Reprinted 2002

This edition published 2007 by
cru Investment Management
Harlech House
20 Cathedral Road
Cardiff
CF11 9LJ

To George, Harriet and Frank
Only one thing in life is important – only one.
All my love, Dad

ABOUT THIS BOOK

The Justi Plan was first conceived in 1990. It married two global issues into a novel that has become startlingly prophetic. The need to protect and preserve rainforests has become ever more acute, whilst the countries that own the forests continue to face real financial hardship and this impacts greatly on their peoples, particularly their children.

First published in 1998 the book made little headway. In 2002 a second edition was published privately for political purposes, and discussions were entered into with over 30 rainforest countries to seek an alliance that would make *The Justi Plan* a reality. Many of these nations wanted Brazil to take the lead and so the author visited the country on three occasions in 2003. The Plan was very well received and he met with Marina Silva, then the Environment Minister in December 2003. Silva fully endorsed the Plan but failed to get it agreed by her government because it was concerned about confronting the United States.

More progress was made in 2005, when ten rainforest countries finally formed an alliance called the Rainforest Coalition to implement the Plan. *The Justi Plan* is becoming a politically powerful novel.

ABOUT THE AUTHOR

Jon Maguire was born in Newark-on-Trent in December 1960. His father was a Baptist minister and his mother a midwife. He was educated at Fitzmaurice Grammar School in Bradford-on-Avon, Wiltshire. He works in investment management and continues to pioneer economic strategies to help solve the injustices of poverty and disease.

He has three children, George, Harriet and Frank, and three step-children, Lucy-Ann, Liban and Hannan. He lives in North Devon, an area of rugged and romantic coastline and one that features in the final chapter of the novel.

A PERSONAL VIEW

The Justi Plan is a book that just won't go away. I have watched the world wake up to the reality of climate change and politically the theme of this book will soon be centre stage. Do not believe that carbon-dioxide emissions can only lead to global warming – because they could lead to precisely the opposite. Climate change is the best description of what is currently taking place.

I was tempted to revise this third edition of *The Justi Plan* but decided against it. It is a prophetic book and I believe God at times guided my pen. I can also tell you what we must do to reverse climate change and stabilise the planet: we must start to reforest the planet and compensate rainforest countries for doing so. The *only* reason they chop down the trees is economic, so if we pay them to maintain the forests we will achieved a valuble objective. Mass reforestation sucks the carbon dioxide out of the atmosphere and stores it again in the trees. The rainforests grow trees quickly and to great heights, creating a massive carbon bank.

I hope you enjoy the book and that it helps you see that there *is* an answer to this very big problem. I also wish the Rainforest Coalition every success and encourage Brazil herself to join it. *The Justi Plan* stands as the way forward for them to achieve massive economic advancement.

Jon Maguire
April 2007

CHAPTER ONE

A small boy burst into the lean-to shanty hut, one of thousands that hugged the hillside overlooking Rio. 'They're coming! Did you pay them?'

'No. I haven't been paid myself,' replied a boy of similar age.

'Run then. They'll kill you else. I'll stay and tell them you're out.'

The boy stood up. 'Meet me by the church tomorrow?'

'Yes. But go. They're coming up the hill.'

The boy took off into the night, cutting his foot on a piece of tin that had been discarded by the entrance to the hut. He ignored the pain and ran for his life up the muddy paths, then turned to scramble across a wide area of wasteland. He dropped down the wall at the far side, hardly even noticing the trail of bloody footprints he left in his wake. He ran hard, not daring to look back, through the park and across the street. In his haste he fell, turning too quickly into an alleyway. Picking himself up he limped along, tears coursing down his face, before jumping down into the deserted basement of a tenement. He banged on a wooden shutter.

'It's me – Luis. Hurry!'

The shutter opened and he dived inside. 'The mob want me,' he panted. 'I haven't paid them for the crack. And I can't pay them because I've sold it and they wouldn't pay me. Now they'll kill me.'

He started sobbing again. A girl of no more than eight years old put her arm around him.

'Luis. Don't worry, you can live with us now.'

He looked at her and she saw the terror in his eyes. 'We sleep in front of the church,' she told him. 'You will be safe with us there. The priest says so.'

Luis' sobs quietened, but he still shook with fear.

A boy of about thirteen emerged from the shadows. 'Did they follow you?' he asked.

Luis shook his head. 'No – I don't think so.'

'Come on then. Let's get to the church.'

There were twelve children in the group. They scrambled out of the basement and, hugging the shadows, made their way along the streets to the church. They curled up together in the portico.

●

It was three in the morning. A blue transit van with blacked-out windows pulled into the street facing the church.

'Ready?' asked the driver, turning to three other men. They nodded.

'I'll wait here. You'll find them in front of the church, at the top of the steps.'

The three slipped out of the van and looked around. The street was empty. They pulled on hoods and walked quickly across the street and up the church steps. The children slept soundly.

'Vermin,' one of the men muttered.

'Do them!' exclaimed another.

They walked over to the children.

'I'll take these,' the first man continued, pointing to four of the children to the right of the group. 'You the middle.... You those there.'

They nodded. Each man took a pistol from his jacket and immediately the sound of automatic fire crackled in the air. Luis looked up for the last time.

After fifteen seconds the men stopped.

The leader of the group kicked the corpse of a five-year-old. 'Vermin,' he grunted.

They turned and ran back to the van, which sped off into the Rio night. Some local residents pulled back their shutters to see what the commotion was about, their eyes finally drawn to a growing pool of blood from the children who lay dead in the portico.

CHAPTER TWO

The view from the twenty-first floor wasn't as impressive as Anna Hughes had imagined. True, it was a long way down, but on a grey October morning the view across central London struck her as a mere urban sprawl. All those cranes, she thought to herself. The city couldn't keep growing skywards forever. She turned from the window and strolled over to the sofa.

'Sir Anthony has asked me to apologise – he's been running late all morning but he should be available in about five minutes. Can I get you a coffee?'

'Thank you. Black, no sugar please.'

Sir Anthony Duce's secretary rose from her desk and moved towards the small kitchen that lay just off the reception area.

Anna sat down. She flitted through the array of titles on the table in front of her. Quite an empire Sir Anthony has put together, she mused. As part of the world media elite, his business interests embraced newspapers, radio and television across the globe. His work was his life. It had been that way since the accident on a suddenly fog-bound M25 that had claimed the lives of his wife and three children. Sir Anthony had been seriously injured, with extensive burns to his face and hands, his legs shattered, his pelvis broken, and the left side of his face crushed. His appearance was now hideous. The finest surgeons had done all they could, but his face and hands were distorted and puckered. Sir Anthony hated his reflection in the mirror. He refused to believe that anyone could really look at him and not feel revulsion; he had become a total recluse. His world was Floor 21. Nobody could remember when he last ventured beyond it, and very few were ever invited to it.

Anna was completely in the dark about why she had been invited into the sanctuary. At thirty-five, her rise to political editor of *The International Times* was widely considered nothing short of meteoric. Her looks had provoked plenty of speculation about how she had made it to one of newspaper's most prestigious jobs, but to everyone who had ever worked with her, Anna's unique journalistic talent was evident. Few could match her ability to open up a story. If one source dried up she always seemed to have another to turn to.

Coffee arrived, but just as the cup touched her lips Sir Anthony's door opened.

'Miss Hughes. It is good to meet you.'

Anna quickly placed the coffee cup and saucer back on the table.

'The pleasure is all mine Sir Anthony,' she said as she rose to her feet. She was unsure whether to offer her hand in greeting but noted that he had made no move to offer his. She deliberately diverted her eyes from him, taken aback by his appearance. She found herself worried about the meeting itself; she couldn't avoid looking at him then. She steeled herself to be as natural as possible.

Sir Anthony turned slightly, showing her into his office. Anna picked up her coffee, entered the doorway and then stopped. The room was vast. The windows had been painted black and the half light came from a myriad of tiny spotlights recessed into the panelled ceiling. The furnishings were ultra-modern. Four abstract sculptures were grouped in the centre of the room, dominating the office. Huge paintings lined the walls, all of them in just three colours: deep blue, scarlet and black.

Sir Anthony passed her and moved to his desk. 'Do come in then.'

'Thank you. I was admiring your office,' Anna replied as she moved across the room to take the chair he was offering.

He studied her. She was certainly beautiful. Tall – at least five foot ten he thought – slender but shapely, very different from the waiflike girls that his own magazines celebrated as fashion icons, whom he abhorred. Her hair was swept back over her shoulders and as she drew closer he noticed the detail of her face – the high cheekbones, the smooth complexion, the penetrating green eyes.

Sir Anthony took his own seat. 'So how are things at *The International*?' he enquired.

'Fine,' she responded. Then thinking that perhaps she was there because he didn't think things were at all fine, she added hastily, 'At least, I think fine.'

'Well, the reports I have are all first class, so fine it is.' He glanced at her before continuing. 'I guess you're wondering why I've asked to see you?'

'Some are wondering more intensely than me, Sir Anthony.'

'Ah yes. I suppose some would. Michael Turner wouldn't happen to be among them?'

Anna shrugged her shoulders.

'Mr Turner worries too much,' continued Sir Anthony, 'which is laughable because – as I'm forever telling him – he's the best editor I have. And he could walk into a job on practically any newspaper in the world. No, I wanted to speak to you about something not entirely relating to *The International*.'

Anna shifted uncomfortably in her chair. Sir Anthony looked hard at her before continuing.

'My business interests are, as you know, extensive. The backbone of it all is news, and I have always believed that our success stems from our ability to find stories before others. Well you know all this, you're doing it all the time.' He looked at her questioningly as he continued.

'Have you ever wondered how some of our biggest stories come to us as exclusives?'

Anna thought for a moment. Her own paper had enjoyed its fair share of scoops. 'Strength in investigative journalism,' she replied.

'In part that's true.' Sir Anthony leaned back in his chair. 'But sometimes we receive a helping hand, particularly in political matters.'

'Government department leaks?' enquired Anna.

'In a way,' he answered. 'But sometimes more than just a leak.'

'How can you get more than a leak?'

Sir Anthony paused. 'If you receive a leak you are only receiving information about, say, a policy statement or future legislation. Try to think one step further. Imagine we were actually part of that government decision.'

Anna interrupted. 'How can we be part of it? We're journalists, not politicians.'

'Ah, but perhaps the government might like to know how its policies will be treated by our newspapers, radio stations, TV stations.' He waited for her to respond, watching carefully for any sign that she was reacting negatively to the direction the conversation was taking.

Anna was struggling to understand exactly what Sir Anthony was saying. He swung his chair away from her slightly, enabling him to look across the sweep of his office.

'What do you think about this then, Miss Hughes? Say they made me part of the decision itself. Then how could I or anyone else in my business criticise government policy?'

Anna found the thought disturbing. Sir Anthony turned to look at her again, but she avoided his eye as she worked out the implications of what he had just said. She thought back to her student days – those heated exchanges in the debating society as to who actually ran the country: on the one hand the media dictating to public opinion, on the other public opinion dictating to a democratic government. She had to check that she had understood correctly – that he really meant he was involved in establishing government policy rather than simply debating the matter as she had while she was a student.

'Are you saying you're actually involved in setting government policy, Sir Anthony?'

Sir Anthony looked at her with approval. 'I'm getting myself a real drink,' he announced. 'Would you care for one?'

'Oh, no thanks.' Her voice trailed away slightly as she glanced at her watch and wondered who could face drinking this early in the day. But then again, what was day and what was night on Floor 21?

He kept talking as he walked to the drinks cabinet and poured himself a cognac.

'Media is a funny old business. As the empire grew, more and more politicians fêted me. They asked about matters of policy and I gave them my views. If they ignored them it was only natural to take an antagonistic editorial line throughout the empire. Then I realised just how much power I was building, how much influence I could exert. Of course, at the end of the day it's down to the government to decide, but we do enjoy a kind of partnership.' He returned to his chair, swilled his cognac round the lead crystal glass, and held it to his nose, breathing in deeply.

'Sir Anthony, aren't you concerned ... well you know?' Anna was struggling to find the precise words. She didn't want to cause offence, but she wanted to explain that in her opinion it was plain wrong to get too close to the government.

'Aren't you worried about the impact of your partnership on the democratic process? I mean, how do you know what you think is right....'

'... Stuck up here day and night, week after week, month after month,' he interjected somewhat dismissively, as if being right or wrong mattered little. 'Isolated from the real world. Completely out of touch with most everyday lives. Yes, indeed. How do I know what is right?' He leant across his desk and pressed the intercom.

'Maureen, bring in the Foreign Office file.'

Anna did her best to smile, but she was becoming increasingly apprehensive. What was this all about? Firstly, it was not entirely about newspapers. Secondly, it had something to do with government policy. Now it seemed to be connected to the Foreign Office. But the biggest question forming in her mind was entirely personal – why her?

Sir Anthony's secretary walked in and handed him a file. He opened it and removed a letter from the top of the pile of papers. Anna sipped the last of her now-cold coffee. Sir Anthony pushed the file to one side and placed the piece of paper directly in front of him.

'This is a letter I received yesterday from the secretary of state at the Foreign Office. Its contents are covered by the Official Secrets Act. You need not know all the matters covered by it, but you do need to hear some extracts that are relevant to you.'

He looked up again at Anna – the opportunity for her to comment was thus offered. Anna, however, continued only to stare impassively at the letter.

'Our friends at the Foreign Office need our help,' he explained, and began reading aloud.

'Dear Sir Anthony,

As you are aware, there has been considerable civil unrest in Brazil in recent months. The weakness of the Brazilian economy is without doubt the principal cause. Her problems in servicing her foreign debt has led to a severe austerity programme, forced on to her government by the World Bank. This programme necessitated a withdrawal of many government subsidies to industry, a withdrawal of welfare benefits, and a sharp increase in personal taxes.

Regrettably this has caused deep resentment amongst the Brazilian people. There have been massive public demonstrations and finally, as a consequence of an indefinite national strike, the government was forced to dissolve the National Assembly. Consequently, a general election has been called and is scheduled for 15 November 2006. This is now only three weeks away and early opinion polls suggest a landslide victory for an independent candidate, Mr Roberto Justi.'

Sir Anthony paused again. 'What do you know about Justi?' he enquired.

Anna visibly relaxed. Thank God for that, she thought. She had been invited as a political editor to give her opinion about a potential leader of South America's most influential nation. There was nothing more to it than that. She would tell him all she knew about Justi – which wasn't much anyway – and that would be it. End of letter. End of meeting. Grab a sandwich and straight back to the office. She should be there by 12.30.

Sir Anthony noticed that for the first time she sat back in her chair.

'Justi is one of life's more intriguing politicians,' she stated. 'The Brazilian people have grown tired of the faction fighting within parties on both the right and left. The military are sensible enough to keep well out of it – at least they know a no-win presidency when they see one. Justi has come from nowhere and caught the public's imagination. He takes a strong Nationalist stance and is running a single-issue campaign – people before debt payments. He's playing the role of people's champion.'

'You and the secretary of state are therefore agreed on Justi,' nodded Sir Anthony. 'But the secretary of state is concerned about what kind of Brazil we will be contending with if Justi succeeds and becomes president.'

Anna interjected. 'There's nothing new about Justi's politics. He thinks he can solve Brazil's debt problems by simply not paying. But we've had debt moratoriums from Brazil before, nineteen eighty-seven was the last serious one. But then, as now, the politics of not paying investors their due interest on national debt are inherently self-defeating. Foreign capital input is banned by the World Bank, selective punitive economic sanctions are applied by the United Nations, and finally the Brazilian people discover that it's cheaper to make the debt payments than try to opt out of the world economy.'

Sir Anthony swilled his cognac. He turned a page and Anna followed his eye. He was missing out entire paragraphs of the letter.

'Ah yes. Here we are.' Sir Anthony cleared his throat.

'We are concerned about Mr Justi's campaign for a number of reasons. Firstly, unlike other politicians who have in the past campaigned on cancelling foreign debt payments, Mr Justi has been quite comfortable in promoting his manifesto to both the national and international press. A number of American networks have interviewed him at length with particular reference to the debt-moratorium crisis suffered by Brazil in 1987. Mr Justi appears to be in agreement that there is no prospect of success for any policy made along similar lines to those pursued in 1987. Our concern centres on the following statement from Mr Justi, which concluded an interview with NBC. "I am not saying that Brazil will cease making debt repayments. Brazil will fulfil its obligations by introducing to the world economy new factors that will benefit the Brazilian economy, to the extent that the burden of foreign debt from which we currently suffer is greatly reduced."'

Sir Anthony put the letter back down on to his desk and, leaning back in his chair, he stared up at the ceiling. Silence fell. Anna studied him carefully. His face was really grotesque. The left side of it reminded her of a crumpled paper bag. His skin seemed to fall off his face in some places, while skin grafts around his jaw seemed stretched so tight she felt his face might rip apart. She considered briefly what drove him on, devoid of human company, lacking nothing that money could buy, trapping himself in the twenty-first storey of a skyscraper in the centre of London. Where was the life in all that?

He turned back to the letter and, still studying it, he asked, 'What does the man mean by "new factors"?'

Anna hadn't the faintest idea and felt it rather out of her area of expertise to offer any opinion.

'I'm no economist I'm afraid. What does the Treasury or the Bank of England make of it?'

'They say he's bluffing.'

'Well maybe he is then. Maybe he's doing what all politicians do – promise manna from heaven, and then when in power preach patience as the virtue most needed to receive it.'

Sir Anthony picked up the letter again. He searched for another paragraph. 'The Foreign Office continues thus:

'The cost of Mr Justi's campaign is by any standards a most significant spend. For a Brazilian election, the level of advertising is unprecedented. Our estimates are that by the conclusion of his campaign he will have spent well over US$35 million.'

'How much?' Anna interrupted.

'Thirty-five million US.'

'Heavens, that's a lot. Where can Justi find that sort of money?'

Sir Anthony raised his hand to silence her. 'The secretary of state continues....

'Our sources in Brazil have confirmed that Mr Justi's personal wealth extends to a mere $200,000, most of which is tied up in a modest villa in São Paulo. They have also confirmed that his advertising was only

14

accepted by payment in advance — to date Mr Justi has paid out in excess of $18 million to various agencies.'

Anna was becoming increasingly interested. Brazilian elections were rarely of much interest to the British public, but an eighteen-million dollar spend by a political unknown, when it couldn't possibly be his own money — now that was possibly something. She needed to conclude the meeting with Sir Anthony and get on if she was to make copy for the following day. Reuters would have a picture of Justi. The NBC interview — she'd need a transcript. Who might know who Justi's backers were? Perhaps some of his opposing candidates would have an idea. Her mind was racing.

'Sir Anthony, I'd like to run this story tomorrow. I don't wish to appear rude but I'm already cutting it fine for copy and….'

Sir Anthony raised his hand. 'No story yet I'm afraid, Miss Hughes.'

'But what if a competitor is on to this as well. You know what this game's….'

He interrupted her again. 'Believe me, no one else has this story.'

She felt on edge again. Why tell her all this about forming government policy and letters from the Foreign Office and worries about Justi? What was the point of this meeting if what they were talking about wasn't to be published? She decided to bring things to a head.

'If you don't want me to run the story, why are you telling me?'

He deliberated for a moment, and drained his glass before replying.

'It's a rather delicate situation. We – I mean, Britain – want to know who's backing Justi and why. So also do our friends in America, Germany and Japan. Between us Brazil owes our banks about two hundred and seventy billion dollars. If she managed to walk away from her debts we would almost certainly see some major banking casualties and we're concerned about chain reactions. So, we have decided on joint action to get to the bottom of Justi's game plan. However, we need a credible front player – someone who won't attract unnecessary interest, someone who won't arouse suspicion. Someone like, say, the political editor of a well-known and much-respected British newspaper.' He offered her a wry smile.

Anna looked aghast. 'Are you suggesting that I go under cover on behalf of the US, German, Japanese and British governments?'

Sir Anthony laughed disarmingly. 'Don't make it sound like that. There's no double-o-seven to it or any of that sort of nonsense.'

'Well I'm not sure,' she replied cautiously. She knew she must play this carefully, given Sir Anthony's position as proprietor of her newspaper.

'Aren't you asking me to work for the government, governments even? Isn't that way beyond my work as a political editor?'

Sir Anthony leaned forward in his chair and met her head-on.

'Perhaps I've been too honest with you. Maybe I should have phoned Turner and told him to order you out to Brazil to work on the Justi campaign. You'd have been none the wiser.'

There was an uneasy silence, an impasse that Anna felt put her under immediate pressure to resolve. She sighed inwardly. Was there a clear enough story to justify Sir Anthony's position? Was she sufficiently interested in that story as a journalist? Was it a problem if her work was used by third parties?

'I can go to print eventually?'

'Of course. When we're confident that Justi's threat, if any, is containable then sure, go to print. The publicity then will be most useful.'

Anna looked at Sir Anthony. He looked at her. Could she trust him? Even if she couldn't trust him, did it matter? Could she look after herself? Well she'd always managed in the past.

'You appreciate that I have to publish in the end?'

'I do.'

The room fell quiet again.

'Can I think on it?'

'Well, I'd rather you didn't. Time is moving on.'

Anna still felt uneasy. 'It's difficult. I'm not sure.' She started to think out loud. 'Don't you feel it's a step too far? I mean, isn't there someone they could use who's more familiar with this type of work? Why me? I'm just a political editor.'

Sir Anthony interrupted her, a slight hint of irritation creeping into his voice. 'But this is a very political assignment.'

He stared at her; her eyes roamed across his office. She felt a career-defining moment had arrived. If she refused she would be finished with *The International Times*, that was for sure. Sir Anthony was ruthless, she knew that. If she accepted she would be thrown into a world way beyond her comfort zone. A rock and a hard place, she mused.

'I'm very unsure,' she stated slowly.

He stared at her impassively. 'I think, Miss Hughes, you should accept.'

There seemed no way out. 'Are you saying I have to go?'

'It is your choice,' he replied.

No it isn't, she thought. She looked past him. 'Very well. I'll go.'

'Excellent. I had hoped you would accept.' He pressed the intercom.

'Maureen, please have my chauffeur take Miss Hughes back to her office.'

He rose from his chair and walked towards the door. Anna felt snubbed – the conversation had been terminated so abruptly. She remained seated for a moment before standing up and moving slowly back towards him.

'Thank you, Miss Hughes. Turner will be given the arrangements. Remember, he must believe this is just a straightforward assignment and it's down to you to keep him thinking that way.'

She walked coolly past him.

'Good luck.' He awaited her reply but now, on a point of principle, she determined not to. She saw Sir Anthony turn on his heel and walk back towards his office before the lift doors closed between them.

CHAPTER THREE

The phone rang in Anna's room.

'Alo? Senhora Oogeeze?'

'Hughes. It's Hewzz!'

'Si. Si. England now okay.'

Unlikely, Anna thought to herself. The line crackled for a few seconds, then finally she heard a click.

'Hello. Is that Mike?'

'Anna – how are you?'

'Oh everything is just delightful! I thought you said the staff here all speak English?'

'Well that's what the travel agent said. I didn't think much about it. With a name like the Hotel Victoria I imagined it would be more English than England itself.'

Michael Turner smiled to himself. Anna's trip was a complete waste of time as far as he was concerned. The loss of a key member of his editorial team for more than two weeks just to cover a second-rate election was very much against his better judgement, but Sir Anthony had insisted so there was little he could do about it.

'Is it raining in London?'

'No.'

'Are you sure? Because it's blue skies over Rio, golden beaches, warm seas, bronzed boys. This is a tough assignment.' She lay back on her bed and looked up at the cracked ceiling.

'Well, here's hoping that your air conditioning collapses and a colony of those extra-large Brazilian cockroaches arrives to keep you company. Pen ready?'

Anna already had a pen and notepad in her left hand.

'No,' she replied sarcastically as she clasped the phone between her shoulder and tilted head, enabling her to write and still remain lying down.

'0061 223 4314 or 4722.'

'And a contact name?'

Turner looked down at his notepad. 'Yep, it's here somewhere. Manuel Justi, International Press Officer, older brother to the aspiring president.'

'Mike, what city is that code? It's not Rio.'

'Hang on, let me see now.' He paused for a few moments. 'Quite right, Anna. Looking at a map I'd say about five … no, more like six hundred miles north north west of where you're staying.'

So she was in Rio and Justi was in Brasilia. Great.

'Well thank you Mr Editor-in-Chief. Next time you toddle off to the Tory conference in Brighton remind me to fix you up with a nice little bed and breakfast I know in Edinburgh.' She sighed. 'What a complete shambles.'

'What was that, Anna? Do I have a copy of Justi's itinerary?'

'Oh, he's found that Edinburgh B and B already, has he?'

'He's in Rio for five days, seventh to eleventh of October.'

She cursed him under her breath.

'And where is he today?'

'On the beach, of course. You've probably already met him. Bronzed boy, I think you called him. Apparently he's putting his suit on to talk to the holidaymakers at eight-thirty this evening.'

'Where would I be without you, Michael?'

'London, in the House, where you know you should be. Run me through it again. What was it Duce felt was so important about Justi?'

'Michael. You're missing me! It's very, very touching to be missed so soon.'

'Well you can smile, but he wants daily reports.'

'No he does not.'

'No joking Anna. I quote, "It is essential that Miss Hughes reports to me personally on a daily basis". Fax from Duce dated yesterday, October seventh.'

Anna went quiet. Sir Anthony had never mentioned anything about daily reports.

'Seriously now Mike. You're having me on aren't you?'

'Serious as you like, Anna – it's for real. Shall I fax you a copy?'

'He's really asking for daily reports?'

'Yes.'

'Can't you tell him that your editors don't do that? I'm not going to get back here at whatever time of day or night and start writing reports. In any event, what if nothing happens – do I just send him a blank sheet?'

'Anna, I agree with you, but it's not my paper and you know what Duce can be like if he doesn't get his own way. You have his phone number. He's probably just fallen in love with you. Don't take it all so personally.' Michael did not want to get drawn into a discussion about whether his political editor should accede to the wishes of the owner of his newspaper.

'Anyway, I must dash – drinks appointment at six so I'm already late.'

'Sure,' she replied.

'Hey, don't worry Anna. Look after yourself now.'

'Okay. Bye now.'

She held the phone to her ear for a few moments after Mike replaced the receiver. The trip had never excited her. She looked at her rather austere bedroom, its dark furniture creating a sense of foreboding against a backdrop of equally dark painted walls, flaking in places. A rubber plant with fading yellow leaves stood in a cracked plastic pot in the corner of the room. What was she doing here? She began to feel as depressed as the plant. Get out of the hotel, she thought to herself. Get on with life and things will sort themselves out.

As she was leaving the room, Anna touched the leaves of the plant. Spontaneously, she picked it up and moved it on to the desk beside the window, where it might get a little light. She poured a whole bottle of mineral water over it to help speed its recovery.

She felt a little better.

●

Michael Turner stood alone at the bar of The Bell public house, a favourite haunt for a few beers after work before his train home to Richmond. He was there to meet an old friend from university days, who had called just that morning to suggest meeting up as he was in town for the day to visit his stockbroker. He had announced, with a certain smugness in his voice, that he had come into a rather large inheritance. Michael wondered idly if this meant he would not have to pay for the drinks. An academic question, he chided himself. He had already had to buy his first drink, having made the error of arriving first. He would now have to greet his old friend with drink in hand, and it would be rude not to offer to buy his friend one, after the usual pleasantries of 'How great to see you – you haven't aged a bit', 'Nor have you', 'Crumbs, it's as if time stood still'. The pair of them would then stand there, with their receding grey hair and paunch stomachs, and relive the past, remembering old so and so, and not forgetting so and so....

He sipped his lager and turned his thoughts to the nagging question of Anna and the Justi assignment. Sir Anthony had never taken this kind of interest in a story before. Why was he so keen on this Justi piece? And why was Anna so important to it? After all, he had plenty of excellent investigative journalists as well as a wealth of freelance talent he could tap into. Something didn't quite fit. He unwrapped his Henri Winterman half corona and lit it from the matches placed on a London red brick on the bar. He drew on it, held his breath for a few moments and then, pursing his lips tightly, blew the smoke high into the vaulted ceiling. He watched it swirling away from him. Perhaps he should carry out a few enquiries of his own. Very discreet enquiries. After all, Sir Anthony had deliberately left him in the dark. Roberto Justi, Anna Hughes, Sir Anthony Duce ... what an unlikely trio.

He heard his name called across the bar, interrupting his reverie.

'Mike! How great to see you.'

'Ted! Crumbs you haven't aged a bit. What's your tipple?'

Anna decided to spend the afternoon investigating the exact details of Justi's rally, which would take place that evening. She hailed a taxi outside her hotel and asked the driver to take her to Copacabana Beach. The ride was even more frightening than the one from the airport had been the previous evening, and she gave up looking ahead for the sake of her sanity. The driver was in his early fifties, short and stocky with receding black hair swept back from a swarthy face. His left arm hung permanently out of his open window, and each time the cab came to a halt his left hand started to tap out the same repetitive tune on the outside door panel. His shirt pocket was bulging with a packet of Marlboros, one of which seemed to permanently hang limply from the corner of his mouth. Anna wasn't even sure it was lit.

'Do you speak English?' she enquired tentatively.

He turned round, shrugged his shoulders and smiled.

'Nao entendo Senhora.' The cigarette moved up and down with each word; she wondered how it didn't fall out. It was a shame he didn't speak English. It was an equal shame she couldn't speak Portuguese, she mused. He appeared to be a typical Brazilian, and as such she would have been interested to know what he thought of Justi.

'Roberto Justi?' She did her best to make it sound like a question.

The driver looked at her in his mirror. 'Quem? Senhor Justi?'

Anna nodded. The driver thought for a few moments, drawing on his cigarette as if to prove it was lit.

'Senhor Justi,' he pronounced in a slow deliberate voice, watching for her response in his mirror.

'Si,' she replied.

'Senhor Justi.' He repeated the name while taking both hands off the wheel to clap.

Much to Anna's relief one hand returned to the wheel, while the other started banging the door panel.

'Jus-ti.' Bang, bang, bang.

'Jus-ti.' Bang, bang, bang.

No wonder the opinion polls were predicting a Justi landslide, Anna thought to herself as the taxi swung a final left.

'Copacabana, Senhora.' He pulled over and Anna handed him an American ten-dollar note.

'Obrigado Senhora. Obrigado.' He gave her Rio's biggest smile of the day. The domestic *real* notes had become practically worthless. Inflation was running at thirty-five per cent a month. Hard currency was king.

Anna crossed the carriageway, strolled over the promenade with its palm trees swaying slightly in the gentle afternoon breeze, and stood at the edge of the beach. It was on a much grander scale than she had expected. The white sands swept away in a classical crescent, framed by the sea on one side and the beach drive – Avenida Atlantica – on the other. Thousands of brown bodies hugged the water's edge, merging into a solid line into the distance, as if to underscore where the beach stopped and the ocean began. She looked across the Avenida to the skyscrapers that formed a parallel crescent, and beyond them the backdrop of the mountains. Above everything towered Sugarloaf, its sheer granite cliffs rising majestically from the city below. Anna leant against the promenade railings and turned to face the sun. She closed her eyes and felt the warmth of its rays on her face. So this is what made Rio, Rio she thought to herself. The cold, dank grey of London seemed far away; for the first time she felt positive about the trip.

She turned again to look across the beach. Finding the Justi meeting was not going to be difficult. There, in the very centre of the beach, was a large stage with an enormous Brazilian flag draped over the scaffolding behind it. In front of the stage was a platform; she guessed this was for the press, and she could just make out a number of camera crews already setting up there. She wondered if NBC would be turning up. Perhaps she could find the reporter who had conducted the Justi interview. Maybe Justi had elaborated on his 'new factors' off the record.

'Press office?' she enquired of a tall man wearing only a pair of well-bleached shorts and a fluorescent yellow cap, on which ROBERTO JUSTI was inscribed in large green letters. He pointed towards a canopy at the side of the stage, under which were half a dozen trestle tables. A few rather hot-looking journalists sat around them. Press badges lay on one of the tables, behind which sat a pretty Brazilian girl in her late teens.

'Do you speak English?' Anna enquired.

'Certainly,' she replied. 'Were we expecting you?'

'I'm political editor of *The International Times*. Anna Hughes.'

'Have you just arrived in Brazil?' asked the girl, running her finger down the press list.

Knowing that her name would not be on the list, Anna opened her shoulder bag and took a business card from the flap inside her diary. She passed it to the girl.

'We've been using copy from Reuters but we've now decided to run our own,' Anna explained, ignoring the girl and picking up a press badge. 'Where is Manuel Justi?'

The girl added Anna's name to the press list before looking back up at her. 'He's not here yet.'

'Well, when is he briefing the press on what to expect this evening; a copy of the speech, keynote points?'

The girl stared at her before replying somewhat smugly. 'Senhor Roberto does not write speeches, so there are no copies. Senhor Manuel does not give press conferences. Senhor Roberto will speak to the people of Rio this evening. You can listen if you want to and take notes.'

Anna searched for a quick reply. She hesitated, and the girl looked down at the list again. The moment for a cutting response had gone.

'Are NBC here?'

'Behind you, Senhora Hughes – in the red shirt.'

Anna turned. The man being pointed out was looking towards her from only a few yards away.

'Having a few difficulties?' he enquired in a soft American accent.

'Are you NBC?' asked Anna.

'Sure am. Al Parks, NBC News.' He offered his hand.

'Pleased to meet you. Anna Hughes, *The International Times*.'

'Pleased to meet you too, Miss Hughes. Miss? Mrs?'

'Anna will do fine,' she replied.

'Were you looking for me?' Parks continued, lighting a cigarette. He looked up. 'Smoke?'

Anna shook her head. 'I'm trying to find one of your reporters – the one who interviewed Justi about his "new factors".'

'That's me,' Parks replied.

The heat was getting to her; her throat felt parched.

'Where can you get a drink around here?' she asked.

'Drink? Sure, there's plenty of bars on the Avenida.'

'I'd value a chat with you about Justi. Can you spare me any time?'

'No problem. Let me buy you that drink.' He gave her a friendly smile and took a notepad and pencil from the jacket he had slung over his shoulder. 'I'll just scribble a note for my crew.'

He handed the note to the girl at the press reception desk. 'Tell them I'll be back within a half hour,' he instructed.

He turned back to Anna and pointed the easiest way off the beach.

'It was just above freezing when I left London yesterday,' she told him as they walked slowly off the sands. 'I'm obviously not acclimatised to the heat yet.'

'Hey, you'll soon find your feet. Nothing that a good ol' drink can't sort out,' he responded, helping her up the flight of steps that led to the Avenida.

There was a small bar on their left and they sat down under the welcome shade of a palm.

'What'll you have?' Parks asked.

Anna watched the bartender crushing limes, then adding ice and a teaspoon of sugar before whisking the mixture and pouring it into two highball glasses for a young couple who were deep in conversation on the other side of the bar.

'What's he just given them?' Anna asked.

'Oh that's caipirinha. Damn popular it is too, kinda like their national drink. Wanna try it?'

'Well the ice should cool me down fast,' she answered, dabbing her forehead with a paper towel from the bar.

The bartender came over.

'Dois caipirinha, com pouco acucar, por favor,' ordered Parks.

'How much Portuguese do you know?' asked Anna, as the bartender turned away from them to make the drinks.

'Years ago I took a year out of college and spent it working down this coastline. It's funny how quick you pick it up if you've gotta use it all the time. And you?'

'Just French and a little German, which isn't going to help me much in Rio is it?'

'No way,' he laughed, lighting up another cigarette. He drew on it hard before continuing. 'Now what do you wanna know about Justi?'

'Well we don't have that much on him so I'm here to dig, and I'm interested in what you make of him. You did a couple of interviews with him, didn't you?'

Parks nodded.

'Well, what do you think of him?'

The drinks came. Anna took a long sip.

'Like it?' asked Parks, as he tasted his own.

'Very refreshing,' she replied, smiling and taking another.

'Hey, stick a vodka in it next time and then feel it kick.'

'Well I'll probably need a few of those during this assignment,' Anna told Parks as he ordered her another.

'Now, what do I make of Senhor Roberto Justi?' He paused. Anna had already warmed to him. He was in his late fifties, with a well-heeled but personable American manner. His hair was greying at the temples, his blue eyes greying slightly almost in sympathy.

'Well I've followed more elections than I care to remember but this guy's unique.' He tapped his hand on the bar. 'Yeah, absolutely unique.'

'In what way?' interrupted Anna.

Parks paused again for thought. 'He's kinda genuine, not interested in playing politics, not the usual party figurehead. In fact, he hasn't even got a party.'

'So what's his motivation then? If he's not interested in the power game, why on Earth would he run for office, particularly with all the problems associated with the office he's after?'

'Exactly. I think he's kinda worked up about the poverty that's everywhere in this country. And the street kids. They say there's about fifteen million of them, living out of boxes or down sewers. It's a terrible state of affairs here. You know, kids of four or five living in crumbling sewer channels underneath the streets of Rio. Abandoned by parents from shanty towns and outlying villages.'

Nobody had mentioned anything about Justi's concern for street children to Anna.

'Isn't his manifesto centred on the economy and the debt burden?' she asked.

'Sure. But when I've spoken with him, there's a passion, sort of deep-seated, talking about the impact of the debt burden on poverty. It's like his own personal manifesto. The election hype is about the debt thing but it isn't really, it's just a screen, like a means to an end.'

Anna leaned back in her bar stool and looked across the Avenida. Parks followed her gaze.

'You won't see any there,' he said, guessing she was looking for signs of these street children. 'No way they come out during the day. And if they came anywhere near here, my God, they'd get a proper kicking from the police.'

'Where are they then?' asked Anna.

'Away from the tourists. It's a plain embarrassment for the authorities – they make sure they're well out of sight.'

Anna turned back to play with her straw, making shapes in the crushed ice of her drink.

'Well I suppose if you can remove a few hundred billion dollars worth of debt, you could then afford to remove the poverty,' she mused, still looking into her glass. 'Does Justi come up front much about the children issue?'

He stubbed out his cigarette.

'Nah. Never heard him mention it once in public. It wouldn't be wise. Brazilians don't much care for the kids anyway. They see them as little thugs, terrorising decent folk. I mean some of these kids, they carry weapons. Not just knives … you've got kids of nine with handguns, committing armed robbery. And they'll shoot you dead if you get mugged by one of them and you don't give them your watch, cards, rings. You name it, they'll have it off you.'

Parks looked out across the beach to the azure of the Atlantic, a deep shimmering blue beneath a cloudless sky.

'Justi never said to me, "Hey Parks, tell America I wanna help those street kids", but when I did my first piece with him I kinda felt that they were the real issue behind his agenda.'

He turned again to speak directly to Anna. 'It was me who actually raised the subject with him, asking him about the homeless and hopeless plight of millions of these little Brazilians. I was expecting the usual answer: "Well it's a very serious issue high on my personal agenda. I'll set up a commission to look at the problem but there are no easy solutions", etcetera, etcetera. Not Justi. No, he just went quiet on me for a few moments, like he couldn't quite find the words. I knew I'd hit a nerve, though – you could feel it. Like a flash of pain, hurt in his eyes.'

'What did he say then?'

'Quite an awkward moment. I didn't like to ask again so I left it a while and then repeated the question. He simply replied that he was running a single-issue campaign to sort out the debt problem. He just plain shut up shop on the kids.'

'So you're none the wiser?'

He shrugged his shoulders and with a slight shake of his head picked up his drink.

'Not as if he has any kids of his own either,' he added. 'I mean I've got three of my own and my heart feels for these kids here, but that's a parent speaking, not a single guy.'

Anna could see no more headway on the street-children front.

'What about these "new factors" then?' she asked, lifting the tone of the conversation. 'In the last interview you did with him, Justi spoke of them, that he was going to introduce them into the world economy to the benefit of Brazil. What was he talking about?'

Parks finished his drink and placed the glass back on the bar.

'I pushed him hard on that "new factors" stuff, but no go. He won't breathe a word more on it, and that's the bit that's got our lot jumpy.'

'What, NBC? What's their worry over "new factors"?'

'No, the White House, Anna. I've been doing this number a long time. Some of our most senior congressmen are good friends. I've had it on good authority that the White House is taking Justi seriously. I'll bet the CIA are working double time, digging around him, trying to figure out if he really has something up his sleeve.'

Anna thought back to her meeting with Sir Anthony. So here was confirmation of what he had told her. It wasn't just Britain interested in Justi.

'You have any ideas?' he enquired of her.

'Well, I've tried taking what he said at face value,' she replied. 'I've asked our economists to see if they could think up some miracle cure for Brazil. They ran through it all. What if Brazil had found massive new reserves of gold, oil, copper, iron? But even then they said it wasn't going to make much of an impression on a two-hundred-and-seventy billion dollar debt mountain.'

'Plus, how would Justi know about any new reserves?' Parks added.

Anna finished her second drink.

'Exactly,' she said, resignedly. 'How would he know?'

Parks looked at his watch. 'Gotta go,' he announced as he stood up from his stool. He turned to Anna.

'Thanks for letting me have a drink with you. My crew, well they're ugly as sin.' He smiled warmly and held out his hand. Anna shook it firmly.

'Can we meet again?' she asked, feeling that even if Parks became light on information he might have an instinct for Justi that could prove useful.

'A proposition? At my age?' he replied. They both laughed. 'Well unfortunately it's my last day on the Justi trail. NBC have me down for the news desk for a few weeks so it's home time. See if my wife still recognises me.'

Anna thought quickly.

'If you were me Al – you know, trying to get to the bottom of what Justi's about – what would you try?'

He looked across the beach to Justi's stage. He wanted to give her a few words of advice that might prove telling. She was anxious to succeed.

'If I were you....' He paused. 'If I were you I'd ask the military about Justi and Justi about the kids.'

'Why the military?'

'Because my guess is they're paying for his campaign, that's why.'

Anna was startled.

'How do you know that?'

He gave her a knowing look. 'Just a hunch. Mind how you ask them, though.'

'Well I'm not likely to be able to ask them,' replied Anna, aware of the difficulties in gaining meaningful high-level access to the Brazilian armed forces.

'Anyway, best of luck,' he said, giving her a small wave as he turned to walk back to his crew.

She watched him as he made his way back to the staging. How was she supposed to talk to the military? And what if Justi clammed up over the street children, just as he'd clammed up to Al? Worse still, what if she couldn't even secure an interview with Justi? She felt the odds being stacked against her.

CHAPTER FOUR

The scene before Anna was pure carnival. Copacabana was alive with the sound of samba; Brazilians of every shade of white and brown thronged the Avenida Atlantica and poured on to the beach. The evening was warm and humid, the atmosphere charged with nationalistic fervour. Justi caps, Justi t-shirts, Brazilian flags – they were everywhere. It had taken Anna more than an hour to travel two miles from her hotel. In the end she had given up, paid the taxi driver and walked the final half mile, carried along by a sea of people. As she stood at the edge of the beach she thought of hazarding a guess at the size of the crowd, but she soon gave up; there were people as far as the eye could see, and they were still coming.

Fortunately, the rally was already running late. Eight-thirty had come and gone but no one seemed to care. She fought her way through the crowds to the press platform. A security guard tried to prevent her crossing the rope that kept the main crowd away from the press platform and the stage itself. Anna found herself so squashed by the crowd that she was almost unable to move. Eventually, however, she managed to turn sideways and show the man her press badge. He helped her under the rope and she walked to the back of the platform to sit on one of the few remaining chairs. A steel band was playing on stage, the vast crowd before them swaying to the music. Some fifteen minutes later they stopped and left the stage to great applause.

The lights went out and, sensing Justi's arrival, the crowd quietened. From where she was sitting Anna saw a lone figure walk on to the stage and face the crowd. She picked up the headset in front of her, which offered an English interpreter for Justi's speech. She waited for the introduction – 'Ladies and gentlemen, please welcome your next president of Brazil' or something similar.

It didn't come. Instead, the stage lights were suddenly turned back on. There stood Roberto Justi, alone with just a microphone on a stand in front of him. The effect on the hundreds of thousands of Brazilians facing him was electrifying. The crowd erupted into a chant.

'Jus-ti!' Clap, clap, clap.

'Jus-ti!' Clap, clap, clap.

'Jus-ti!' Clap, clap, clap.

Anna was grateful for her headset, as the noise of the crowd was deafening. Justi simply stood there impassively, a tall man with strong features, the jacket of his yellow linen suit hanging loosely from his shoulders, his arms clasped behind his back. He was positioned before an enormous Brazilian flag that formed the backdrop to the stage itself.

'Jus-ti!' Clap, clap, clap.

'Jus-ti!' Clap, clap, clap.

Anna timed it. It lasted a full four-and-a-half minutes. She turned and looked across the crowd, a vast sea of noise and colour. Nearer to her, where the crowd pressed up against the security rope, she noticed tears in the eyes of some of the old men. What a burden it must be to carry their hopes, she thought to herself.

Eventually Justi signalled for silence. Anna's headset burst into life.

'Friends, our beloved Brazil stands at a crossroads.'

The crowd fell silent. Justi paused.

'There are those who say we should go straight across. Let us for a moment do just that. Let us for a moment join those who believe Brazil has been moving in the right direction.' He stood back from the microphone and shaded his eyes with his left hand. Then moving forward again he continued.

'But wait my friends, wait, wait, wait.' His voice trailed off. 'Wait with me. I can see a signpost.'

He shaded his eyes again with his hand. 'Shall we read it? Shall we?'

The crowd erupted again. 'Si, si, si!' they chanted back. Here was Justi, their champion, pointing their hopes, their lives, their country in the direction of self-determination, of prosperity.

He beckoned the crowd to quieten again.

'You see the signpost at the crossroads facing our great country is pointing straight on, straight on to the World Bank.'

The crowd jeered automatically.

'Senhor World Bank,' stated Justi, his voice just audible above the crowd. He lifted his left arm and slowly began to wave. 'Senhor World Bank. Goodbye.' He thundered the words out.

Up went the chant again.

'Jus-ti!' Clap, clap, clap.

At this rate he's only going to say about four lines, Anna thought to herself. No wonder they don't bother with scripts for his speeches – memorising it was not going to be difficult.

As crowd quietened, Justi began speaking again.

'Our beloved country has for too long suffered at the hands of Western capitalists. We have borrowed too much of their money. They willingly lent it. We cannot afford to now pay the interest, let alone ever repay the loans. But it need not be this way.' The crowd applauded but Justi beckoned again for their attention.

'Who says that the World Bank runs global trade? Who says that the World Bank controls the potential of our economy? They do not – they just control countless hundreds of billions of dollar loans. We will turn the tables on them in these areas, placing into their world factors that will change the balance of power. Their stranglehold will be broken. Brazil will be free.'

The speech continued in a similar fashion for a further twenty minutes. Justi extolled the virtues of a strong and free Brazil – free from the clutches of the pinstriped foreign bankers who were bankrupting his great nation. He, Roberto Justi, knew how to deal with them. He would play them at their own game and win. Brazil would be transformed from a world debtor to a world creditor.

Anna was disappointed with the speech. He had said hardly anything of substance. There had been nothing on child poverty, no attempt at an explanation of the 'new factors'. Great theatre, yes, but then again, her agenda was very far removed from that of the crowd, who had clearly loved every second of it.

The band came back on. Justi struck up the first bars of the national anthem. It was as if the ignition of some great engine had been turned, roaring into life and sweeping in song all before it. The crowd became a mass of waving flags, a sea of yellow and green. Anna looked across the crowd. It was an incredible sight. All these dreams, she pondered to herself. What if Justi couldn't deliver? How cruel was the deception to all these people then? Was he promising something that he knew deep down he could never really give them? Perhaps he was economically naive, perhaps he did not understand the complexities of a modern economy, the dependence of the Brazilian economy on the rest of the world, the necessity of open markets for Brazilian exporters, the need to attract foreign capital to boost investment into industry and improve the country's infrastructure. Was Justi on a tightrope? Even after listening to him she was none the wiser.

Justi took his leave to tumultuous applause. The band continued playing and carnival descended again. Members of the press began packing up and one by one they melted into the crowds, the foreign television crews to NTX – Brazil's commercial television station, which would satellite link their recording back to their home stations – and the journalists to

40

find a telephone from which they could download copy before retiring to a bar for the remainder of the evening.

Anna recognised the girl from behind the press table earlier, making her way towards her.

'Senhora Hughes – for you.'

She handed Anna an envelope. Anna had left a note for Manuel Justi before the rally requesting an interview with his brother. She felt unusually nervous as she opened the response. She wanted to believe that Justi was just another politician – patronising and predictable. She wanted to treat this as another run-of-the-mill election, but she felt under pressure. Both the election and Justi were more important than that, as Sir Anthony had made very clear to her. America, Japan, Germany, Britain ... they were all expecting her to come up trumps regarding Justi's 'new factors' and his unseen backers. What if Justi wouldn't see her? The question seemed to repeat itself in her mind a thousand times as she opened the envelope. She read with considerable relief the hand-scribbled note:

'Senhor Roberto Justi will be pleased to meet you at an informal reception for guests and friends to be held tonight at the Villa Maranon. 10 p.m. till late.'

'Yes!' she exclaimed quietly to herself. Justi was within striking distance.

●

The Villa Maranon was not quite as she had imagined it to be. Throughout most of South America money and power went hand-in-hand in politics, but this villa suggested neither. It stood in a long, narrow road in a middle-class suburb, among other similar properties. There was a small garden to the front but, being built into the hillside overlooking the city, there was no garden to the rear. The rendering at the front was cracked and the paint was flaking. Cars sprawled all over the pavement. As she approached, Anna could see people crowded into brightly lit rooms, the shutters still wide open. It would be difficult to talk to Justi in a crowd, she mused. She listened to the sound of many happy voices, punctuated by laughter, coming from the villa.

She walked slowly past it, wondering whether it was even worth going in. People were still arriving, and she noticed that the majority were still wearing their Justi caps and t-shirts. Anna had gone via her hotel, where she had quickly changed into a cocktail dress. She felt very out of place. And an even worse thought had struck her. Suppose Roberto Justi could not speak English? What then? She could hardly ask someone to interpret – it was, after all, supposed to be a party.

She leant against a garden wall a hundred yards along from the villa and looked out across the twinkling street lights of Rio. On the one hand she felt conspicuously overdressed, incapable of speaking even a limited amount of Portuguese and needing an interview, not a drinks party. On the other hand, this could be her one and only chance of getting to Justi. She took a deep breath and walked purposefully back to the

Villa Maranon, turning through the small open gate and up the path to the open front door. She thought about knocking but there seemed no point – the hall was crammed with guests already. She squeezed past them into the front room, which was just as crowded. Despite her physical discomfort, she began to feel more relaxed about her dress; it was practically impossible to see what anyone was wearing in the crush.

She caught sight of a tray of drinks passing within reach.

'May I?' she asked, smiling at the elderly man who was carrying them.

'You are English?' he enquired kindly.

'Yes. Can you speak English well?' she replied, hoping that she might at least have a potential interpreter if the need arose.

'No. A little.' He smiled again and then left Anna to continue his tricky job of offering drinks round.

'Aha. I heard the sound of English as spoken by an English lady.' The voice came from just behind her. She turned to see a tall, middle-aged gentleman, slightly balding and with a large, boisterous face, wearing what she could just about make out as a rather smart black blazer over grey flannels. He was squeezing through a small gap in the crowd to join her.

'Manuel Justi,' he announced, shaking her firmly by the hand. Anna smiled, despite the fact that his strong grip was hurting her.

'Anna Hughes, from *The International Times*. You speak English then?' she enquired.

'My dear girl. I've lived in England,' he replied jovially.

'Thank goodness for that. I was worried that, having asked to meet you, you wouldn't speak English,' replied Anna, with an obvious sense of relief. 'Unfortunately, I cannot speak Portuguese. And Senhor Roberto?'

'Yes. He speaks English too.' Manuel leant on Anna and reached out to snatch a drink from another passing tray.

'Do excuse me, only I think we've over-invited and we might well run dry shortly. I should drink that one as fast as you can and grab another quick.' He downed the glass of sparkling white wine in one swift movement. Wiping a drop from his lip he continued.

'You haven't finished yours yet, Miss Hughes? Miss?'

He was like a whirlwind, Anna thought to herself. Large, personable, irrepressible.

'Still Miss.'

'Ah, but plenty of suitors no doubt,' he charmed, studying her carefully and finding her looks most agreeable. 'Now tell me, how is London these days?'

'As busy as ever. A little too much crime, particularly in the West End. Did you have any area of London specifically in mind? Where you lived, perhaps, when you were over there?'

'Oh!' he exclaimed. 'I lived all over. Generally wherever I could stay with friends or even mere acquaintances. Anywhere, as long as it was free. But it was the Swinging Sixties – marvellous. You'd find a party and stay for a week.'

'Well, it's changed a lot since then.' Anna smiled and took a very small sip of her wine. It was warm and sweet, and tasted dreadful. 'It's all a bit serious these days. I think we work far too hard. But then people need the money, London is so expensive.'

'I think that's becoming the same the world over. Even here, people struggle to get by. We need to put a few more hours in the day, that would help. Take today, for instance. What was it? Oh that's it. I forgot to get all the papers delivered here this morning for Roberto to read over breakfast. Plain trivial nonsense to get worked up about, but he did. Bearing in mind that I didn't get to bed until gone four last night, how am I supposed to remember everything?'

He leant on Anna again while taking another drink from a passing tray.

'You still haven't finished that first drink. You'd have been no good at a Sixties bash,' he joked, then abruptly changed the subject. 'Are you enjoying our election?'

'It was quite a show this evening,' she replied. 'Did you expect that kind of turnout?'

'It's the same everywhere.' He swilled the drink in his glass then held it up to Anna's. 'What is it you Brits say? Ah yes. Down the hatch!' He tilted his head back a little and dispatched his wine in one go. Anna feigned a sip of hers.

'What was I saying?' he asked her.

'"It's the same everywhere" were your last words, before the "down the hatch" bit,' she reminded him.

Manuel liked her. She was fun ... witty, alive, beautiful and fun! What a great girl, he thought to himself. Shame he wasn't twenty years younger – alas, he was old enough to be her father.

'That's right. You've reminded me. Jolly well done.

Yes, wherever Roberto goes they turn out in their thousands. It's incredible.'

'What is his appeal then, Senhor Manuel?' she asked, weighing her tone carefully so she should not put him on edge, and attempting to finish her glass at the same time in an effort to please him.

'You've finished. Bravo! I'll grab you another as soon as I see one pass by. His appeal you asked. Well he's giving everyone hope. Yes, it's hope that Roberto gives every single Brazilian. Before Roberto came along there was such a sense of desperation, in the papers, on radio, on television. Desperation. Most of all you could see the desperation in the eyes of everyone in this country. But Roberto talks of a new Brazil, he speaks the language of hope for a better future, the language of people's dreams.' He grabbed two drinks from a passing tray and, handing one to Anna, he concluded, 'The result is as you see.'

'And can he deliver?' asked Anna. She thought she saw Manuel's eyes flash and instantly regretted her clumsy comment. It had slipped out. He had been relaxed, leaning against a wooden dresser, smiling as he talked. Now he stood tall, the smile gone.

'We do not give false promises, Miss Hughes.'

Her heart sank. She had not meant to antagonise him; he was her only chance of getting a meeting with Roberto Justi.

'Senhor Manuel. Did I offend you? If so, I am most sorry,' she said quietly, touching his right arm gently.

He looked at her. She had such a sincere look. It made

her appear even more beautiful than before. He held up his hands momentarily,

'Nonsense my dear. It is I who must apologise. The Latin temperament, I'm afraid.' He was leaning against the dresser again, a smile beginning to flutter across his face. 'Roberto keeps telling me to slow down a bit, but this thing has a pace of its own. I'm needlessly touchy, too sensitive by half probably. Then, at the same time he says slow down, he gets worked up about things like the breakfast papers.'

'Well,' replied Anna in Manuel's defence, 'you're doing a great job. The opinion polls give you over seventy per cent of the vote.'

'And rising,' beamed Manuel. 'If only the damn election was tomorrow ... Still – not long now, eh?'

Anna glanced around her. 'Senhor Manuel. Is there any possibility of meeting with Senhor Roberto?'

'Ah, yes. Well I did get your note, as you know, which after all is why you're here. He is up to his eyes at the moment, as you can imagine. Plus there are certain political constraints.'

'Such as?'

He leaned towards her and, still smiling, replied, 'Well we don't believe we have many potential voters in Britain.'

Anna was ready for this one. Her reply came immediately but with no hint of forethought.

'Senhor Manuel, you surprise me.' She took a sip of her drink before continuing. 'The election is won. Seventy per cent and rising, as you said. I felt sure you would already be looking beyond it, to post-election Brazil, to the international community and to Britain's considerable influence.'

She watched him carefully. Surely Roberto Justi had a confidant in his brother. She had just presented the international community in the traditional sense – a community that Brazil would usually have to court favour with, to support and at times submit to. What would be his reaction?

'My dear girl,' he countered, his voice low, 'we've been looking at post-election Brazil for a very long time now. Do we see a different international community? Will Britain have influence? Perhaps. Will America, with all her military might, will she remain strong? Will the dollar, the yen and the euro – your pound even – will they be the power currencies of the world's economy? Possibly.' He spoke with a quiet confidence. It was deep-seated in respect of the outcome of Justi's election success and the implementation of his policies, whatever they were.

'But how do you change the international community?' Anna asked.

He noted again her sincerity. She was not asking with the contempt that so many foreign journalists had displayed.

'Tell me, Anna…. May I call you Anna?' She nodded. 'Good. Then please call me Manuel.' She nodded again. 'Now tell me. Do you believe that revolution can change the international community? Can it change the world?'

'Well, not in the historical sense of the word, no. Lenin tried it but even his success secured less than one-third of the world and all of that has practically collapsed again now.'

'We agree then.' He touched her arm. 'I do hope I'm not boring you, only I read History and Politics, and I love talking of these things.'

'You're not boring me in the slightest. Really, not at all.'

'Marvellous. Well think about this then. Revolution, as you say, will not change the world. This is because revolution is promoted by the "have nots" against the "haves".'

He paused for Anna's agreement and, eventually realising this, she nodded.

'Right. Splendid. To succeed, the "have nots" believe that they have to violate the laws of the "haves".'

She interrupted him. 'But that's only because the laws of the "haves" were designed by the "haves" to stop the "have nots" getting what the "haves" have.'

Manuel laughed, and Anna laughed with him.

'I'm on my fifth drink,' said Manuel, raising his glass into the air. 'And I'm finding these "haves" and "have nots" damn confusing.'

'Have not what?' she asked jokingly.

'Have not a drop,' he replied to their mutual amusement as he downed his drink. 'But you are quite right, my dear. You can understand the thinking of a revolutionary, maybe even sympathise. But if you are serious about change – world change – you have to learn from the mistakes of others.'

'So no Justi revolution then, Manuel?'

Manuel stared at her. His brain was dulled by the wine ... he had to be careful, he reminded himself. She was very beautiful. She was lovely company, really lovely company.

She was also sincere. He sighed deep within himself as he thought that, alas, she was not Brazilian. She stood for the 'haves', he stood for the 'have nots'. He searched for the right words.

'We are talking revolution.' He paused again. 'But revolution without violation.'

He felt he had said enough. Anna waited, hoping he might talk further.

'Call our Brasilia office tomorrow morning,' he said as he kissed her on both checks. 'I will set up a meeting for you with Roberto. It has been a great pleasure, Anna. Do stay and enjoy the party.'

'Thank you, Manuel,' Anna replied. 'You have been most kind.' She smiled at him as he turned away. The villa was still crammed, the guests were having to speak increasingly loudly to each other to be heard. She was not really in the mood for socialising. She pushed her way out into the hall and then back out on to the pathway that led to the street. A taxi drew up with more guests and she acknowledged them politely.

'Hotel Victoria?' The taxi driver nodded.

Anna stared at the unfamiliar streets as she was driven back to her hotel, wondering about her chances of sleeping when her mind was racing. Roberto's 'new factors' ... Manuel's 'revolution without violation' ... what was the meaning of it all? Would she be able to find out? And what on Earth was she going to report to Sir Anthony?

CHAPTER FIVE

Roberto Justi sat down at the breakfast table. Still yawning, he poured himself a coffee. 'See, Roberto – all your precious papers,' chided Manuel as he pointed to an enormous pile of them, stacked with the locals on top. The nationals lay beneath them, then the principal international papers, but as these tended to be a day behind the campaign they frequently went unread.

'Did they like it?' asked Roberto.

Manuel sifted through the pile and found the *Jornal do Brasil*, Brazil's biggest-selling national paper. He handed it to his brother. Roberto studied the front page with considerable interest. It was dominated by his picture, in full colour, waving goodbye to the World Bank from the stage at Copacabana. He sipped his coffee as he read the headline: *Justi Pledge: Goodbye World Bankers.*

Smiling, he flicked through the copy – the report was favourable. He turned inside for the editorial. So far very little editorial comment had been supportive of his campaign, most was noncommittal, but today it was dedicated to his manifesto. He read it carefully.

'There can be little doubt that Roberto Justi is destined for the presidency. Anyone who witnessed the scenes in Rio yesterday evening cannot possibly imagine how Justi can fail.'

This was fantastic, he thought to himself. Coffee cup in hand, he read on. He felt sure they would retain some criticism for his lack of detail on the main policy, but on reaching the end of the editorial, he realised there was no criticism at all.

'Manuel, have you read this editorial?'

Manuel was reading the sports pages of one of the local papers. 'The General is doing a very good job for us, Roberto,' he mumbled in reply, resenting the intrusion into his own reading.

Roberto read the piece again. 'It covers our weak spot well, Manuel,' he pressed.

Manuel gave up reading his paper and sat back in his chair, resigned to the fact that his brother would now want to read it aloud to him.

'Come on then, Roberto. Read it.' He sighed, reached for the coffee and poured himself another cup.

'But it's fantastic Manuel. Listen.

'Justi's opponents claim that when in power he will not be able to fulfil his promises, that on the detail behind his debt pledge he should put up or shut up. But Justi is right to box clever. If this was a military conflict, no one would expect detail to be published prior to a strategic strike. In this new millennium, economic conflicts will increasingly be won by the element of surprise. This is Justi's position and it is credible. Whether in power he wins or loses the economic battles ahead, he has

an advantage over all other candidates in this election: he carries the affection and loyalty of the Brazilian people. Facing the future united may well prove decisive.'

Roberto looked up at his brother.

'Like I said, well played General,' responded Manuel.

'Yes, well played indeed,' pondered Roberto. 'When are we expecting him?'

Manuel had started to read the sports pages again and ignored the question. Suddenly the paper was whipped away. He looked up to see Roberto staring at him.

'I said when are we expecting the General?'

Manuel glared at him. It wasn't yet ten o'clock. He didn't really wake up properly until after ten on a normal day, but today he also had to contend with a dull, thudding headache, a legacy of the previous evening's excesses.

'I don't know. Tomorrow I think,' he replied, leaning across the table to retrieve his paper.

'What's the score for today then?' enquired Roberto.

Manuel stood up. It was useless. His brother was not going to leave him in peace. He moved to the window and picked up a pile of correspondence, memorandums and notes that had built up on the large white-painted sill, and then returned to the table. He sipped his coffee, which was now not hot enough for his liking.

'Do me a favour, Roberto. Pour me a hot cup of coffee while I sort out your life for you.' He held his cup out. Roberto took it from him and poured the contents down the sink before refilling it with hot coffee from the percolator. Manuel was busy rifling through the papers, making two separate piles. When he had finished he picked up the pile to his right, tapped the papers on the table to align them neatly, and then placed them directly in front of him. He pulled the top paper from the pile.

'Right. This afternoon you visit a factory that makes computer terminals. Then you move on to one of the hospitals.'

'And this morning?' interjected Roberto. He was tiring of such visits.

'Free,' replied Manuel.

'This evening, free as well?'

'Free, but....' Manuel paused, flicked through the pile and withdrew a note from the middle. 'But I nine-tenths promised an interview and....'

Roberto cut him short.

'Manuel, I thought we'd agreed – no more interviews. We don't need them, we already have a game plan which we stick to. Okay?'

Manuel took the notepaper with Anna's details on and moved it to the bottom of the pile.

'Okay, okay. I hadn't forgotten. I'll phone her and say no.'

'Do that,' replied Roberto. 'You heard the editorial in the *Jornal*. We've done the hard part.'

'Fine. Just fine,' Manuel responded.

'Anyway, why did you promise it?'

'Well she's not from the Brazilian press. She's British.

Political editor of *The International Journal* or something like that. One of their good broadsheets anyway.' He decided to repeat Anna's line from the previous evening. 'It's all well and good us thinking about winning elections Roberto, but perhaps we ought to start thinking about things after the election. And she's a smart lady. She's already pushing for what we're likely to be doing when the presidency is won. We could learn from people like her – what to say, where to say it, how to say it.'

Roberto sat, wondering about the interview his brother had more than half arranged. 'Thinking about what we'll be doing is one thing. Telling people is something completely different.'

He noticed his brother looking somewhat disappointed.

'Don't feel let down.'

'Well I do a little,' replied Manuel despondently. 'She's a lovely girl, a real treat of a lady.'

'She's still a journalist Manuel. She's looking for copy while you're looking into her sweet brown eyes.'

'Green,' interjected Manuel. 'Her eyes are green.'

The room fell silent. Roberto leaned back in his chair and looked at his elder brother. Perhaps he was being a little hard on him, but Manuel had a tendency to forget agreements when he felt like it. Roberto had seen this weakness cause Manuel problems all his life. The problem was, you could never fully rely on him. Three marriages, three divorces. Friendships made, friendships lost – a life littered with broken relationships. Even his own children now paid little attention to him. True, they were grown up and had families of their own, but they never made contact with him and Roberto did not blame them. Manuel had a fearful temper, especially when drinking. Most of the time he would be the life and soul of the party when drinking – charming, fun, full of laughter and stories that could keep guests enthralled for hours. But once in a while, and for no obvious reason, drink would make him aggressive, even violent. Roberto could handle him like this, but no one else had ever managed to cope with more than a handful of such outbursts before they left him. Three wives, three divorces. That said it all, Roberto thought. Should he concede and give this interview? He began to soften on the matter. Last night had been a great success and much of that had been down to Manuel.

'All right. But if I see her, you have to promise me that this is the very last interview.'

'Absolutely the very, very last Roberto,' Manuel assured him. 'You'll adore her.'

'Unlikely Manuel. It is you who has the weak spot for the ladies, not me. I'll see her here at eight. Tell her no more than half an hour.'

'Leave it to me.' Manuel rose from his chair to leave the message for Anna.

'Don't go yet,' Roberto asserted. 'I need to know a few things. All I have at the moment is that she's British with green eyes.'

'Ah yes. Well what sort of things do you want to know?'

'Have you talked to her much already, for instance?' He was so close to victory, nothing was to be left to chance now. A slip of the tongue, a contradiction and tomorrow it could be on the news stands in Britain. That might not seem important, but the day after it could be headlines in Brazil, that was the danger.

'I've told her nothing more than the usual. You worry too much my dear younger brother. Even if we told all now I don't think it would make much difference.'

Roberto sighed. 'How many times do I have to tell you that the reason we're not giving the specifics of our policies is not only to do with winning the election. It's also to do with the need to keep the world at large in the dark so that we give them no time to make contingencies.'

'Ah, yes,' muttered Manuel. 'Still, that's why you're going to be president and not me. I'd be quite useless.' He chuckled. 'I'd never be able to remember what I could say to whom.'

'Nor what you said the time before either,' added Roberto. 'Does she know I've lived in London?'

'No. In passing I told her that I'd spent a little time there back in the Sixties. But she never asked anything about you, except of course that she wanted an interview.'

Roberto picked up the editorial page from the *Jornal do Brasil* again.

'Can she speak Portuguese?'

Manuel shook his head.

'That's a pity,' said Roberto. 'I could have given her this.'

'You're not expecting any problems are you?' enquired Manuel, sensing his brother was growing edgy about the interview.

'No. It's just the London thing gets me a bit concerned. Five years was a long time. If she started digging back there it could....' He trailed off. 'No. You are right. I worry too much.'

Manuel walked over and put a reassuring arm round him.

'Roberto. You *do* worry too much.' He patted him a few times on the shoulder and left the room to make his calls.

'Still on the subject of worrying,' Roberto called as Manuel was almost out the door. 'What's happening on the advertising?'

'The final blitz begins tomorrow,' Manuel replied. 'Television, radio, hoardings, papers. The agency contacted me yesterday. Everything's ready to go. You'll be better known than the pope at the end of this.'

'And the funding? Everything all right?'

Manuel sighed. His brother was no hostage to fortune, unlike himself, who preferred to hope things would work out and worry about them when they went wrong – as they invariably seemed to do in his own personal affairs.

'Like I said earlier, the General comes tomorrow.'

'What were the other things we had to sort out with him?'

'For God's sake Roberto, relax,' responded Manuel, opening his arms in exasperation. 'You know, you mustn't be so intense. It makes you very difficult to be with when you get this tense.'

'I'm not tense,' stated Roberto calmly. 'I merely want to get on top of things, that's all.'

'Fine,' Manuel sighed, then paused to try and remember why the General was coming the following day other than to discuss the advertising.

'The General is coming to detail the front for the funding of the advertising and also to advise us on our obligation to the existing constitution. Now are you satisfied?'

Roberto nodded.

'Now I'm going to make some calls.'

'And her name?'

'Whose name?'

'The lady journalist's name. It might help if I knew it before she arrived.'

'Senhora Hughes. Senhora Anna Hughes.'

He ignored Roberto calling after him again about the timings for the afternoon visits. He instructed his campaign headquarters to tell Anna to come to the villa for eight, then changed it to a quarter to, which would give him fifteen minutes with her. She really was rather beautiful, he thought, as he looked blankly out of the lounge window at the blackening sky. Why shouldn't he steal her for fifteen minutes? After all, he was the International Press Officer and she was definitely International Press.

There was a deep rumbling of thunder in the distance. He looked at the parched grass and hoped for rain.

●

It was ten to eight when Anna arrived at the Villa Maranon that evening. She was finding it difficult to get timings right in Rio. The traffic was unpredictable, and so too was the speed at which taxi drivers could pick their way through it. She had spent most of the morning trying to phone Justi's Brasilia office; it was almost permanently engaged but eventually she had managed to get through. Lunch had been more pleasant. The Hotel Victoria had a pavement café and she had enjoyed sitting there, watching the hustle and bustle of Rio pass her by. She'd tried a caipirinha again, this time with a shot of rum. Two more followed in the afternoon but from the comfort of the hotel bar instead, as the rain fell in torrents outside.

She felt quite relaxed about meeting Roberto Justi as she walked up the little path again, breathing in the warm smell of earth in the air that followed the rain after a long dry spell. She had decided to dress on the safe side, in a pale blue trouser suit and navy shoes that she had purchased from Harvey Nichols' Heathrow store on leaving for Brazil. She knocked on the heavy wooden door. Manuel opened it and greeted her warmly, as if she was an old friend. He looked pleased when in response to the offer of a drink she asked for a caipirinha with rum.

By the time Roberto realised that Anna was not late at all, but in fact had been waylaid by his brother, it was fully quarter past eight. He became impatient and on investigation was aggravated further by the sound of them talking merrily in the lounge. Manuel was in the middle of a tale about how he had once been dared to swim across the Thames. Unable to fight the current, he had floated down past Tower Bridge, scrambled out the same side, crossed the river on foot, and then appeared triumphantly on the other side, to the amazement of his friends.

Roberto stood in the doorway, waiting for him to finish.

'Ah, Roberto. I was wondering where you were!' Manuel exclaimed, seeming both surprised and delighted to see him.

'If you recall, I agreed to meet in the breakfast room,' said Roberto, ignoring Anna, who had risen to her feet, awaiting an introduction.

'I'm wrong again,' smiled Manuel disarmingly. 'Anyway, Roberto this is Anna.'

Roberto held out his hand to Anna, his face expressionless.

'Senhora Hughes. I apologise for the informality of my brother,' he said curtly.

'Nonsense,' Manuel responded. 'We are as friends.'

Roberto ignored him.

'If you will follow me, Senhora.' He turned and left the room, not waiting to see if she was behind him.

'Don't worry about him. He's always a bit straight-laced,' whispered Manuel as they followed Roberto through the hall and into the breakfast room.

'Welcome to our campaign nerve centre, Senhora,' said Roberto as he offered her a seat at the table. Anna smiled as she looked around the sparsely furnished room. Other than the table and four chairs, there was only a small wooden chest pushed into the corner; the room was lit by a single bulb that dangled from a lopsided shade in the centre of the ceiling.

'Perhaps it all happens at your Brasilia office?' she replied.

Roberto did not respond. He sat facing her, almost looking through her. The atmosphere was awkward, but she had experienced worse.

'Well, what do you want to know?' he asked abruptly.

She took her pocket recorder from her handbag and placed it on the table between them.

'Do you mind?' she enquired, glancing at the recorder.

'No, I don't mind.'

She pressed the record button and, sensing his resistance to any further pleasantries or small talk, she decided to get straight to the point.

'I notice you have a substantial commitment to advertising. Are you paying for it personally?'

Roberto showed not the slightest flicker of concern at the question.

'Why do you ask?' he deflected the question back to her.

'Well, can you afford to personally cover the cost of it all? Some estimates suggest your final spend could top thirty-five million US dollars.'

Roberto laughed. 'Sure. Look around you. Money no object.'

'So it's not your money then, Senhor Justi?'

'No, it's not my money. I have very little money. But I do have my supporters Senhora Hughes.'

'Who are they?'

'They prefer anonymity. The other candidates do not detail their funding. Even in your own country certain parties go to great lengths to ensure funding is as discreet as possible.'

'But the opposition parties here, and all the main parties in Britain, have a clear, broad manifesto. Manifestos that detail what measures they intend taking to achieve their aims. However, your manifesto is narrow in the extreme and you have continually resisted providing the detail, which makes me wonder if your financial supporters know far more than the public at large.'

Roberto looked at her dismissively. It irritated her. He ignored the question and broadened the interview.

'Just like the public, my supporters know that nations such as your own are screwing us – if you will pardon the phrase.'

She looked at him intently. He spoke quietly, his wide brown eyes holding hers for a moment, then flitting to look at the wall behind her, or the doorway to the side of the table, or the tape recorder. They were more disinterested than in any way shifty.

'Nations such as your own are thrusting poverty on us,' he continued. 'They are trampling our future under their bankers' feet. Just like the public, my supporters believe that I can turn the tables. Unlike the public, they also have money and so they support me – so would millions of others, if only they had the means, but I can't say to people "Give me a dollar towards an election advert" when their children are going hungry.'

'But do they know how you intend to sort out this oppression you keep talking about?' she pressed.

'Perhaps. Is that a problem?'

'Will they be expecting some sort of payoff? Why else would they stump up thirty-five million?'

Roberto paused. 'I think we're going round in circles, Senhora,' he stated calmly. 'Perhaps you have some other questions for me?'

Anna wondered whether to give the funding issue one more go, but it was clear that he had no intention of speaking further on the subject. She changed tack.

'In an interview you gave to NBC you talked of introducing "new factors" into the world economy to solve Brazil's debt problem. What are these new factors?'

'Well they won't be new any more if I tell you,' replied Roberto, smiling broadly, knowing that she was finding the interview increasingly hard going. She waited for him to continue, then realising he did not intend to, she pushed him further.

'Leading economists dismiss your claim, and say that you have nothing new to resolve Brazil's economic problems. Why should you be believed? Why won't you just say what it is you intend to do, then we could evaluate it?'

'What do leading economists know?' he replied with quiet mocking. 'And why should I tell you what my plans are? I am asking the Brazilian people for a mandate. If they give me it then I will gladly tell them, and you, and the rest of the world what my plans are. Then you can evaluate it as much as you like Senhora.'

Anna was trying as hard as she could to find a chink of light in what he was saying, but she was becoming increasingly despondent. She had made no progress at all. She recalled Al Parks' words: 'Ask the military about Justi and Justi about the kids.' She might as well ask Justi about both. She watched him carefully as she spoke.

'Are the military funding your campaign?'

He paused. 'That is a question too far, Senhora.' he replied.

Anna regretted asking it. She had hoped he might have been caught off guard and compromised himself, but he had replied within the bounds of common decency. Some questions were over the mark, and with nothing to support it she knew she had gone too far.

'I apologise, Senhor Justi. Really, it was a mistake to ask such a question.'

Why couldn't he be like Manuel, she thought to herself – warm, personable, easy to get on with? The contrast was so marked. Here was Roberto, ten years younger then his brother, cold, aloof and distant. A handsome man, true … a man with presence and conviction, but very much a closed book. The interview was useless. She wanted to get out.

'You have been most kind to give me your time,' she said, reaching across the table and picking up her recorder.

Roberto stood up and walked across the room to the door back into the hall. As Anna replaced the recorder in her bag she thought she would have one last go.

'What do you want to do about the children living in the streets and sewers in Rio?' she enquired casually.

'As I say, if we solve the debt problem so many of my people will be better off, the street children included.'

Al Parks had said Justi was vulnerable on the issue; he had obviously learnt how to handle the question since then, Anna thought to herself.

'Goodbye Senhora Hughes,' Roberto shook her hand.

'Thank you for your time' she replied with an unconvincing smile. She heard him close the door before she had even reached the gate.

She decided not to flag down a taxi. A sense of failure had

settled upon her and she preferred to be alone with her thoughts as she walked the mile or so back to the hotel. Not only was the Justi campaign different in substance to anything she had ever encountered, the style of their campaign was different, too. It relied entirely on mass publicity. There was no election machine behind Justi, no canvassing, no analysis of support by region, no obvious strategy at all, she thought. And only one policy. That was the most incredible thing about it – with only one policy and absolutely no detail behind that one policy, Justi was going to sweep to power in a landslide victory.

She decided to walk along the backstreets, where she could think more easily. She strolled slowly along the pavement, passing a few bars, avoiding the stares of small groups of elderly men who sat outside drinking beer and playing cards.

The trip had been entirely fruitless. The only thing she could tell Sir Anthony was that an NBC reporter reckoned that the military were funding Justi's campaign. Wow, she said to herself, it was hardly worth reporting, especially as this information had backfired on her less than half an hour ago in the Justi interview. She tried to think of something else worth remaining in Brazil for. There would be no further opportunity to meet Roberto Justi; even if there was, she was not likely to get any further with him than she had earlier. She sighed deeply. She would have to return to London and tell Sir Anthony that she had blanked. As she walked up the final steps of her hotel, Anna wondered if her lack of success on the Justi assignment would damage her career.

The concierge called out to her as she passed across the foyer to the lift.

'A message, Senhora.' He handed her a small note then turned to deal with an irate guest whose laundry had not been returned on time.

Anna shrugged her shoulders as she looked at herself in the mirror of the lift that took her to her room on the fifth floor. Her feeling of isolation and loneliness returned as she entered her depressing room. She felt so down that she no longer cared if her career failed.

She opened the envelope without much interest.

'Please phone Michael Turner as soon as possible.'

Anna stared at the phone and then again at the message. She left the piece of paper by the phone and drew the curtains, slipped out of her suit and went to bed. Pulling the sheet tight round her she flicked off the room light by the switch above her bed and sought the sanctuary of sleep.

●

She awoke just after seven and had a quick shower. She had not eaten the night before and, feeling hungry, she decided to have something more substantial than her usual continental breakfast in her room.

In the hotel restaurant she devoured two orange juices, cereal, two eggs poached with smoked fish, hot croissants with butter and strawberry jam, all washed down with a pot of tea. She started to feel better and the depression of the previous evening lifted. She was looking forward to returning to London. Sir Anthony could not be too hard on her; after all the British, American, German and Japanese governments had been unable to get to the bottom of Justi's policy so she could hardly be branded a failure.

She asked the receptionist for flight times to London, and was told that because it was still not nine o'clock, no travel agents were open so only the airport could give flight times. The airport was permanently engaged so it would have to wait until nine. As soon as they had the information they would phone her in her room. Anna turned away to make for the lifts.

'Senhora Hughes?' called another of the receptionists. She had an envelope in her hand.

'For me?' Anna replied.

'Yes. A fax.'

'Thank you.'

She opened it in the lift. It was from Turner. She read the facing page.

'Anna — tried contacting you and hope you got the message. Don't worry about phoning now. Read the enclosed. You may find it of interest. Please keep this confidential. You are the only person I'm giving it to. Treat it carefully. See you soon and take care. Mike.'

The lift doors opened at the fifth floor and she stepped out, flicking through the remainder of the fax. It was a copy of an article, covering seven pages. She entered her room and sat down at the desk to read it properly. She stared at the title on the first page:

'The Market Economy – a Future View'

What on Earth had Mike dug up, she asked to herself. She looked at the bottom left corner. The author was someone named Angela Felton. Next to her name was the date – July 1986. Anna thought hard if she had ever heard the name before, but she could not even recall an Angela, let alone a Felton. She read on.

Twenty minutes later she called the receptionist and cancelled her request for flight times. She was desperate to speak to Turner. She looked at her watch, it was now eight-thirty, but just three-thirty in the morning London time. She couldn't phone him, she'd have to wait until lunchtime.

She read the article again and smiled to herself. So here then were Justi's 'new factors'; now it all added up. Anna maintained a wry smile as she read the article a third time, confident that a second meeting with Roberto Justi would now be conceded by his campaign team ... and that it would be very, very different from the first.

The morning seemed to drag on relentlessly. Anna had tried hard to keep herself occupied in the hope that this would kill time faster; she had read *The Times* in under ten minutes, skipping through articles, unable to concentrate.

She had tried the crossword, but had thrown the paper to one side after a few moments. The only thing that interested her was the Felton article and the list of questions she had penned for Turner.

At just after noon she phoned her office, only to be told that Turner had a breakfast meeting and would not be in before ten. The afternoon seemed to stretch out even further than the morning. She had to find something to do for three hours.

Taking a taxi, she went to Copacabana – the beach deserted except for a handful of dog walkers at the water's edge, under a grey, threatening sky. Mist shrouded the mountains; Sugarloaf was almost completely lost to it. Anna walked along the promenade, pulling her coat more tightly around her against the chill of the stiffening breeze, past the bar where she had first talked about Justi with Al Parks. It was closed, the shutters pulled down tight and fastened with large brass padlocks on metal rings concreted into the floor.

Looking out across the sands it was hard to imagine the scenes of two evenings ago – the euphoria of the rally, the sense of hope spilling over so easily, so naturally, into carnival. She had warmed to Roberto that evening. He had a heart for his people, she thought to herself. Yet the man she met at the Villa Maranon last night was a different person. Perhaps he didn't so much care for Brazil, perhaps he had a personal vendetta against the rest of the world. He had spoken to her with a quiet aggression. Maybe it was because she was not from Brazil, because he felt she represented the very system he had vowed to fight against. She was not certain. She cast her mind forward. Would he agree to meet her again? If she was right about the Felton article, he would be a fool not to. What would be the outcome of that interview, she wondered. Would he still be so cold when his world was under threat of being torn apart? Perhaps she would get to meet the real Roberto Justi and be invited to understand him and the issues that drove his life. She felt a few drops of rain and saw a café that appeared to be open on the other side of the Avenida. Pulling up her hood, she walked quickly across the carriageway as the rain fell more heavily.

After two cups of coffee the rain was still falling. The owner, a white, middle-aged lady with a kind, freckled face, phoned for a taxi.

'The rain is no good for the skin,' she said, raising her hands to her cheeks, an array of gold rings on her fingers. 'Staying in the dry. This is how I have kept my complexion all these years.'

Anna smiled and, leaving her a larger tip than usual to cover the cost of the call, she thanked her for the advice and did her best to not disappoint as she ran, hunched over with her coat draped over her head, to the waiting car.

On returning to the hotel she paced round her room, distracted only once when she noticed that the rubber plant, which had looked so sad on her arrival, had rewarded her kindness with a shiny new leaf, uncurling itself from a small bud at the top of the main stem.

At last three o'clock came. She phoned her office again.

'Yes, he's in, but not at his desk,' replied one of her subs.

'I'll hold,' replied Anna.

Half a minute passed.

'Anna?'

'Mike!'

'Anna. How nice to hear from you. How's it going? Was the article any use?'

She was concerned about the discussion she wanted to have with him – the newsroom was open plan.

'Mike, could you take this call in a meeting room?'

'Sure,' he replied. 'Is everything okay?'

'Oh yes. No, everything's fine. I just want to talk to you about that article.'

Turner called over one of the subs and asked the call to be put through to him in the meeting room on the far side of the office.

'Anna?'

'Good. We can talk now?'

'Yes. Door's closed. No problem.'

'I've a whole list of questions about that article you faxed. It's dynamite Mike. I think it'll blow Justi to bits.'

'Well I wasn't sure why you were in Brazil but I thought it might be interesting background stuff for you.'

Anna hesitated, mindful of Sir Anthony's instruction that Turner was not to be made aware of the background to her assignment. She thought quickly about what she should and shouldn't say. She decided to keep as much as possible to herself, but she would have to let Mike in on a few things – she needed his support.

'Mike. I think there's something you should know. Sir Anthony sent me out here to try to get to the bottom of what Justi's about. He's concerned about him. Actually, a lot of people are concerned about Justi.'

'People like who?'

She thought of telling him about the link to the Foreign Office but she was worried about how much of her assignment was covered by the Official Secrets Act. She felt she had said enough.

'People like him, I guess,' she replied evasively. 'He didn't actually name names, he just said a lot of people. Fellow media magnates, I guess.'

Turner detected a little hesitancy on her part.

'It's quite important I know, Anna. I've thought from the beginning that Duce's involvement was unusual. But if there's someone else involved too, I really need to know.'

Why might that be? She thought fast. She appreciated his concern but why was he pushing for information he had no obvious need for? She stood her ground.

'Like I said Mike, I don't know. Duce didn't name names.'

Turner was anxious for her. He was worried that the Felton article may have pushed Anna's assignment beyond the scope of journalism and thus Sir Anthony's involvement needed clarifying. After all, it was Sir Anthony who had instigated the Brazil trip in the first place.

'Well just remember I'm concerned about any possible tie-ups beyond Duce, Anna. It doesn't quite all stack up you know.'

Too true, she thought to herself.

'Anyway because of the "ifs" and "buts", I did some digging,' he continued.

'Who is Angela Felton then?' enquired Anna, seizing the opportunity to move the conversation away from Sir Anthony.

'She was Roberto Justi's girlfriend back in the Eighties.'

'You're joking!' she replied in disbelief. 'If that's true Mike, then Justi's had it. I was confident enough on pinning him down just on the back of the article. But now he's connected to the author, he'll have no chance.'

'What do you make of the article then?' he asked.

'It's mind-blowing.' She paused. 'Just mind-blowing.' They were the only words to describe it.

'Come off it, Anna,' replied Turner. 'It's a pipe dream, that's all.'

'If Justi comes to power, he has the geographical infrastructure. He has the rainforest,' Anna countered.

'And then we're to ransom?' he interjected. 'I mean, can you really start charging for air and water as if they're some sort of new commodity? Of course you can't. The rest of the world is just going to say it's extortion ... blackmail.'

The line went quiet. To Anna the magnitude of what the world was facing was overwhelming. She was struck by Turner's dismissive attitude.

'Just say he did try it Mike. Say the world couldn't stop him? Could he then break the banking system? If the deal was to cancel Brazil's debts, how many banks would go under?'

'God knows! But it's all conjecture, Anna. Imagine if we threatened to start poisoning the sea with tonnes of ghastly chemicals, something capable of threatening the world's entire ecosystem, and then said to the world, "Pay up or we'll poison". It's just a non-starter. The world won't stand by and let it happen.'

'But it's not like that. He's not going to poison anything. It's about Brazil's own forests and what Brazil wants to do with them is surely up to Brazil itself,' she replied.

'But you can't just chop down rainforest on that scale. Just think of the implications. Like Felton said, Brazil's rainforest provides one-fifth of the world's water and one-third of the world's oxygen.'

'Precisely,' Anna interrupted, with a hint of exasperation. 'That's the whole point. Why should Brazil just give the world all that water and all that oxygen? Why shouldn't we pay for the air that we breathe and the water we drink? For nothing, yes, Felton's right. Why for nothing?'

Turner took time to respond. He wondered if Anna was becoming a bit unbalanced over the Justi assignment. Surely no sane person could argue for charging for the things that were the necessities of life. The air was carried by the wind from where? Who could say who owned it? Didn't the water also come with the wind? No one could own it, and yet here was one of his most capable editors suggesting that it was possible.

'Mike. Are you there?'

'I'm just thinking that's all. Look Anna, I think you're off the pace on all this, I really do. If you take Justi's position, how level-headed do you think you can be in covering this assignment?'

'What do you mean by that?' she demanded. 'Just because I

think someone has a valid point doesn't mean I report issues in a biased way. You know that, for pity's sake.'

'I'm just flagging it, that's all. No need to get uptight.'

'It's not blackmail,' she continued, returning to the Felton article. 'If that's what you think, then it's you who's off the pace. More importantly, what can the world do about it? That's the real point.' She did not invite a reply. 'Where is this Felton woman now? Is she still part of the Justi show?'

Turner quietened. He'd made his point and he knew, at the end of the day, he could veto copy. Whatever her private view it wasn't going to find its way into his paper.

'I don't know. I should be getting more info tonight. Phone me tomorrow morning?' his tone was somewhat frosty.

'Who are you talking to then?' she asked, running her pen down the list to the question that read 'How did Mike get hold of the article?'

'I can't say.'

'So can't you say how you got this article? I mean, it's almost twenty years old,' she pressed.

'No, I can't say. Tomorrow then?'

'UK time, yes?'

'Yes. And what do you propose to do in the meantime? Have you met with Justi yet?' he asked.

'I met him last night, which was obviously before I received your fax. So I got nowhere.'

'Are you going to see him again?'

'I'm not sure.' She could think of no reason not to. Someone had to confront Justi.

'Well just go careful, Anna. We're only newspaper writers. These people are playing for much higher stakes.'

She hadn't thought much about her own security. She was running a risk in confronting Justi. Suppose the military *were* backing him – what might happen to her before she could leave Brazil?

'I think I have to see him,' she replied. 'But you're right. I need to watch myself. Where would it be best to see him, do you think?'

'Why don't you just phone him? Does he know where you're staying?'

'No. I've always had to contact them.'

'Well phone him then, but not from your hotel. Do it from a payphone somewhere.'

He was right. She mustn't run unnecessary risks, but she felt disappointed. She had so wanted to actually be there when she talked to Justi – to see his reaction, to witness the moment when his campaign landed on the rocks.

'Okay,' she replied, slightly subdued. 'I'll phone him.'

'One last thing Anna. Duce says he's yet to have a single report from you. Is that right?'

'Yes. I don't want to just give him a report saying I've nothing to report.'

'Well you know he wants to hear from you. I think you ought to fire one off to him quickly.'

'All right. I'll do one later.'

'And take care Anna. I mean it.'

'I will.'

She tapped the disconnect button with her left index finger and, still holding the receiver in her right hand, telephoned Justi's Brasilia campaign centre. This time she got through first time. They would not give her the phone number for the Villa Maranon. She demanded that they phone Justi for permission to release it to her. They would not. She told them in the interests of his campaign they should contact him immediately and advise him that Senhora Hughes had in her possession an article by Angela Felton, that she would ring again in half an hour for the Villa Maranon's phone number and that, if she was refused it, then she would be publishing Felton's article in Britain the next day. She hung up.

When she called back some forty minutes later she was struck by how cooperative the Brasilia office had become. Of course she could have the phone number, it had been a regrettable breakdown in communication earlier when it had been withheld. Yes, Senhor Justi hoped she would call.

CHAPTER SIX

The atmosphere at Villa Maranon was extremely subdued. Manuel had broken the news to Roberto that Anna had connected him to Angela Felton and that – worse still – she had a copy of an article written by Angela. They had run through their options for fully two and a half hours. Angela had written many articles, but only one could really damage them. Suppose she had some fairly harmless piece about a moratorium on felling the rainforest, with the consequential rise in timber prices to Brazil's ultimate benefit? Roberto remembered Angela writing that one and her excitement at its conclusion. 'Roberto, listen to this then!' she had gushed. He had listened with as much enthusiasm as he could muster and, while her student contemporaries had hailed it an economic blockbuster, it had been destroyed by a one-minute flick through the OECD's report on the state of Brazil's economy, showing that timber represented just one and a half billion dollars of gross domestic product. An article like that could be brushed away quite easily.

But just two months later, Angela had penned 'The Market Economy – A Future View', a variation on the same theme, except this time she cut the trees down. Not just a few to supply the world with timber, but the whole forest. Timber was not the forest's real priceless commodity to the world at large – it was the air that the world breathed and the water the world drank. This was Angela's argument: that just as the world placed a price on an ounce of gold, or a tonne of grain, or a barrel of crude oil, or a kilo of cotton or beef, equally there should be a price placed on a cylinder of fresh air or a gallon of fresh water. In a world that actually paid for these 'commodities' – these essentials of life – Brazil, with its vast forests the size of Western Europe, would be a major global economic force. The Arabs did it with oil, she reasoned. Brazil could do it with rainforest.

If Anna had this article then there was no hiding from it, and for the Justi brothers this was definitely the worst-case scenario. They would have to do something – merely hoping for the best could end in complete disaster. If the world understood what their only policy really entailed they could have the leading nations threatening military action against Brazil. His support would melt away under the threat of air strikes, naval bombardments and land-force attacks. A vote for Justi would be portrayed by his opponents as a death wish. But what could they do to prevent her printing the article? What could they offer her? Money? A role in their government? Head of Brazilian state television? Neither of them felt Anna would be interested in these options. They were backed into a corner and they knew it. All they could do now was to find out just how much she knew, and then talk to her, reason with her, argue if necessary, and hope to persuade her not to publish. Manuel felt it would be better if he spoke to her – he had got on well with her and felt that Roberto had alienated her. But Roberto would have none of it. If their campaign was to collapse he wanted to be there when it happened. The responsibility was his. Manuel had no choice but to accept his brother's decision but he still felt it was an error.

'She likes me, Roberto. I could explain things as to a friend,' he argued.

'Liking will have nothing to do with it.' It was Roberto's final word on the subject.

They sat in the lounge facing the telephone. In the silence of the room they each thought of the moments that had brought them so close to victory, along with new thoughts about the uncertainty of their futures. What would happen if they lost the race for the presidency? There were no contingencies – there never had been. That morning, Roberto had lain in bed, watching the first rays of dawn glimmer through the shutters, thinking of the twenty years of planning that had brought him this far, to the point where victory seemed inevitable, where a new world order would be ushered in and history would be rewritten. Vain thoughts. Vain thoughts indeed.

The phone finally woke them from their reveries. Roberto let it ring four times.

'Senhor Roberto Justi,' he announced.

'Senhor Justi. It's Anna Hughes from *The International Times*.'

'Ah, Senhora Hughes. Thank you for calling. My Brasilia office said you might be getting in touch.'

'Yes, well there's been a development since our interview yesterday. I have received from my London office a copy of an article by an Angela Felton. Do you know her?'

'A long time ago, yes I did know her. But let me see now, that was almost twenty years ago. Is that the development?'

His voice remained calm. Manuel felt he was coming over far too business-like.

'I believe she was your girlfriend at one time, Senhor Justi.'

'Is this relevant?' he replied.

Anna paused deliberately before continuing.

'I'll come back to that if I may. The main reason for phoning you concerns an article she wrote in nineteen eighty-six. "The Market Economy – A Future View". Are you aware of this article?'

She wondered what Justi was thinking right at the moment she named the article, knowing that the secret of his campaign policy – his only policy – was out.

Roberto placed his hand over the mouthpiece. 'She has the article,' he whispered to Manuel.

Manuel had been staring intently at his brother for the duration of the call thus far. He turned away and, sighing deeply, stared down at the floor instead.

'Senhora Hughes. I am aware of that article,' replied Roberto.

'And she was your girlfriend when she wrote it?'

'Yes. Yes she was....' His voice trailed off.

Anna wanted to make her position clear.

'You see, that article talks of "new factors" and how they could solve the Brazilian debt crisis. It threatens the world with the destruction of your rainforest. And you see how close you were then to the article, Senhor Justi. Too close to it, I'm sure you would agree.'

'Could you hold the line for a moment? I would like a word with Manuel.'

Anna wondered what they could be discussing. There was no way out now for Justi, she thought. What could Manuel do to stop her reporting back to Sir Anthony and destroying Justi's campaign by going to print.

'Anna. It's Manuel here. How are you my dear?'

'How are you Manuel? I think that is the question. And what's happened to your brother?'

'Oh, he's still here but I thought it was time I spoke to you, as I do see you as something of a friend.'

Anna felt she could not let go – not now, not when Justi was so clearly in difficulty.

'Manuel, I think Roberto needs to talk to me. This matter strikes at the very heart of his campaign for the presidency. People have a right to know.'

'Perhaps you could come here to talk to us?'

She wondered if this invitation was a trap. Her own safety and security had to be considered. Going to the Villa Maranon was just too risky. Any face-to-face meeting was too risky. She leant against the side panel of the payphone.

'I can't Manuel.'

'Why ever not?' he persisted. 'We could arrange for a lift if you can't get a taxi. In fact, why don't I come and pick you up personally. Then we can have a good chat about things.'

'It's not that simple Manuel. Please try to understand.'

'Well then, can we come and talk to you? Where are you, anyway?'

'I can't say Manuel. I really do think it best if I can just ask Roberto a few more questions.'

'But Anna, Angela's article. You must not print anything about it. This is so important. Please, I urge you.'

Anna heard the gentle pleading in his voice, it made her feel uncomfortable, almost disloyal. But she could not turn back now.

'Manuel, if Roberto will not talk to me I will publish. The article will be printed tomorrow morning in Britain.'

Manuel turned to his brother who was standing at the window looking out across the city. He did not attempt to cover the mouthpiece.

'Roberto,' she heard him say. 'She will publish tomorrow if you do not speak with her now.'

Roberto stayed silent. Manuel waited for some ten seconds.

'Roberto,' he called again quietly. 'You're going to have to talk to her.'

Roberto turned and walked slowly back to the coffee table. He took the phone from his brother and decided to brave it out.

'Senhora Hughes. Please, I have little I can say to you. I cannot stop you publishing, despite the difficulties I would then face. It is not so much about the outcome of the election – Angela's article was an outline if you like – but the detail has been refined considerably, and I don't believe I would necessarily lose if you published.'

'I think you probably would,' Anna interjected. 'I think if Brazilians knew that you were planning on running the risk of holding the whole world to ransom and cutting down their entire rainforest, they'd probably drop you like a stone. Your opponents would have a field day. They'd suggest a military response from the rest of the world to stop you in your tracks and they'd have world leaders queuing up to agree with them. You'd be history.'

'Believe me, I say again that I am not concerned about the risk to my campaign. Brazilians do not care for their rainforest Senhora Hughes. They'd rather see it put to the saw in any event. At least then it might be of some use to them. As for any military response, well I think that is an extreme position you are taking,' he bluffed. 'As I say, Angela's article is old and lacks the detail. The threat of you publishing is not to me. No, it is certainly not to me.'

'Who is it a threat to, then?' she responded impatiently.

There was a brief silence at the other end of the phone.

'You are worried for your safety, Senhora Hughes? Is that why you won't meet us?'

'Perhaps,' replied Anna, aware that her question remained unanswered.

'On what conditions would you meet with me then?' he continued. 'Perhaps have a fellow journalist present or someone from your own embassy. Maybe we could fly someone of your choice out from London?'

'Why is a meeting so important?' she persisted. 'What can you tell me face to face that you can't tell me now?'

'There is something I need to show you. Something you have to see for yourself. Please, before you publish?'

She noted the hint of resignation in his voice. She thought about conceding to a meeting. What risks was she running? Would they really do anything to her? Could she minimise the risks even if they did intend to harm her?

'Senhor Justi, I would consider meeting with you, but only on these terms.' She paused. 'Firstly, I meet with you alone.'

'Agreed,' replied Roberto.

'Secondly, that you understand that the Felton article, the details of this call, and the time and place of our next meeting will be sent within the next half hour to my parents in England, with instructions that they should pass the information to my paper if they do not hear from me within four hours of our meeting.'

'Agreed.'

'Finally, that I set the venue for the meeting.'

'That is not possible, I'm afraid. You will not know how to find what I want you to see. You will have to trust me.'

'Where are we going then?' she asked.

'When you left me yesterday you asked after the welfare of our street children. I want you to meet some of them, Senhora Hughes. You need to meet them.'

So Al Parks had been right, Anna thought.

'Many live in the sewers beneath the city. To meet them we have to go to them. There is no other way,' continued Roberto.

Anna considered the risks of such a meeting. Justi had agreed to enough for him to be completely compromised if anything happened to her. In addition, she had felt for the plight of the street children when Al Parks had mentioned them; meeting them would satisfy her own interests, too.

'Okay,' she conceded. 'What do you propose by way of arrangements?' she asked.

'You agree to meet, then?'

'Subject to arrangements I'm comfortable with.'

'And you won't publish until after we meet?'

'No. You have my word,' she assured him.

'Perhaps if I drive my own car and pick you up somewhere. Your hotel perhaps?'

She did not want to give away her hotel name; she struggled to think of somewhere that they would both know and that Roberto could drive to without being mobbed by adoring voters.

If it was early enough in the day the Copacabana area should be quiet enough, she thought.

'At eight o'clock tomorrow morning I will be on the promenade by the Avenida Atlantica. I'll be standing directly adjacent to where you had your stage for the rally.'

'I'll be there,' replied Roberto.

She replaced the receiver. She was ninety per cent sure she'd done the right thing. There were always some risks with journalism – it went with the territory – but this was far bigger than anything she'd been close to in the past. Perhaps she was out of her depth completely and just didn't realise it. She felt anxious as she returned to her hotel room, her fears only slightly allayed after speaking to her father, who confirmed that the file had been received but who had been naturally disturbed by the accompanying instructions should she fail to make contact by seven o'clock the next morning. After all, they didn't normally get up until seven-thirty. At least she was the only one worrying, Anna thought as she ordered an avocado salad and a bottle of Chilean dry white wine from room service, before sending the briefest of reports to Sir Anthony.

> *'To: Sir Anthony Duce*
> *From: Anna Hughes*
> *Apologies for not reporting earlier. Am making no progress yet;*
> *will advise you the moment there are any developments.'*

The 'message received' icon flashed on Sir Anthony's monitor. He selected it and muttered 'How disappointing' to himself, as he compared Anna's report to that of the senior MI5 officer responsible for the team of four agents who had been operating round-the-clock surveillance on Anna from the moment she had arrived in Rio.

○

'Where's that piece on Christmas retail sales forecasts?' asked Michael Turner of Piers Ridell-Saunders, his City editor. It was six-thirty in the evening and he had to be at the Royal Garden Hotel in Kensington to meet his contact from the Foreign Office at seven. Time was against him and it had been a particularly trying day, spent mainly with lawyers preparing a defence against a libel suit from Dwight Dart, the leading rock star who had instigated proceedings after *The International* had described his night in a hotel room with four young ladies as a 'romp'. Dart now claimed that he had been taken ill after eating some undercooked seafood and the young women were all nurses. Turner had hired a private investigator who discovered that Dart's nurses were all part-time strippers working during the day for an escort agency called '4s, 5s, 6s'. The mind boggled. But having to defend these cases remained an irritation. Was it even possible to damage the reputation of slugs like Dart anyway? With more concern for their fees than the case, the lawyers felt it was very much in the best interests of the paper to defend all libel suits.

Ridell-Saunders waded through piles of broker reports, articles and correspondence.

'I was waiting for a fax from UBS with their forecast,' he explained, as the pile finally gave way and a mass of papers slipped like a ship's launch over the edge of his desk.

'Balls,' he muttered. 'Can't it wait until tomorrow?'

'The point is, Piers, you believe that everything can wait. Our City pages look like yesterday's copies of *The Times* and *Telegraph*.'

'Nonsense!' retorted Ridell-Saunders. 'I get my fair share of scoops and you know it.'

'When was the last one then?'

Ridell-Saunders sat back in his chair. It had been yet another fine lunch. The claret had been especially good, and he had stayed at the Balls Brothers Carey Lane branch – the City's leading wine merchants – all afternoon. He couldn't really think about anything, he concluded to himself.

'I will make a list and present it to you tomorrow morning,' he flapped.

'Well if I don't see copy on Christmas retail sales in tomorrow's edition then that list had better be pages long,' replied Turner, scooping up the pile of fallen papers and dropping them in front of Ridell-Saunders.

He turned to his assistant editor and gave him a ten-second debrief while putting on his coat, and then left the office. He had to wait five minute for a cab; the journey from Docklands to Kensington was at least twenty minutes on a good run, but as they crawled bumper to bumper along the Embankment he realised it was going to take at least thirty. As they arrived at the hotel, Turner paid the fare and ran up the steps to the entrance two at a time.

His Foreign Office contact was seated in the comfort of a large sofa facing Hyde Park, flicking through the *Financial Times* with a vodka and tonic already half finished in front of him.

'Harold. Terribly sorry I'm late. Traffic was dreadful.'

Harold Treeby, assistant permanent secretary at the Foreign Office, rose to greet him.

'No need to apologise Michael. I've only just made it myself.'

Turner looked at his half-empty glass and thought otherwise. Treeby was something of an enigma. Turner had first come across him when he was a fairly undistinguished middle-ranking manager of the advisory committee to the Treasury. He had watched him progress from there, to

Turner's mind never seeming to achieve very much, yet rising swiftly through the ranks of more capable peers to his current position. But the connections were all there – Eton, Oxford, his father a former Conservative cabinet minister in Heath's ill-fated government of the early 1970s, and now appointed to the 'other house' as Lord Treeby of Atworth. Wheels within wheels. Talent was only part of getting on, and an increasingly smaller part the higher one rose.

A waiter took Turner's coat, along with his order for a scotch and water.

'So how are things at the Foreign Office, Harold?'

'Oh, very much business as usual,' replied Treeby genially. 'Did you get the Felton article?'

'Yes. Thank you very much Harold. Most helpful. Most illuminating.'

The waiter returned with the scotch. Conversation ceased while he placed it in front of Turner on a paper coaster with a small jug of water to the side.

'As I said on the blower, we've got the wind up on this one Michael. Right proper to-do I can tell you.'

Turner poured half the water into his scotch.

'We are off the record?' continued Treeby, suddenly anxious.

Turner looked up from his drink. 'Harold,' he chided, smiling. 'How many times must I tell you – it's always off the record unless I ask you if it can be on. It's that way round.'

Treeby picked up his drink and leant back into the sofa.

'Oh yes. I apologise, but they're not all like you, Michael. Well you need no reminding about that,' he said, diverting his attention to his drink to avoid Turner's eyes. He recalled the horror of the phone call that had initiated his connection with Michael Turner, editor of *The International Times*, and now personal confidant over certain delicate matters that could have been the end of him both professionally and socially. He was forever in personal debt to Turner's discretion over that 'affair'; it had struck him as a frightfully generous gesture by Turner to purchase exclusive rights to the sorry tale and then not to publish. In any matter that he could help Turner in return, he felt a strong obligation to do so.

'As I was saying, the winds are blowing proper storm force. Not just us either,' continued Treeby. He spoke in a hushed voice that made even simple statements such as 'I'll order more drinks' appear clandestine.

'They've all sent the balloons up over it. America, Germany, Japan … and its going to get nasty.'

'Balloons up over what?' asked Turner.

'That Felton piece of course!' exclaimed Treeby, 'All that tree-chopping stuff. We don't like the sound of it one little bit.'

Turner looked at him in quiet disbelief. Treeby was speaking as gravely as he had ever heard him. Surely he wasn't taking the Felton article seriously?

'But it's nonsense, Harold. It's just a complete non-starter.'

'Well we're not taking any chances Michael. If this Justi fellow wins, it may not be such a non-starter as you think.'

'You're kidding,' Turner replied with growing incredulity. The Foreign Office must be mad, he thought to himself. They were making this Felton-Justi stuff sound plausible.

'No kidding. Now, I have the information for you. It's the Felton file. Poor girl. Still, when your number's up and all that....' He passed a brown envelope to Michael.

'What are you saying Harold? Is Felton dead?'

Treeby looked around him. A couple of Arab businessmen were sitting at a small table behind them. He nodded at them while pressing his hand discreetly on the envelope.

'It's all in there, Michael.' He finished his drink and rose to his feet. 'I'd better be on my way. Dinner party at eight old chap. Daren't be late.'

Turner looked at the envelope.

'Thanks Harold. One last thing, does the Foreign Office have any dealings with Sir Anthony Duce?'

Treeby paused in thought.

'What – your boss? No, not to my knowledge, but there's always a lot going on and I wouldn't necessarily be told.'

'Could you make some enquiries for me?'

'No problem. No problem at all. If I find anything I'll let you know.'

'It would be much appreciated, Harold.'

He looked at the envelope again. 'Perhaps lunch next time?'

'Look forward to it. Know a great new wine bar. Marvellous place. Lovely girl serving.'

Turner smiled. 'Well I'll be in touch then.' He shook Treeby by the hand.

After Treeby had left he ordered another scotch and opened the envelope. There was far more information on Felton than he had imagined. That troubled him slightly.

CHAPTER SEVEN

Roberto Justi swung his hired Ford saloon on to the Avenida. The urgency of the situation had distracted him all the way from the Villa Maranon. He had to stop Anna Hughes from publishing. Everything else was in place. General Valto, commander-in-chief of all Brazil's armed forces had, after a number of delays, met with the Justi brothers the previous evening. He confirmed that the military had formed fifteen offshore unquoted companies to front its funding of Justi's campaign. Their date of incorporation was backdated to cover monies already paid over in campaign advertising expenses. The companies and funding were in violation of the constitution, but the military had decided that in this case it was permitted on the grounds of national interest. 'Or hopefully abolition of it,' Manuel had quipped.

The General had not got the joke and, after staring at Manuel for a few moments, he had continued to explain the constitutional position on the funding. This seemed to hinge on two key points: firstly that no one should ever find out, and secondly that if anyone ever did then they would not live long enough to spill the beans. Given the General's straightforward attitude to political threats, Roberto had decided against revealing their potential problems with Anna. The General had also confirmed that the entire Brazilian press was now supporting the Justi candidacy. Roberto avoided asking how this had been achieved; he did, however, have visions of editors receiving visits from sinister small gangs carrying automatic weapons and delivering death threats against the panic-stricken editors' wives and children. He dismissed this vision as extreme.

After the General had left Roberto had the usual argument with Manuel about the involvement of the military. Manuel had always been against it, principally because of its historic role in Brazilian politics. For Manuel, democracy was a concession by the military and tended to last only as long as the military felt it should. 'They will take over everything Roberto. You will become their puppet,' he had often warned. Roberto agreed the situation was not ideal, but argued they had little choice. Who else would fund the campaign – all thirty-seven million US dollars of it? Who would provide vital influence in the media? And if he came to power, how could he ever achieve his aims without the positive support and active involvement of the military machine? He had been surprised by their keenness to become involved. He thought back to his first meeting with General Valto. Did ending Brazil's debt mean more money for tanks, planes and frigates? The deal was done in an instant.

Roberto glanced along the Avenida and saw Anna, a lone figure, a few hundred yards away. He pulled up alongside her.

She walked around the car to the passenger door, which he had opened for her.

'Good morning, Senhor Justi,' she said, slipping into the passenger seat.

'Good morning,' he replied, his head turned back over his shoulder as he pulled out into the light traffic.

'You are wearing clothes you don't mind ruining?' he enquired without looking at her, as the car turned left, away from the beach and towards the centre of Rio.

'I wouldn't say I don't care for them, but it won't matter that much,' she replied, looking down at her Dior jeans.

'I have overalls for you,' continued Roberto, 'and rubber boots too.' He pointed behind him, and Anna turned to see some faded green overalls and black wellington boots on the back seat.

'And you know they'll fit?'

'No,' he replied. 'No, I could only guess.'

They drove the rest of the way in silence. The smart areas of Copacabana gave way to increasingly poorer areas, high tenement buildings towering above them, washing strung across rusting balconies on every floor. Men, young and old, sat in the morning sunshine, leaning against graffiti-covered walls; mothers and grandmothers struggled with shabbily dressed children on their way to school.

Roberto took a final turn into a deserted cul-de-sac with derelict houses on one side and rough open ground on the other. He pulled over and parked.

'This is it.'

They got out of the car and Roberto opened the rear door to remove the overalls and boots.

'What size shoe?' he asked, checking the soles for a size number. Anna looked at him; he stood over six feet tall, whereas she was five foot nine.

'The smaller ones I guess,' she replied. 'I'm sure they'll do.'

He held out the smaller pair while Anna put on the overalls. They were at least two sizes too big. She turned up the legs and rolled up the sleeves; it was manageable, she thought to herself. To her relief the boots actually fitted. Justi fetched two torches from the car and gestured towards a manhole cover in the middle of the street.

'Ready?' he enquired, as he tested the torches. She nodded and followed him to the cover. He bent down, gripped the pull-bar, lifted it up and then sat down on the edge. He shone his torch down into the tunnel below.

'It's a drop of about five feet, Senhora Hughes. I'll help you down.' He dropped into the tunnel, then looked up at her. Anna sat on the edge, turned round and slithered into the hole. Roberto handed her a torch, then leaned outside to replace the cover.

Anna fumbled to turn her torch on. It was now pitch black and the smell was overpowering. She placed her hand across her mouth and nose, trying to breathe through her mouth to cope with the warm stench of raw sewage, running some six inches deep around her feet. The smell still gripped her; the gases were choking and inescapable. She began to feel she couldn't breathe.

'Are you all right?' she heard Roberto ask. Anna concentrated on breathing normally but her stomach wrenched. Vainly she tried to stop it, embarrassed about her reaction, but she retched again. Bending forward she vomited four times, unable to catch her breath between each lurch of her stomach. She needed air. Half-choking she gasped for breath.

'Senhora Hughes. Shall we return above ground?' Roberto was clearly concerned.

'I'm sorry.' Anna coughed, the stench cutting the back of her throat but no longer choking her. 'I'm very sorry. Most embarrassing.' She spluttered the words between small bursts of coughing while she fumbled for a tissue in her pocket. She mopped her brow gently and wiped her mouth.

'I'm feeling okay now. Please, let's go on.'

'The smell can be overpowering. It took me a few visits before I could really cope with it,' consoled Roberto, touching her arm gently as he did so.

'Quite,' she replied.

Roberto shone his torch along the tunnel and Anna saw the brickwork of the walls fading away into the darkness, the sewage flowing between them like a tiny polluted stream.

'We'll go this way,' he said, as he moved off to follow his torchlight.

They walked in silence, with just the sound of their boots wading through the sewage. Anna looked around her but there was no relief from the rows of bricks – standard-sized bricks in poor condition, chipped at the edges with flaking, discoloured red and brown fronts and crumbling pointing.

After five minutes Justi stopped. The channel ran into a small square chamber, where the ceiling was higher and numerous tunnels ran off in different directions. Anna stretched her neck, stiff from stooping. Roberto shone his torch into the start of each tunnel. In the half-light of his torch's side-beam Anna noticed something move in the far corner. She swung her torch in the direction of the movement and the light caught the staring eyes of three large rats, gorging themselves on a sanitary towel.

Roberto had turned towards a tunnel on their right.

'Did you hear anything then?' he asked her.

'Nothing,' she replied.

'Listen again.'

Anna tilted her head. She heard the quiet trickle of the sewage flowing around their feet.

'Voices, Senhora Hughes. From down there,' he whispered.

She listened again. Yes, there was the sound of voices, high pitched.

'Children's voices?' she enquired quietly. He noted the surprise in the question.

'Yes.' He swung his torch around the chamber. 'Countless children, for whom this is their home.'

They stood silently. Anna found it almost too difficult to believe that children could ever be found in such appalling conditions, let alone that these putrefying sewers could be their home. Roberto moved off down the tunnel. Anna waited a few moments before following. How could anyone live here?

She struggled to take in the dark enormity of it. It was surreal.

After a few hundred yards Roberto stopped to listen again. The voices were quite close now. He beckoned to Anna to come closer to him.

'Please stay near me,' he whispered. 'Some of them are already murderers. Violent crime is a way of life. Please, even if you think they are just children remember this. Eight-year-olds carry weapons; it is another world.'

Anna was struck by his matter-of-fact manner that neither condoned nor condemned. They moved closer. She could make out some of the voices, babbling away in Portuguese; a boy, a girl, then another girl and another. The tunnel curved round to their right. Suddenly the voices died and Roberto signalled Anna to stop.

'We are not the police – we're from welfare,' he called out in Portuguese.

A boy's voice called back to them from the darkness.

'What did he say?' asked Anna.

Roberto smiled at her. 'He says they have knives and a gun.'

They moved forward around the bend in the tunnel. Their torches picked up a long pile of bricks that had fallen into the sewer floor. Four pairs of little dirty legs dangled from a ledge in the space left by the fallen brickwork.

'Ola!' Roberto called.

The face of a young girl appeared from the wall, blinking in the torchlight. She dropped barefoot from the ledge to lean against the tunnel wall, staring intently at them. She had a harrowed expression, her eyes deep-set, her cheeks hollow, her short black hair dirty and knotted. Anna looked at her tattered dress; it was nothing more than a torn, oversized and badly stained yellow t-shirt. She could only have been ten years old.

'Have you any money?' the girl asked in Portuguese. Anna tried to understand, once again feeling the desperate gulf of differing languages. Justi took a bar of chocolate from the inside pocket of his overalls and held it out to her. The girl turned to the other children and gabbled in Portuguese. She walked forwards, staring more at Anna than Roberto, and took the chocolate. Returning to the others, she ripped off the wrapper and, after taking half the bar for herself, passed the remainder to the other children on the ledge. Justi moved very slowly towards them, speaking softly.

'This is Senhora Hughes. She works for a newspaper and would like to write a story about you.'

One by one the children leaned forward – not the smiling faces of children, but faces with adult expressions, where hope had long since died. They stared intently at Anna as she followed Roberto to finally stand in front of them. The same girl to whom Roberto had just given the chocolate pointed at Anna.

'Have you any money?' she asked.

'She cannot speak Portuguese,' replied Roberto. 'She only speaks English.'

The girl did not understand.

'She speaks like Americans,' he explained.

The girl nodded. Roberto turned to Anna.

'Have you anything for them?' he enquired.

'I have some money, but it's dollars. Will that be any use?'

'No. No one will accept dollars from them. And they won't use them either. They'll be picked up immediately by the police, who will say they must have robbed a tourist to get them.'

'I don't have anything else, I'm afraid.'

Roberto explained the situation to the girl. She stared at Anna with an uncomfortable gaze, then spoke again to Roberto, pointing at Anna's neck.

'She wants your necklace,' Roberto told her. 'If you want them to talk to you, you'll have to give them it.'

'But it's worth over five hundred pounds. Don't you have anything? I'll settle with you later.'

'I'll try.'

He spoke again with the girl for about a minute. Anna smiled at the other children. They simply stared back at her.

'They won't settle for anything less than your necklace. The girl wants it for herself; there is a boy she loves who doesn't care for her. She says that with that necklace he'll love her.'

Anna looked at the girl. Was the interview really worth that much? The girl would probably only swap it for a few cruzado-reals. Reluctantly, she removed it and handed it to the girl, who held it up for the others to see.

'Ask them their names,' Anna requested.

'Paulo, Sofia, Maria and Christi,' replied Roberto in his role of interpreter, pointing to each child in turn.

'Why do they live here?'

'They say that their parents deserted them and they tried living on the streets but a friend of theirs was shot as he slept in a doorway, so they feel safer living down here.'

'What do they do about going to school?'

Roberto turned to her, not even bothering to ask the question.

'What do you think, Senhora Hughes?'

She felt awkward again. It was hard to think what to ask them. What did they want to do when they grew up? Where did they want to live? What were their favourite games? The reality of their circumstances began to hit her. They would not grow up. Not here. They would all perish; none of them would live to see adulthood. The terrible truth of their plight dawned on the darkness of her conscience. She looked at them in their dishevelled rags; four little lives devoid of hope, bereft of a future. She saw how much wider their eyes had become, living in the permanent darkness of the sewers. They were always staring, staring at her as if she was some strange creature, some odd exhibit in a shop window. They had no fear for they had nothing to protect. Their eyes had no pleading in them – this was their lot. Not for them the happiness and innocence of childhood, the love and care of a mother and father, the friendship of brothers and sisters, the doting affection of grandparents. Not for them the freedom of fields, rivers, parks and pools, of the eternity of the sky and the infinity of the stars. This was their lot, before hunger or disease or a police bullet took them from it and they passed into a world where their spirits could find again the freedom that their current lives had so comprehensively crushed.

'Senhora Hughes? Any more questions?'

Anna shook her head.

The girl, Sofia, who was still clutching Anna's necklace, started talking to Roberto, pointing up the tunnel.

She wants you to see her friend, a little way from here,' Roberto told Anna. 'Will you go?'

Anna nodded. The slight figure of Sofia moved off into the darkness of the tunnel, leaving the other children perched on the ledge. Anna gave them a little wave, but they stared as impassively as ever back at her. She shone her torch away from them, leaving them again in the darkness of their continual night and followed the girl and Roberto.

Every now and then Sofia would call out her name – a kind of unofficial password in this underworld of all underworlds – as they approached other groups of children sitting or lying on similar ledges above broken brickwork. There were hundreds of them as they continued to move slowly up the tunnel. Some were in complete darkness, others had small candles burning demurely in the blackness. Some of them were so small, they could not have been any older than four years old, thought Anna.

Sofia finally reached her friend. She was a girl of about thirteen, Anna guessed – evidence of breasts swelling under a makeshift dress consisting of a small green raincoat. Unlike the other children, she was pacing up and down the tunnel, her bare feet treading through the sewage with no more concern than if she had been paddling in a clear stream in the open air. She was clutching a bundle of rags.

There was a short, heated exchange with Sofia, culminating

in tears coursing down the girl's cheeks as she hugged the rags closer to her. Roberto listened attentively to the two girls.

'It's about her baby.' Roberto turned to Anna. 'Sofia is telling her to come with us and see a doctor because her baby is sick, but she won't come. She's worried that if she leaves the sewers the authorities will take her baby from her.'

'Her baby is that bunch of rags?'

'Yes.'

Anna could not believe it. Children were actually being born into this environment; it surely wasn't possible. But here, right before her, was the evidence. A young mother, a child mother even, bringing life into this stinking filth, this abject deprivation. She looked with an aching heart at the pathetic sight in front of her; the love of a mother for her child persecuted by a world above of winners and obliterated by a rat-infested, disease-ridden world of losers below. She checked herself. No. These children were not losers, they were never given the opportunity to win, denied the oxygen of opportunity, the elixir of hope. Anna thought of the arguments of economic necessity, of austerity programmes to reduce a nation's debt and encourage enterprise. Enterprise? She recoiled from the thought she had for years so readily embraced. Enterprise that creates this? Winners and losers were one thing, but should these children really be the losers? And if this was losing, who could stomach the guilt of winning? She bit her bottom lip to control the tears filling her eyes.

'Senhor Justi. This is tragic.' Her voice quivered.

'She wants you to look at the baby. It's a little boy. Sofia has now told her you're a doctor.'

Anna took the bundle of rags from the young mother. There was hardly any weight; his eyes were closed. She pulled back the pieces of cloth that covered him. The tiny creature's skin hung from his little frame as he lay lifeless in the cradle of her left arm. She felt his cheeks; they were cold. Alarmed, she felt for a pulse on the his wrist, but she could not find one. She placed her ear to his chest, but could hear no heartbeat. The child was dead. Anna sighed deeply, submerged by a sense of complete desperation, and finally the tears began rolling down her cheeks. She looked at the young mother and lost herself in the desolation of her eyes.

'The little boy is dead,' she pronounced quietly, handing the baby to Roberto, then holding her head in her hands. She could hear Roberto speaking softly to the young mother. She heard her plaintive cry and looked up to see the child kneeling in the trickle of sewage, tenderly kissing her dead baby.

Can this be life? thought Anna, as she watched her own tears fall into the raw sewage around her feet. Could the purity of her tears make this putrid brown stream run clear? But the tears became as polluted as the sewer itself the moment they touched the surface.

She looked at Roberto, his arm around the young mother, offering the consolation of a father. Her heart went out to him. At least he had a passion for change – for humanity. He understood winners and losers. She knew she could no longer win when losing took people to such depths of despair and heartache. Publish against Justi? Never. Her heart had gone completely from the assignment.

'I think we have seen enough,' Roberto said to her quietly. They walked away from the young mother, still clutching her baby. Sofia was talking to her, the other children gathering round, listening.

Roberto and Anna did not retrace their steps completely. He located a different manhole cover and, feeling for gaps in the brickwork, pulled himself up to remove it. Anna turned away from the blinding daylight. Gradually, she focused to see Roberto reaching down from the street above. She took his hand and felt him haul her to the surface.

'Stay here, I'll fetch the car,' he said.

He returned a few minutes later to find Anna with her overall and boots already removed.

'If you don't mind I'll just grab my shoes and find my own way back,' she told him, offering a weak smile before opening the passenger door to reclaim her shoes from the foot well.

She looked at Roberto. His face was drawn, knowing that he had run out of time to talk further with her, to cajole, to persuade her on the subject of the article.

Reading his thoughts, Anna made her feelings clear.

'I would like to help you, Senhor Justi.'

He held out his hand to her. With her shoes in one hand she had to cross hands to take his. He clasped it gently.

'Please Senhora Hughes, if you want to help them, please do not publish.'

'Don't worry. It would be the wrong story,' she replied.

She had decided to return to England on the next available flight. She would tell Sir Anthony that she had got nowhere with the assignment. She was too choked to explain her intentions to Roberto; she was unable to tell him anything at all. She smiled sadly, withdrew her hand, put on her shoes and walked away from him.

CHAPTER EIGHT

'Coffee, gentlemen?'

'Most kind, Sir Anthony,' replied Mark East, the US embassy security secretary.

The German and Japanese security secretaries nodded in agreement. Maureen poured. 'White with'; 'Black with'; 'White without'. Sir Anthony's was poured without questioning. She left his office.

'Not good, gentlemen,' said Sir Anthony, pulling two files in front of him from their previous position to the right of his desk. 'Miss Hughes has rather gone against us I'm afraid.'

He passed a stapled report to each of them.

'You will see on page one copies of her daily reports.'

A copy of Anna's note was provided, along with the final report sent after her visit to the sewers, which announced that she had found nothing of any value, had no prospect of meeting Justi and was therefore returning to England.

East laughed. 'So what was she doing in Rio?' he commented.

'That's on pages two to six,' Sir Anthony replied.

They turned and flicked through the reports from MI5. Meetings with Justi were all detailed. Times, places, any conversation capable of being recorded. Transcripts of all her phone calls from her hotel room. A transcript of her conversation with Justi from the payphone, in which she revealed she had the Felton article. They had been unable to record what Justi had said, but enough could be gleaned from Anna's side of the conversation in any event.

'I think it fair to say that Miss Hughes has been somewhat minimalist with her reporting. And we need to consider if her return to the UK under a clear pretence is now an escalation of our current problem over Justi. I know my government is fast losing patience.' Sir Anthony leaned back in his chair. 'Where are yours on this now?'

The German secretary, Teit Langer, replied first.

'Clearly they have not seen this document, Sir Anthony. But they will be most alarmed by it. The election is now days away – not weeks or months any more – and we know no more than we did a week ago. It is a growing crisis.'

'More importantly, we now have Anna Hughes as a potential convert to Justi's cause. This report proves she now knows about the Felton article and that she's met Justi over it,' added East. 'I mean, look at this transcript of her call to Turner, page four. She actually believes Justi has a case!'

He waited for them to find the extract before reading selected pieces out loud.

'Listen to this. Second para – and I quote her –

'If Justi comes to power, he has the geographical infrastructure. He has the rainforest.

'And a few lines further down….

> *'Just say he did try it Mike. Say the world couldn't stop him. Could he then break the banking system? If the deal was to cancel Brazil's debts how many banks would go under?*

'Well, at least she doesn't understand whose banks we're really worried about. But again, next para, just listen to the woman.

> *'But it's not like that. He's not going to poison anything. It's about Brazil's own forests and what Brazil wants to do with them is surely up to Brazil itself.'*

Sir Anthony interjected. 'It actually gets worse. Look at what she says towards the bottom of the page.

> *'That's the whole point. Why should Brazil just give the world all that water and all that oxygen? Why shouldn't we pay for the air that we breathe and the water we drink? For nothing, yes, Justi's right. Why for nothing?*

'And then a few lines later….

> *'It's not blackmail. If that's what you think, then it's you who's off the pace, Mike. More importantly what can the world do about it? That's the real point.'*

The room fell silent.

'And next she denies all knowledge and returns to the UK.' East took the words out of Sir Anthony's mouth.

'That's the long of it, isn't it?' continued East, looking at each of them for agreement. They all nodded.

'So now what?' He waited for a response from the others. None came.

'Well, what do you reckon, Teit?' he asked.

'I think our options are now extremely limited. Hughes was our last roll of the dice. Are the military funding Justi? We still don't know. Are they aware yet of our investigations? How long before Hughes tells Justi of our interest?'

'It would appear that the Brazilian military is still unaware of our interest,' replied Sir Anthony. 'MI5 report very little security around Justi. They also mention that this concurs with the CIA's findings.'

East motioned to him to continue.

'I think if we take a look at our options now, gentlemen, we are in a corner. Hughes is a major threat. All she has to do is tell Justi that we have some kind of covert action running and his security net will tighten to the point that we can't impregnate it.'

The Japanese secretary, Takito Yashmani, spoke up.

'Sir Anthony. You know the position of my government. We do not believe that we can support every option, particularly the option I believe you are now suggesting.'

They all listened to him carefully, making sure that they heard him correctly as he struggled phonetically to speak in English.

'What do you suggest?' replied Langer. 'Do nothing? I

mean, just sit back and let Justi bring us all to our knees. Is that an option?' He turned directly to Yashmani.

'How many banks can you afford to lose? Let's say that the Justi thing escalates … that he actually pulls off his little stunt. What then if the US can't afford to pay the interest on her debt? How many banks will you have left? The problem with this is that Justi might – and I only say might – bring the whole financial system down. Frankly, he has to be stopped. We just can't run that sort of risk.'

Yashmani went quiet. Japanese institutions had invested trillions of dollars in US treasuries. If the US could not service interest payments on this, he knew their banking system would collapse. He looked at Langer. Germany, too, could not survive that.

'It's the same for you,' he replied curtly.

'I know that,' replied Langer, his voice increasingly strained. 'Yes, we will have no banks left. None, repeat none. We'll have queues of depositors just like in the Thirties; but there'll be nothing to pay them with this time. It won't be a run. They'll raze them to the ground this time.'

Sir Anthony sought to calm things down, although he admitted to himself that his guests had every reason to voice such concerns. Justi spelt disaster to global financial markets.

'If I may be so bold as to bring our minds back to a solution to the Justi issue,' proposed Sir Anthony. He waited for the room to quieten. 'We have no choice left now.'

East nodded.

'But we all have to agree to this,' Langer responded, looking at the Japanese secretary.

'Do we have your support?' enquired Sir Anthony of Yashmani, who was still flicking through the report, looking for an alternative to the apparent *fait accompli* being presented to him. None appeared, but this was a report from the British. Was it to be trusted? If it was an exaggeration, or a fabrication even, then what? The election was a matter of days away now. There was no time to substantiate it; neither was there time left to sit back and do nothing. If Justi became president, if the military was backing him, then the world would be held to ransom. But Justi was so crucial to his own success. That was the point.

'You all still agree that without Roberto Justi this threat is hot air?' he asked.

'If the military is behind him then that's the long and short of it. They won't understand all the economics of Justi's plan – not the politics of it all on a world stage – they'd never front it,' Sir Anthony replied.

'And Manuel Justi?' continued Yashmani.

Sir Anthony and East laughed mockingly, amused by the idea of Manuel Justi running anything, let alone a national state, and a national state about to take on the world at that.

'I think you can assure your government that the best possible outcome is for Manuel Justi to succeed his brother,' said Sir Anthony, smiling broadly.

'He's a wine sop as well. If his brother was taken out he'd slip over the edge in no time,' East added.

'And your Miss Hughes?' asked Yashmani as they were

shown to the lift some twenty minutes later.

'We have no options there either,' commented Sir Anthony matter-of-factly. 'Unless any of you can think of something else for her?'

They were still smiling at this thought as their chauffeured cars returned them to their embassies.

○

Anna awoke to the sound of her own voice being played back on the answerphone. She fumbled for her bedside lamp and, after a few attempts, turned it on. It was six-thirty in the evening. She still felt very tired; the jet lag had not worn off and she had only been asleep for four hours. She pulled the duvet round her. The flat was cold, as the central heating timer was still set for her usual work pattern, which involved returning from the office at about eight. Still, it was good to be home she thought as she hit the playback button. The tone came. Turner started speaking.

'Hello Anna. Hope you've returned home safely and this hasn't disturbed you. Anyway, now you're back I don't know if you're still running with this Justi thing, but I have the Felton information for you and....'

She picked up the phone extension by her bed.

'Mike, it's Anna.'

'Ah, you're back!'

'And tired,' she replied yawning. 'I've only had four hours sleep in the last thirty. Anyway, I'm sort of interested in the

115

Felton stuff but it's more of a personal thing now.'

'Did you meet Justi again?'

'Yes.'

'And?'

'And I don't think he's half the threat I made out to you on the phone the other day.'

She had already decided to play Justi down to Sir Anthony and anyone else who showed an interest until after the election.

'I'm pleased to hear it,' Turner enthused. 'I was getting worried that you were going down a dead end over it all.'

'Yes. Still, there we have it. Back to real politics tomorrow,' she replied.

'It's PM question time and it should be a cracker. Labour are in a lot of trouble over yet another defence order.'

Anna tried to show interest but it was difficult. Who cared about British politics, or any run-of-the-mill politics for that matter? She knew she had to, but the politics manifested in Roberto Justi still dwarfed her thinking.

'Can't wait,' she responded with a yawn.

'You ought to get some more sleep. But guess what happened to Felton?'

'I give in.'

'She died two years after that article. How about that then?'

'Dead? Angela Felton is dead?'

'Yes. Fell fifteen floors from a hotel room in New York.'

'Fell?' Anna repeated.

'Well there was nothing to suggest otherwise.'

'Did the balcony give way or something?' asked Anna, her

adrenaline level rising rapidly and bringing her wide awake in an instant. She sat up in bed half waiting for Turner's reply, thinking about the implications of Felton's death.

'No. She was in New York to address a UN conference on the economics of the rainforest economies. She fell on her first night.'

'So she never spoke at the conference?'

'Not according to the records. But what's the big deal?'

Anna checked herself.

'None really. Just a bit of a shock to hear that she met her end so tragically. We all live forever and all that.'

'Yes. Funny old life. Oh, and she was Justi's wife, not his girlfriend. Still, you'll be in tomorrow?'

'Yes.'

'Go back to sleep Anna. You'll feel better for it.'

'Yes,' repeated Anna, replacing the receiver and staring blankly at her bedroom wall.

Angela Felton had been Justi's wife? She was dead? And she had met her end in circumstances that Anna thought to be more than a little suspicious. She grew worried about the risks she was now running. Could Angela Felton have lost her balance and toppled over a balcony? What were the chances of that? A million to one – probably more than that. So, say she was pushed, or thrown?

Anna's mind started racing. She shook her head, struggling to think of how anyone could pick up a fellow human being, man or woman or child, and throw them in cold blood to their death fifteen floors below. She shuddered at the thought of it, the horror of that moment to Angela Felton: the realisation of the intent of her assailants; the terror of going over. What would you think in those final seconds, as the Earth rushed up at you, as though you were not moving but death's arms were reaching out to you so fast, too fast to even think your farewells to friends and hugs to your loved ones? She tried to imagine the sensation, but she was overtaken by an overwhelming sense of fear for her own safety.

If Felton's death was not an accident it could only have been planned – but who would have the motivation? Surely only the security forces of the US. Or Germany, Japan or Britain, she added to herself, mindful of who Sir Anthony had listed as Britain's 'friends'. After all, these were the people most threatened by Felton's position on economic power. And what a coincidence to be denied the platform for her theory the day before she was due to speak.

Another, more chilling thought seized Anna. If the security forces of the US, or Britain, or any other member of the Western Alliance, were involved in Felton's death then they must have read her original article.

She felt suddenly quite helpless, fighting something she could not see, could not talk to. Something that was as anonymous to her as it must have been to Angela Felton. Something that you met with only when there was no other way out.

Her mind still racing, she again thought of Angela as she opened the sliding doors to her balcony, stepping out on to it to admire the view over Manhattan, then feeling powerful hands grabbing her legs at the knees and throwing her over the edge in an instant. If they had acted then because of Felton's views – because of her article – then they must still know about it. They must already have made the connection to Justi.

'So Duce knew,' Anna whispered to herself. She thought back to her original meeting with Sir Anthony. The Foreign Office letter must have been a fake. So why had they sent her out to Brazil? What was the missing piece that they needed? The name of Justi's backers? It could only be that – there was nothing else to know.

She lay in bed, racking her brains for a reason why this information would be so important. Slowly it dawned on her why the Foreign Office was so interested. If Justi did not have the backing of the Brazilian military then the West could influence military leaders to oppose him. But if he did, there was very little they could do to destabilise him internally – and external influence was risky if it involved outright action. And the reason they could not overtly enquire about the military's position on the Justi issue? Suddenly it seemed blindingly obvious. She sat up in bed and thought back to her exposure to Justi – the Copacabana rally, the party at the Villa Maranon, the personal interview the following evening, the visit to the sewers. There was one common denominator. Justi was not protected. He had no security.

'You bastards,' she said to herself, biting her lip. 'You disgusting bastards.'

With trembling hands she lifted the telephone receiver and dialled Roberto's number in Rio. The phone was engaged. She tried Brasilia, and heard the same tone. She kept trying both numbers. Engaged, always engaged. With a rising sense of panic, she scribbled on a sheet of notepaper.

'For the immediate and personal attention of Roberto Justi.
Phone Anna Hughes in England
+44 207 633 9776
It is absolutely urgent.'

She set the note on her fax machine, entered the Brasilia number and, hugely relieved that the fax at the other end responded with a ringing tone, she pressed 'Send'. The note passed through. She requested a status report, which indicated 'OK'. There was nothing more that she could now do. She was too alert to sleep, despite the physical fatigue. Perhaps a bath would relax her.

She walked through to the bathroom and started to fill the tub. She raised the drawn blind to access the wrought-iron handle of the casement window, opened it slightly for ventilation, and looked out across the narrow garden below, typical of the Georgian townhouses of central London. The lights from the ground-floor flat lit the south-facing patio and then faded across the lawn, turning the trees and shrubs at the end of the garden into dark shadows. Beyond the wall was a small unlit lane, providing vehicle access to the garages and car ports at the back. As she stared into the darkness of the lane her eye was caught by a movement in the shadows. Heart hammering, she tried to focus on the lane, but she couldn't see anyone. She tried laughing at herself but found her own insincerity hollow. As she let the blind down again she suddenly stopped and hesitated. Perhaps she ought to take another look. Turning off the light, she eased the blind back to peer out from the side of the window.

A shiver ran down her spine. Behind the lilac bush in the far corner of the garden crouched a figure. She studied the silhouette for a few moments. Whoever it was stayed motionless, making no attempt to get closer to the building.

Anna moved away from the window and went into the lounge. She pulled back the curtain a fraction and looked across the square to the front. At first she saw nothing unusual, but then her eye caught sight of a man at the end of the terrace. He was of strong build, casually dressed in a bomber jacket, jeans and trainers; he was strolling somewhat aimlessly towards her front entrance.

Panic gripped her. What was she to do? She could not run away – they were already covering the only exits. The idea of fighting them was ridiculous. She had to hide. But where? A small part of her suggested she was reading something into nothing; that she was just jet-lagged and not thinking straight, but these self-ridiculing thoughts held sway for just a second. The roof space was her only chance.

Grabbing a stool from the kitchen she stood on it and slid the loft-access cover to one side. With her left foot caught under the seat, she pulled both herself and the stool into the roof space. She replaced the cover and waited for her eyes to grow accustomed to the darkness.

A few glimmers of light from the street outside shone dimly through the gaps in some misaligned tiles. In the darkness she could just make out a water tank about twenty feet away, to her right. She crawled across the rafters, feeling her way carefully to avoid putting her hand or foot through the ceiling boards, trying to prevent the legs of the stool clattering against the joists as she dragged it behind her.

She eased the lid off the tank. It would be a tight fit but there might be enough room. But what about the displaced water? She checked for the overflow, then placed the stool in the tank and climbed in herself. She felt the water rise around her legs until the overflow was reached. Catching her breath as she submerged herself further, she tried to manage the displacement into the overflow pipe which, fortunately, found its way into a large drain at the end of the terrace, out of sight and hearing of the MI5 officers now closing in on her.

The water was freezing. Pulling the lid down on top of her she knew she would not last in it for more than about twenty minutes.

From the silence beneath her she heard a quick flurry of footsteps. 'Get out of my flat!' she wanted to scream. She listened to the footsteps moving around her apartment. There were definitely two people moving systematically through every room.

Huddled in the cold water, the feeling of fear suddenly left her. She felt as though she was past the point where she could fight against death. There was nothing more she could do; only fate knew her destiny now.

As the minutes passed, she tried to think back over the small chapters of her life, but the images passed fleetingly as though reluctant to stay with her. She thought about God, hoping for a sense of inspiration or comfort, but there was nothing. She only had the same nagging questions about a deity that would allow the world such pain and suffering, yet still be God and saviour. Perhaps if He had made man in his image then it was man's fault, not God's. Increasingly, though, the one thought that transcended all others was that she was becoming numb with cold. She began to worry about hypothermia.

Anna heard footsteps pass under the roof-access cover again, and hoped beyond hope they would miss it. But the steps finally stopped in the hall, right beneath the cover. Her heart sank. She rolled on to her side and curled up in the furthest corner of the tank. She tried to stop shivering, but breathing was becoming difficult too. She worked the foam insulation cover beneath the lid back into place and then lay perfectly still, her head tipped back so only her nose and mouth protruded above the surface of the water. She heard someone pull themselves up into the roof space. She closed her eyes. If she lived, she lived, if they found her she was probably dead.

A man's voice, low and quietly spoken, came from the hall.

'Anything?'

Another man replied, his voice so close to her that fear again gripped her.

'It's pitch black up here. Is there a torch?'

'No. We didn't think we'd need one. FK reckons they cut your mobility down by as much as twenty per cent.'

'Really?' replied the MI5 officer from the roof space. 'Well next time we hit a thirty-five-year-old girlie from civvy street, tell FK we could probably cope with twenty per cent less mobility. It's pitch up here. It's mobility minus the lot now. You're sure she's actually in?'

'We thought we saw her from the back but we're not sure.'

'Leave it then. She's probably out screwing some boyfriend she hasn't seen for a week. After all, we know she didn't get laid in Rio.'

The man in the roof space laughed. 'All I've got up here is a water tank. I'll check it out and then we'll stake the place from the car.'

Anna listened intently to his footsteps picking their way over the joists to the tank. When his hand clasped the lid she breathed in deeply and then silently lowered her head as far below the surface as possible.

The man had his pistol trained on the tank. He peered into the tank, but could see nothing. He pushed away the insulation foam with the end of his pistol. Still nothing. He felt the water.

'Shit – this is freezing!'

Turning, he made his way back to the access cover.

'It's clear,' he said, as he dropped down into the hall.

'Stake it here or back to the car?'

'Not from here. I've done that before. Next thing you know she'll turn up with her mum, dad, granny and six brothers and sisters. Taking that lot out would take some explaining.'

Anna heard the front door open and close quietly. She lifted her face above the surface of the tank and breathed deeply.

A sense of elation passed through her as she climbed carefully out of the tank. She recalled their reference to her time in Rio; sleeping around had never been her thing anyway but they had spoken of it as a point of record. There were so many missing links to it all, so many tenuous connections. But someone had ordered her to be taken out of the picture and in the grey, sinister world that had become the Justi assignment, that answered some major questions. She lowered herself back down into her apartment and crept into the bathroom.

She desperately wanted Roberto to call – he was clearly in very real danger now. She decided to risk using the phone, and dialled his number in Rio again. This time the phone rang and rang. There was no answer. The Brasilia line was still engaged. Turning on her mobile phone, she redirected the land-line to it. There was no choice – she had to leave the apartment.

As she changed her clothes and threw together an overnight bag she wondered what the best exit would be. Having already swept her apartment would they bother to cover the back, particularly when her car – which she supposed they would know of – was parked to the front?

The light was off in the spare bedroom, and from there she could look out over the back garden undetected, if she was careful. There was no sign of anyone, no figure silhouetted amongst the bushes; the garden was clear. She watched the lane for a few minutes, trying to detect any movement. There was none.

Where should she go? She thought about her parents in Devon but decided against it. They might well have that staked out too. Her usual haunts – friends and colleagues – should also be avoided. She decided to check into a hotel in the West End. She would be unlucky to be discovered there amongst hundreds of tourists. But then what?

Anna sat on her bed, suddenly struck by the full force of her future. She had to leave Britain. Whoever these people were, they were not going to just go away. They wanted her out of the Justi equation and would not rest until she was. There was no way back for her now. If she wanted to stay alive she would have to flee the country. And go to where? Only one place suggested itself. She would have to return to Brazil.

Her mind turned again to Sofia comforting her friend in the desolation of Rio's sewers. She looked around her flat in the semi-darkness; she had worked so hard for it all but now it all seemed pointless. Perhaps if she could do something to help children like Sofia she could re-establish the value of her home and her possessions.

She left her apartment, walked slowly down the three flights of stairs to the rear exit and, closing the door carefully behind her, strode swiftly across the garden and into the lane. She met no one and, with enormous relief, she turned into the road behind the square. A cab with its 'Taxi' sign illuminated in bright yellow pulled over as Anna held out her and a short while later deposited her at The Hilton on Park Lane Hotel.

Taking a room on the seventh floor she went straight up to it, glad to be just another person as she made her way to the lifts, through scores of wealthy American, European and Japanese tourists thronging the foyer.

CHAPTER NINE

Anna poured herself a gin and tonic from the mini-bar, using both the small bottles of gin. She downed it in one. Now the adrenaline rush was subsiding, her nerves were causing her to shake violently. She followed the gin with a straight whisky and then studied the display on her phone to test the strength of reception. She was pleased to see all five bars registering. But still no phone call from Roberto.

Suddenly feeling cold again she pulled back the bedcovers and wrapped them round her, sitting motionless, waiting for the alcohol to take effect. Slowly the shaking reduced. She looked at herself in the mirror and sighed deeply. With little else to do, she turned on the television and flicked through the channels. She checked the reception on her phone again. It still showed five bars. She flicked through the magazines in the room: *Johansenn's Favourite Country Hotels*; *London — What's On*; *Finest Hotels of the World*. She could not focus on anything.

Please Roberto, ring, she thought, glancing at her mobile. She flicked through the television channels again, unable to concentrate on any of the programmes. Flicking to the Teletext news, she read down the headlines:

'US demands trade embargo in the Gulf p104
President Hall veto threat over Congress welfare reforms p105
Hull 600 jobs boost from Sony, Japan p106
New Vauxhall Electric steals show at NEC p 107
Bundesbank supports Euro rate rise p108'

It had been more than twelve hours since Anna had eaten and she suddenly felt hungry. She was hesitant about leaving her room, but knew she could not hide there indefinitely. She phoned down to the restaurant for a reservation, threw back another whisky, and headed downstairs.

Insisting on a table in the far corner of the restaurant, she turned her attention to how best to leave the country. She was certain that MI5 would have international departures at all the main airports covered, so her options were limited. She figured her best bet was to take an internal flight to the small Channel Island of Alderney, and from there fly to Paris and then on to Brazil. The chances of Alderney being on red alert to intercept the political editor of a major British paper were fairly remote. She had visited the island a few years previously, noting its independent spirit, its rise in pro-French sentiment and its pan-European aspirations. It may be a mere drop in the European economic landscape, but it was pro-European, pro-French and therefore by definition anti-British. That mattered more than anything else in terms of influence at the moment.

On returning to her room she looked again at the Teletext headlines. A new item was flashing at the bottom of the screen.

'Brazilian presidential candidate's brother shot dead p109'

She re-read it. 'No, please no.' She paged to the bulletin.

'Manuel Justi, the brother and press officer of the leading candidate in the Brazilian election, Roberto Justi, was assassinated as he left a campaign rally attended by over 100,000 people in Maraba, a city in Brazil's poverty-stricken north-east region. The candidate, who was standing next to his brother at the time of the attack, is reported to be unhurt and is now under tight security from the Brazilian military. Roberto Justi tried in vain to assist his dying brother, but a doctor confirmed him dead at the scene. No one has admitted to the attack and a major police investigation is already underway. The assassin, who eye witnesses claim used an automatic weapon, escaped on a motorbike, which was later found burnt out on the outskirts of the city. Roberto Justi is already set to achieve a landslide victory in the election, due to take place on 15 November.'

Anna sat on the edge of her bed and read it again and again, despair overwhelming her. She thought about Manuel – his warm-heartedness, his sense of life and fun, his passion for Roberto's hopes, his dream of a new Brazil. His irrepressible nature had been taken from this world by a bullet not even meant for him.

Too shocked to cry, too numb to even think any more, searched the other channels for more information. CNN only had the same information as the BBC, with a reporter, not even yet in Maraba, talking from a mobile telephone and getting the responses of some local people, but providing no additional insight as to what had taken place.

Anna looked around her room at the prints in their cheap frames, at the mass-produced furniture that ensured no matter where you were in the world, a Hilton bedroom always looked the same. 'Yes, soulless,' she called out to her image in the mirror. She stared at herself. Her mind wandered. So this was the world that in the past she had strived for; a world that now seemed to have no values, no principles, no belief in what was right. Her feelings were now nothing to do with what she had witnessed in the sewers of Rio, they were about what she herself had seen in London, from the freezing cold of her own water tank and now on page 109 of BBC Teletext. And what had these people achieved? She was still alive; Roberto was still alive. All they had done was take the life of a man who she knew meant precious little to them dead or alive.

She drank the last whisky neat. Despair turned to anger. Who were these people that treated the lives of others with such contempt? What right did they think they had to maintain their power by eliminating, in such a cowardly way, their opponents? She picked up the phone and dialled nine for an outside line. To hell with the risks she thought to herself. So what if she died? Her call was answered.

'Sir Anthony?' she enquired.

'It is.'

'It's Anna Hughes here.'

'Oh, Miss Hughes. How nice to hear from you. Nothing doing in Brazil then?' He wondered how she had escaped MI5, but now that Roberto Justi had also survived and was surrounded by security, she was no longer a major threat. He could play this in a very straightforward manner.

'Not really, Sir Anthony. Sorry I didn't call you yesterday but it was all very hectic, arranging flights and things.'

'Think nothing of it. Is there a reason for your call now?'

'Well yes, I do have some really rather good stuff on Justi.'

'Do you?' he replied, managing to sound interested.

'Do you know of Angela Felton, Sir Anthony?'

He wondered momentarily how to reply.

'The name is familiar. Why?'

'She was Justi's wife and wrote about his "new factors" back in 'eighty-six. Apparently she died two years later.'

'I'm struggling to place her. Still, what else might you have?' His tone was dismissive, expressing his disinterest in the 'new factors'. It confirmed Anna's view that Sir Anthony had known all along about Justi's plans. That said, she still wanted to meet with him. Only the funding issue remained.

'I have a micro-film proving he's not being funded by the military.'

'Pardon. Say again?' She knew she had his attention. 'Did you say you have proof that he isn't being backed by the military?'

'Yes. I have copies of numerous documents on film. Memos, company names, even account numbers; they're all there.'

'Who is backing him then? It's extremely important that I know as soon as possible,' hurried Sir Anthony, aware that proof of non-military funding for Justi would enable America, Britain, Germany and Japan to make representations to the

Brazilian military, explaining that Justi's plans would lead to a conflict that Brazil could never win. They could then bring the West's massive media machines screaming to life all around the world, lifting the lid on Justi's 'new factors', suggesting that any attempt by Brazil to hold the West to ransom over its rainforest would meet with overwhelming military force against the country. The Brazilian military would have to support the West by stating that it would not commit itself to a conflict in defence of Justi, whether president or not, as they would not self-destruct in a conflict in which the odds were stacked against them. Sir Anthony clenched his fist. Yes, Justi's campaign could still be stopped.

'Shall I bring the films over to you then?' Anna asked nonchalantly.

Sir Anthony thought about it; she was but a pretty political editor, hardly a threat to his security. And while he knew she had been the subject of an MI5 hit, in all probability she did not. He already knew she had not been at her apartment when they had swept it; she was probably still completely unaware that a contract had been put out on her and that it had now been removed. A counter strike by her directly against him, therefore, was completely implausible.

'Yes. Films you say. Bring them over then. They may be invaluable items Miss Hughes, you understand?'

'And this time perhaps I can have some of that cognac.'

Her tone surprised him.

'If you would like to, by all means.'

'Oh I would like to Sir Anthony. Very much so.'

He wondered if he had mistaken the suggestion in her voice. She sounded alluring. He paused. Say she came over and one thing led to another, one cognac became two and then three, maybe four; supposing then.... He shook his head; what was the matter with him? Had he forgotten his hideous appearance? It was not possible for anyone to even consider him in a physical sense now.

'So I'll just come on over then?' she said quietly, caressing the words into the mouthpiece.

The tone was there again, he thought. It was hard to mistake it, even though it had been years since any woman had spoken to him in that way.

'Well....' He gave a little sigh as he entertained the thought that she just might be interested in sex. 'Well yes. Okay then. But don't come through main security.'

He did not want anyone to know that he had received a visit from a woman after hours, especially if one thing did lead to another. If anything happened between them it was to be strictly private.

'You'll find a red door to the west side of the building, with a security-code lock,' he continued. 'The number is two two zero nine eight. My private lift is through the small lobby. When you get in just press Start. It automatically stops at my floor and will open on to my lounge. I'll be waiting for you. How long do you think you'll be?'

'No more than fifteen minutes.'

'Good. I'll see you then.'

Anna replaced the receiver, grabbed her coat and left her

room. She asked the taxi to take her to Embankment tube station, not wanting to be traced directly to Sir Anthony's offices. A few minutes' walk from the station and she arrived at the red side door. She punched in the code, the lock clicked open and she entered the building. The lift doors were open. She surveyed herself in the full-length mirror, running her fingers through her hair, sweeping it over her right shoulder to expose the nape of her neck. She touched up her lipstick and undid the third button on her blouse to reveal a hint of cleavage. Dressed to kill, she thought with a wry smile as she hit the Start button.

Sir Anthony was waiting for her with a glass of cognac.

'We meet again, Miss Hughes.'

She took the glass from him and raised it to touch his own.

'We do indeed. But please call me Anna.'

'Your health then, Anna.'

'And yours, Sir Anthony.'

She swallowed the warm liquid in one go. He stared at her in both shock and amusement.

'You like it?' he asked with a little laugh.

'It's wonderful,' replied Anna, handing him her glass. He took it and looked at her somewhat vacantly.

'Well, may I have another?' She touched his shoulder.

'Oh yes, um. Certainly. I'll just go and pour you one. Make yourself at home.' Sir Anthony pointed to the sofa as he left the lounge to revisit the drinks cabinet. His mind whirled with images of Anna naked, inviting him on to her. Strange, unfamiliar thoughts, yet irresistible too. He felt a loss of control. He poured the drinks and hesitated a moment to regain his poise. Returning, he found Anna on the sofa. She patted the seat next to her; he felt uncomfortable yet unwilling to distance himself from her. She was a remarkably beautiful woman – he had thought so at their first meeting. But at the time she had just been extremely polite and businesslike. It was a different Anna Hughes before him now. He hesitated again.

'Are you sure, Anna?' he asked tentatively.

'Because you think your accident has left you unseemly – ugly even?'

He was startled, but she held his stare.

'You think no one could possibly find you attractive, don't you? Which is why you cocoon yourself in here. That is true, isn't it?'

He sat down beside her and stared into his glass, finding it difficult to respond.

'Yes,' he murmured.

'Please look at me, Sir Anthony,' she said softly.

As he turned she reached out her left hand and ran her fingers gently down his face, smiling at him as she did so, successfully containing the repulsion she actually felt.

'I find you attractive. A man of such power and wealth. Women find those qualities stimulating.'

He held her hand to his face as her fingers reached his chin, not wanting her to withdraw it. Touch ... someone had touched him. It was a strange sensation, evoking distant memories of his wife and of other women he had known.

'You are most kind, Anna. Most kind.' He let go of her hand and looked away from her. He had almost forgotten the reason for her visit but, distracted as he was, he needed the information she had.

'I nearly forgot. The films. Where are they?'

'Well actually, Sir Anthony, there is only one film. And I've hidden it.'

'Hidden it? Where?'

'Oh, in here somewhere. When you went to fetch me another drink.'

Sir Anthony looked around his lounge. It could be anywhere. Anna lay back on the sofa and giggled.

'An awful lot of good places to hide a little film.'

'Give me a clue?'

'Oh, very close to you.'

He looked at her. Tilting his head to one side, he smiled.

'And how close might that actually be?'

She gave a provocative laugh and sat up.

'But are you up to finding it? Is that your bedroom?' She motioned towards a part-opened door in the corner of the lounge.

'Do you want to go there?' he asked hesitantly, trying to hide a look of excitement, confirming his hope that she did.

She took him by the hand and led him through to it, pulling him round to face her as they entered, running her fingers through his hair. She moved closer and kissed him, feeling his hesitancy, sensing both his desire and his uncertainty. She stroked his face again.

'Anthony, relax. And enjoy,' she whispered in his ear. They kissed lightly on the lips again. He could not find any words; the situation was almost surreal.

She pulled away from him gently and went to his open wardrobe, in which were neatly arranged some twenty suits, all black or navy pinstripes, and a vast number of double-cuffed white shirts. Tie racks were fastened to the inside of the door; ties, hundreds of ties. Anna pulled a few out.

'All silk?' she enquired. He smiled and nodded.

'All yours?' she added playfully. He laughed.

'All mine.'

'And your favourites?'

He came to stand beside her, kissing her lightly on her neck as he pulled one tie, then another, then another until a pile of twelve lay coiled on the floor in front of them.

'I said your favourites, not your whole collection,' she teased, tilting her head back and kissing him. She felt his hand running down her blouse.

'Perhaps you have an absolute favourite?'

'I'm wearing it.'

She took hold of it and, swinging round, she pulled a little away from him so that the tie tightened. She gave it a few small tugs.

'Well, we'd better take it off then.'

She let it go and watched as he struggled with the knot, finally throwing it from him on to the pile on the floor. She scooped them up and strolled over to the bed, running her fingers through them. He followed her with mounting anticipation. She sat on the edge of the bed and placed the ties carefully to one side. He watched as her delicate fingers undid the buttons of her blouse, his arousal growing as she let it fall from her shoulders. He moved to stand in front of her, his hands clumsily fondling her while she first undid his shirt and then his trousers. Pulling him down on top of her they kissed again, passion and lust now swirling through his head. She rolled over on top of him and sat on his chest.

'Games, darling. Games time now. The film, remember?' She smiled at him and he nodded. Taking one of the ties, she secured it to his right wrist.

'Now I wonder if you can find it without using your hands.'

Sir Anthony laughed. Anna kept smiling as she fastened another tie to his left wrist. She turned around, still sitting on top of him.

'And without using your feet,' she continued, wriggling gently and feeling his hands pulling at the zip of her skirt as she fastened a tie to each of his ankles. She slipped off him and stood up at the side of the bed. She pulled her skirt down slowly, hips swaying gently.

'Ready to play?' she asked, unclipping her bra and letting him remove it completely. He fondled her breasts and she pulled his head down into them.

'I said are you ready to play?' She stepped back from him.

He could only smile. 'Ready,' he replied in a whisper.

'Lie down then,' she whispered back, taking the ties attached to his wrists and securing them to the headboard. She ran her fingers all the way down him. He closed his eyes and moaned slightly as her hands moved between his legs. The moment was brief as Anna moved down to his ankles, which she tied to the two posts at the foot of the bed. He lay spreadeagled before her. She moved gently back on top of him and knelt astride his chest.

'How silly. I never undo my own underwear,' she said as she bent forward and kissed him. His mouth was eager.

'Can you help me?' she asked, running her hands over her body and rolling her knickers down gently. He tried to release his hands but could not. 'Please Anthony, perhaps if I get a little closer.' She moved to sit astride his face.

'I'm trying Anna, but your knots are very good,' replied Sir Anthony. She watched as he tried in vain to free himself. The ties held firm.

'But darling, remember the film darling.'

She moved back down him, bringing her face against his, kissing him lightly on the forehead.

'Come on, one last try,' she teased.

She saw the veins of his neck and arms stand up as he strained against the knots of the ties.

'I can't move, Anna. Honestly, I'm stuck,' he said laughing, enjoying the fun of the chase.

Anna got off him and stood at the foot of the bed. He noticed that her manner had changed. She picked up her clothes and dressed.

'Anna? What are you doing?' he asked in sudden panic.

'You sad, sick, ugly *bastard*,' she said quietly, emphasising each word so that it became a statement in its own right.

Sir Anthony still could not quite figure out what was happening. Was this part of the game? He wondered what he was supposed to say in reply. He laughed nervously.

'Oh, Anna – it's part of the game, I see.'

Anna continued staring at him impassively.

'What game?' she replied.

His smile subsided, anxiety creeping across his face.

'Anna,' he said, more loudly. 'Anna. What are you doing? What am I supposed to do now? Why have you dressed? Where is the film? Is this still the game or not?'

'What film?' She picked up the tie he had said was his absolute favourite and moved back to him without speaking. She placed it round his neck and tied a slip knot.

'Oh, it's still the game Sir Anthony,' she stated in barely a whisper, as she tightened the knot round his neck. She stared straight into his eyes as he started to pull in vain against the ties that bound him.

'Stop it Anna. It's too tight, I can't breathe for God's sake.'

She tightened the knot still further. He gasped for breath, his eyes opening wider, his head turning from one side to the other.

'Stop it now!' he tried to scream, his mouth wide open but no sound leaving his lips, his head thrashing. Unable to speak he tried to catch Anna's eye. She had to stop, he thought to himself. She wasn't going to kill him.

She remained strangely calm, watching him writhe, listening to his unintelligible gurgling and wheezing. A minute passed. He grew limp and his tongue hung from his mouth. She watched patiently as he started to convulse, gulping for air, his face turning blue. Finally he stopped struggling and lay still, exhausted, his eyes pleading with her. She watched as he started to slip into unconsciousness, his eyes slowly closing.

'Sir Anthony, you are a murderer,' she spoke quietly into his ear. 'But never mind now because you are going to join Manuel Justi. I believe he is waiting for you on the other side.'

Anna watched until his head fell to one side. She fastened the slip knot and stood up. She looked at him for a further few minutes, feeling neither remorse nor satisfaction. She felt for a pulse. There was none.

She left the bedroom, walked through the lounge and entered his office. She wanted the Foreign Office file. She searched his desk. Nothing. She moved through to the reception area and looked through the three filing cabinets. In the second draw of the third cabinet she found it. Her fax to Justi, sent earlier that evening, was on the top. She read through the minutes of Sir Anthony's meeting earlier that day with the US, German and Japanese security secretaries. The front cover of the file had a date on it – 2004. She went back to the cabinet, there were four other files running in date order: 1988–1990; 1991–1996; 1996–2004. She sat on the reception desk and began reading through them. There were reams of correspondence between Sir Anthony, the Foreign Office and the key embassies in London. She came across Angela Felton's article in the earliest file. On it was a scribbled pencil note: 'M to deal – NY.'

Anna shook her head. She removed papers of interest from the files before returning them to the cabinet, then walked back through into Sir Anthony's lounge and placed them in the inside pocket of her coat.

She left the building the same way she had come in and walked back to the hotel, weighing up the chances of getting the next moves right. It was eleven-thirty when she arrived back at the Hilton.

'I have to leave earlier than expected,' she said to the receptionist. 'I need to get to Southampton airport. Can you arrange a taxi and prepare my account?'

She returned to her room and collected her belongings. Five minutes later the concierge called to say the taxi had arrived. As it drove across Westminster Bridge on to the A3 she stared out of the taxi window. What was she more afraid of? The men who had broken into her flat to kill her, or the fact that she herself had just committed murder? She shrugged her shoulders indifferently. She was a murderer. So what? Who really cared? Sir Anthony had lived by the sword; he died by it. She thought about the following morning. Maureen would hesitate before disturbing Sir Anthony, but she would eventually. Anna glanced at her watch; she reckoned she needed to be out of the country by ten o'clock the next morning at the very latest.

●

'Here we are then.' The voice of the taxi driver awoke her. She looked out of her window. 'Welcome to Southampton Airport' read the sign above the terminal entrance.

The first flight to Alderney departed at seven. The plane carried just twenty passengers and the ticket office, she discovered, did not open until six. She looked at her watch; it had just turned two. She sat down on a metal bench, one of many that stood in neat rows in the middle of the almost deserted terminal. A couple of cleaners were polishing the floor at the far end, slowly making their way across the building. The restaurant was closed, but a vending machine offered hot drinks. Anna walked over to it; both the tea and coffee were sold out. The only available option was beef soup. Against her better judgement she inserted the required fifty pence piece. The machine made various sounds; the clunk of the cup falling on to the vending tray; the dried beef soup powder against the plastic of the cup; the running of the boiling water on top of the soup powder. Anna looked at the mixture, which had lumps of soup powder floating on the surface, and left it on a shelf next to the vending machine.

She slept fitfully on one of the metal benches until six, before buying a ticket for Alderney. She also purchased an onward flight to Charles De Gaulle airport, leaving Alderney that same morning. It raised her hopes of securing a flight to Brazil the same day.

She strolled through customs in Southampton, Alderney and Paris without anyone giving her a second glance. A flight to Rio left Paris later that evening; a direct flight to São Paulo was not available for three days. It wasn't ideal but she could fly from Rio to Brasilia or São Paulo daily; she was certain that Roberto would have now left Rio for his home in São Paulo and that Manuel's funeral would take place there. There was an outside chance he would go to Brasilia, as his office was there and he still had an election to win, but somehow she doubted it. She purchased the Rio ticket. It was now approaching midday. Her eyes felt leaden with sleep, but her mind was still too active. She exchanged some sterling for euros and walked across the concourse to the telephones.

'Mike, it's Anna.'

'Where in heaven's name are you? I've been phoning you all morning,' he exclaimed excitedly.

'Why do you ask? Is there a problem?'

'Problem? It's sensational. Duce is dead. Can you believe it?'

'Dead?' she replied, sounding genuinely amazed.

'Strangled apparently. In his own bloody bed. No one saw anything, no one heard anything. His secretary found him an hour ago; apparently she's really shaken up about it.'

'It's unbelievable. What are the police saying?'

'Nothing officially, but the deputy commissioner spoke with me personally and off the record it's kinky sex. Stretched out apparently and throttled.'

'Heavens no! Can you imagine going with him? It's enough to make you sick.'

'Quite. But anyway I need copy for tomorrow. Well not about how he died, but an obituary. Which is why I've been trying to get hold of you. I need you to do the piece.'

She decided to come to the point of her call.

'Actually Mike, there's something I need to tell you. I'm resigning.'

'Resigning? What on Earth for?' he replied, taken aback.

'I've had enough, that's all. I want a break from it all.'

'Nonsense, Anna. You're just exhausted from the Justi thing. Now come on, get back into the office, pick up the swing of things again. You'll be fine.'

'Not this time, Mike. I'm not fine. My heart's gone from it.'

He detected a tone in her voice he had not heard before.

'Well don't resign. I mean I really do value you Anna. Why don't you take a week or two off and think about it? Perhaps we could meet up and talk things over, eh?'

She sighed. He wasn't relating her resignation to Sir Anthony, that was a relief, but she felt unreasonable in insisting on her resignation – her reason was weak, and they both knew it.

'Okay, Mike. I'll take some time out, maybe ring you in a week or so.'

Her voice was quiet and monotone. He thought she sounded depressed. She replaced the receiver wondering what had become of her life. Within a week the fabric of her values had been shaken by Justi and now her career was over and she had taken someone's life. Was it because of Justi that she could no longer accept the system and its leading players? She felt her mind turning circles, confusing issues and values. She picked up her bag and walked through to the international departure lounge.

Meanwhile, Scotland Yard confirmed to MI5 that strangulation was not uncommon in bondage sex cases; being temporarily starved of oxygen while climaxing apparently heightened the senses. Regrettably in some cases the lack of oxygen could be overdone. MI5 decided to leave the enquiry to the vice squad on the strict understanding that there was to be absolutely no publicity. Sir Anthony had devoted too much of his life to the service of the country to be dishonoured now.

CHAPTER TEN

Roberto Justi's home in São Paulo was even more modest than the Villa Maranon in Rio. A small, box-like affair with a tiny yard behind rusted railings to the front, the garden to the rear slightly bigger and, unlike the Villa Maranon's front yard, boasting a few plants and a patchy lawn. It was a drab place, not helped by Roberto's infrequent visits in recent months.

Military guards were everywhere. The small street to the front was cordoned off and four soldiers were positioned on the villa's flat roof. Ballistics had confirmed that the weapon responsible for Manuel's death was an automatic Bryant 350T, the stock-in-trade weapon of most CIA hits. No matter how remote the chances of a second attempt on Roberto's life, the military were taking no chances now. There were only three days left before polling.

Manuel's death had lifted Roberto even higher in the opinion polls to an unassailable and invincible lead of eighty-two per cent of the vote. Roberto, however, had been more deeply affected by Manuel's death than anyone knew. The brothers had had their moments over the years, and at times

Manuel had irritated Roberto to breaking point. There had been many occasions on which harsh exchanges had taken place, but they had always been close. Manuel had played the caring elder brother to him in his early years, the showman and playboy revered by both Roberto and his friends in their teenage years, as some truly sensational-looking girlfriends were paraded by Manuel in the bars of the small district that was their home on the southern outskirts of São Paulo. The bonds of friendship formed between them in Roberto's late teens as Manuel's marriages failed and he kept reappearing to share Roberto's bedroom in their parents' small home.

Manuel had always been around since then. Since Angela died he had been the only person Roberto could always trust. What he lost from Manuel in terms of his inability to handle the detail had always been more than made up for in terms of unfailing loyalty.

The funeral was due to take place the day before the election, the arrangements kept secret for fear of another attack. Roberto had insisted it should be a strictly private affair – family and friends only. That said, Manuel's children had declined to attend and friends of any substance were practically non-existent. Was he really to be the only mourner at the graveside? He felt again the waves of anguish and loneliness that had beset him in the months after Angela had died. The emptiness, the struggle to get on with life's basics. He hardly felt fit enough to take on a hostile allegiance of leading nations.

Anna alighted from the taxi a hundred yards away from the street cordon. Since her arrival back in Brazil she had tried vainly to contact Roberto; his Brasilia office would not guarantee to pass on any message, verbal or written; nor would they detail his address in São Paulo, although Anna obtained it easily from the Reuters office in Brasilia. She paid the driver and walked slowly towards the cordon. A young soldier leaning against an army jeep watched her approach, his machine gun swinging gently round to point directly at her and cover her approach. Noticing the gun trained on her, Anna offered him her warmest, broadest smile. He grinned back but the gun did not move away. She stopped some ten yards away from him.

'Do you speak English?' she asked him.

He shrugged his shoulders. A few other soldiers moved to stand by him, grateful for a momentary break from the boredom that inevitably crept into round-the-clock blanket security.

'Very pretty,' one joked in Portuguese.

'Voce fala ingles?' Anna asked again.

'Pretty and English,' replied another, again in Portuguese, to the other soldiers.

Hearing laughter coming from the cordon, a short, stocky officer strode down to them. The soldiers noticed him and stopped laughing. He barked an order at them and they each returned to their postings.

'Senhora?' he enquired abruptly of Anna, his head slightly to one side and staring directly at her.

'Voce fala ingles?' she questioned.

'A little. What you want?' he responded in hesitant English.

'I want to see Senhor Roberto Justi.'

'No possible. You will leave.'

Anna looked at him and raising her voice slightly replied purposefully, 'He will want to see me, so I do not intend to leave.'

They stared at each other in a state of impasse.

'Senhora. I have the orders. No possible, no visitors.'

'And do your orders stop you from taking messages?' she enquired. She moved to take her notepad from her bag.

'Do not move, Senhora,' he snapped. She looked up to see the soldiers round the cordon on their knees, their guns trained on her.

'It's only a notepad in here,' she told him quietly. Only one of the soldiers would have to misinterpret a movement for her to be shot.

'Pass the bag. Slowly.'

'Senhor. Do your soldiers understand you? If I lift the bag towards you will they understand?' She stood perfectly still as she talked. He moved towards her and took the bag from her. After searching it he clicked his fingers on his left hand, at which signal the soldiers again stood easy. He handed it back to Anna.

'Thank you.'

'You understand? Security has to, Senhora.'

'Yes. I can understand it.' She scribbled a quick note to Roberto and tore it from the top of her pad.

'Is Senhor Justi at home?' she enquired.

'No can say Senhora.'

'But you will take him the note?'

'Yes, I take the note to the villa.'

'I'll wait right here then,' she stated, holding out the note to him.

The officer looked at her, feeling that there was something about her, a sense of purpose and presence. He took the note, barked his orders to the cordon troops and turned away to Roberto's villa. He passed the two soldiers guarding the entrance, walked through the lobby and knocked on the door of the lounge. Roberto opened it and was somewhat surprised to be handed a note from the captain responsible for his overall security.

'Senhor Justi,
Am at the cordon. I know who killed Manuel. Can we talk?
Anna Hughes.'

He thought for a moment – he wasn't in the mood for visitors, nor was he properly dressed to receive them. That said, he felt obligated. Manuel had a clear soft spot for this English journalist, and if she did know something about Manuel's death....

'Let her through,' he told the captain. He saluted smartly, stepped back, turned briskly and returned to the cordon.

'Senhora, you pass,' he said politely, dropping the red-and-white tape that sealed access to the street. She followed him to the villa's entrance and waited in the lobby as he knocked again at the lounge door. Roberto opened it, thanked the captain and turned to Anna.

'Senhora Hughes. This is a surprise.'

He waved her into the lounge and she took a seat on a faded maroon armchair with sagging cushion and threadbare arms.

'A surprise for me too, Senhor Justi.'

She looked at him, suddenly lost for words. She had no idea what to say; so much had happened. Turning away, she opened her bag and removed the papers she had taken from Sir Anthony's files. He felt her nervousness.

'Perhaps a coffee, Senhora?' he enquired.

'Please.'

He called to his housekeeper for two coffees and then took a seat facing her in a matching armchair that was, if possible, even more the worse for wear than Anna's. One of the arms looked as though it was about to fall off and part of its support to the main framework was broken.

'You say you know something about Manuel's death?'

'Yes. Yes I do,' she replied quietly, somehow unable to look at him. 'Firstly, can I say how upset I was – deeply upset – to hear about Manuel....' Her voice trailed off. She felt strangely shaken as she tried to talk. She fought against sounding emotional in any way but she knew she was struggling.

'It is most kind of you to say so. And most kind of you to come here from Rio.'

'London, not Rio. I've come from London.'

'But I thought....'

'I returned to London after our meeting,' she interrupted him. 'To throw myself back into my work and try to forget about Brazil.'

'But why have you come back then?' he asked earnestly.

She looked up at him, uncertain where to begin explaining what had happened since she left, still confused in her own mind about what she had done and why. Would he even believe her?

Roberto realised there was something different about her. This was not the composed English journalist he had met a few days ago. She was clearly agitated – distressed even.

Coffee arrived, the interruption enabling Anna to regain some of her composure. She took a long sip.

'I'm back because someone tried to kill me. I think MI5.'

Roberto stared at her.

'They tried to kill me, and they tried to kill you, too,' she continued.

The room went quiet.

'I know they tried to kill *me*, Senhora. Well actually the CIA, not MI5. But why *you*? What had you done?'

'Not much. But they'd trailed me out here and they knew I'd met you and I didn't let on that I had. They weren't taking any chances, that's the fact of the matter. It's all in there.'

She passed him the minutes of the meeting between Sir Anthony and the US, German and Japanese security secretaries that concluded with the need to eliminate both her and Roberto. She sat staring at her coffee, drinking it slowly as she heard the pages turn, first one, then two, then finally the third, grateful for the time afforded to sit quietly and gather her thoughts.

'When did you get hold of this?' he asked, re-reading the front page.

'I tried phoning you to warn you – in Rio, in Brasilia. Always engaged. In the end I faxed you.'

'You had this before Manuel died, yes? But it's the same date as he died,' he stated, flitting through the paragraphs again, turning the pages.

'No. I didn't have it then.'

He looked at her.

'So how did you know to warn me, Senhora?'

'I realised that our Foreign Office must already have a copy of Angela's article when I heard about how and when she died. And that meant that they only really wanted to know if the military was backing you, to see if it was actually necessary for them to intervene, if you understand?'

She looked away and ran her fingers through her hair. It was all so difficult to explain, there were so many 'ifs' and 'buts', yet for all that Manuel was dead, Roberto should have been and so should she. That was the sad proof.

'I do understand,' remarked Roberto kindly. 'I do. I've understood from the day Angela died. I've always believed that the CIA murdered her. Of course by the time I got out to New York – you did know she was killed there?'

Anna nodded.

'Well when I got to New York the whole thing was already buttoned down. She'd fallen off her balcony, that was all there was to it. I was shown her room but they'd already cleaned it, there was nothing. They had even packed her case – it was in the concierge waiting for me to collect it. But I knew. I knew they had wanted to silence her from the conference.'

'Were there any threats beforehand?'

'No, nothing. But how could Angela fall from a balcony?' He stood up and walked to the window, where he gazed out across the yard.

'Angela was quite small, about five foot three. The top rail of the balcony was four foot high.'

The room went quiet again. Anna looked at the pencil note on the copy of Angela's article taken from Sir Anthony's office. She turned towards Roberto.

'Perhaps you should see this.'

He looked around and then walked back to her.

'It's Angela's article. I know it backwards,' he replied.

'It's the pencil note on it you may find interesting.'

Roberto took it from her and read the note, 'CIA to deal – NY'.

He sighed deeply and then returned to his chair.

'Nothing surprises me any more,' he stated, his tone subdued. 'They will stop at nothing. They have too much to lose, that is why. And they tried to kill you, Senhora?'

Anna nodded. 'Just an hour or so before Manuel, I think. They came to my flat.'

'And you escaped?'

'Not really. I hid,' she replied, feeling reluctant to talk further. Her experience seemed suddenly trivial compared to what Roberto had gone through. 'Oh, and they have your Brasilia office tapped. I found a copy of my fax to you on the file,' she continued, moving the conversation away from herself and handing him the fax copy.

Roberto read it and called in a guard, who was sent to fetch the captain. Roberto issued instructions to sweep not just his Brasilia office, but all the properties he stayed in.

'What do you intend to do now, then?'

Anna looked at him blankly, unsure what to say. She wanted to help him but she wasn't Brazilian, she was an outsider.

'I'll come back to that then,' Roberto continued. He looked at the papers again.

'Where did these come from? You mentioned your Foreign Office. Are these their copies? I note from the minutes that Sir Anthony Duce represented your government. Are they his papers then?'

Anna had to deflect the question somehow, but it would be difficult – the minutes were too recent. How could she be in possession of them unless they had come from Sir Anthony himself? She looked at Roberto and shrugged her shoulders.

'You know he's dead Senhora? Sir Anthony I mean.'

Anna nodded.

'I'm told he died just a few hours after Manuel. And that fax shows a time of about two hours before Manuel died.'

They looked at each other for a few seconds.

'And until Manuel died you were as much on their hit list as I was,' he continued slowly, working through the times in his mind. And you would have known that.'

Anna did not respond.

'You went to meet with him?'

Anna said nothing. A hush came over the room.

'Did you kill him?' he asked finally.

Anna looked straight through him. She had thought she could cope with that question. She thought she could justify what she had done by what Sir Anthony himself had done in the past. But she knew she must never say it out loud. Was she a killer? She thought of Sir Anthony, spreadeagled and naked on his bed, his hands and feet bound, his anxious look as she walked towards him fully dressed again, Eton tie in hand, slipping it round his neck and then taking his life. It was unreal. she abhorred violence, so what had made her do this? It wrestled uneasily in her conscience. Roberto looked at her and leaned forward.

'Senhora, did you kill him?'

Anna turned away slightly and looked down at the floor. What could she say?

'If you didn't kill him, do you know who did?'

She sat unmoving, unspeaking. He knew from the timings she was more than just strongly implicated. She had a strong motive.

'May I call you Anna?' he asked.

Anna gave a small nod.

'Anna. Whoever killed Sir Anthony, I will always be indebted to them. You understand?'

Anna gave another small nod, moved to tears.

'And if I can help them in anyway ... you understand?'

'Thank you, Senhor.'

'Roberto, please.'

'Thank you, Roberto,' she whispered, wiping a tear away from the corner of her eye.

He thought back to his antagonism towards her at their first meeting; how he had taken her to be yet another pretty journalist fluttering her eyelashes in exchange for copy. He had warmed to her as they spoke briefly before departing after their visit to the street children in Rio's sewers. Now he felt for her. She had kept her promise and had not published against him. Indeed, she had gone further than that – she had covered up for him.

'Are you still working for your paper?'

She still couldn't look straight at him.

'No. I've resigned.'

'Will you be staying in Brazil for a while then?'

'I'm not sure. I guess it depends.'

'On what?'

She felt confused. What did it depend on? She didn't know. Sensing her hesitancy again, he leaned forward and took her hand.

'Anna, you are tired?'

'Yes. Exhausted,' she whispered, sitting back in her chair.

'Why don't you go and have some rest. Let me have a think for you, okay? Let me know where you're staying and I'll be in touch.'

She made no attempt to remove her hand.

'Thank you. But I feel confused. So much has happened.'

'I know, but I would like to help.'

Anna nodded. Roberto stood up, called for a guard and gave him instructions.

'He will take you to your hotel, I take it you do have one?'

'Yes. Hotel Sol.'

He walked her out to the waiting jeep.

'Thank you for coming Anna. And thank you for all you have done.'

She climbed into the jeep and stared ahead into the darkness as the cordon lowered in front of her, the jeep accelerating away. Back at her hotel she slept soundly.

●

Anna returned to her room after breakfast just as the phone rang. It was Roberto's campaign office.

'Senhora Hughes?'

'Yes.'

'My name is Carlos. I am responsible for Senhor Justi's campaign operations. I have a message from Senhor Justi. Is it convenient to talk?'

'By all means.'

'Senhor Justi would like to offer you a position in his administration. Shall I talk further?'

Anna was more than a little surprised. 'Yes. It's not a problem. Please go on.'

'He would like you to become our press officer, taking over the position from his brother, Manuel. You are aware that Manuel Justi was assassinated?'

'Yes.'

'But we must continue. In a few days time Senhor Justi will be president. There is much to do.'

'It is a kind offer. Do you have any terms for the job?' she enquired, trying to sound as professional as possible.

'Senhora, Senhor Justi does not operate that way. You will be well looked after. It is an appointment of trust, an appointment of trust on both sides. You understand?'

She thought she detected a hint of suspicion, which she easily understood. It was not an everyday occurrence for a British journalist to be offered a position at the heart of Brazil's future administration.

'Can I think about it?' she asked, remembering that she had asked the same question of Sir Anthony in respect of her engagement in the Justi investigation.

'The world is moving very quickly Senhora. Senhor Justi has to make an appointment – you are qualified for the role? If not there are countless candidates Senhora.'

'Certainly. But can I think about it for just a little while? Say until first thing tomorrow?'

'I will ask. It is possible. But tomorrow you can give a definite answer?'

'Yes. Yes I can. But it is a little difficult for me. I am English. The appointment is for Brazil. And if Senhor Justi is elected president then I will be at the heart of a government that I have little right to be part of.'

'But you understand our cause?'

'Yes.'

'And you believe in it?'

'Yes. At least I think I do.'

'Then we would be very happy if you would join us.'

She took comfort in his reply, assured that his was not a sympathy statement, nor a misplaced thank you from Roberto for dealing with Sir Anthony.

'Are you sure? I would like to help, but I feel a little awkward. Somewhat an intruder?'

'Nonsense. Nonsense. I understand why you may feel this way, but we do not. Senhor Justi is a wonderful man, a fine judge of people. He would not have offered you the role if he did not think you were right for it. And that you would get on with us all, although in truth there are not many of us to get on with.'

Anna smiled. 'No, I gathered that from your campaign offices.'

Carlos laughed. 'Precisely.'

There was a brief pause before he continued. 'Well I will hear from you first thing?'

'Yes.'

'And if Senhor Justi asks I will tell him you are positive?'

'Yes. I am positive and I would like to help.'

'Thank you then. You know my number?'

'Yes. It has registered on my phone. And thank you for calling. It is a most kind offer.' She replaced the receiver.

Roberto called Carlos towards end of the day, keen to hear if Anna had accepted his offer. He was disappointed to learn she had not, and toyed with the idea of calling her himself. He decided against it. The situation was problematic for both parties. Essentially she was English and her role was definitely not. Would she stay the course? What would she do if the going became really tough? Would she have the commitment to stay with it? If she was Brazilian then her obligation would be clear. But an English lady, what would be her obligation? He left the issue alone, knowing that by midday the next day he would have his answer.

Anna took a walk from her hotel, deep in thought. She knew that if she accepted Justi's offer she would never again work for a British newspaper – the government would see to that. Was it worth everything she had ever worked for to throw her lot in with Justi? She was far from certain. She appreciated his cause, indeed she felt committed to it, but would that cause win through? That was the critical question. Ideas are cheap, she pondered. Could Justi actually pull it off? Then again, what were her options beyond Justi? Nothing grabbed her. She thought again about Sofia. She could almost sense her calling to her, asking her to support Justi, to create a new world – a better world.

She found a corner café with small wooden chairs placed tight against the window, leaving a little space for passers by.

'Coffee please.'

'Si.'

She watched the world pass by. A mother with two small children sat down next to her. She watched the children's excitement as their mother ordered, laughing and happy. When had Sofia last laughed? Did she even know who her mother was? She closed her eyes and leaned back in her chair, tilting her head towards the sun. She listened again to the happiness in the Portuguese babbling of the children at the next table, steeling herself to make a decision. So what if Justi failed, she thought? So what? It was worth the effort.

On returning to her hotel, she phoned Carlos, accepting Justi's offer.

'Senhora, we are all delighted,' he replied.

Roberto later phoned her personally, inviting her for dinner that evening. 'Nothing special, you understand,' he had said. No surprises there, she thought.

●

As Roberto had promised, dinner was a simple affair – grilled fish served with a tomato salad on bright red plates with a yellow floral print. Roberto explained in as much detail as he had thought of how best to put into practice what Angela had only written of.

'It is a tightrope, Anna. It's very much Brazil against the world.'

'Because you control the majority of the world's rainforest?'

'Yes. But it's not so much that we control the majority, it's that we control enough to panic the rest of the world.'

'And panic Brazil too?' she enquired.

'Yes.' He swirled the remaining wine in his glass. 'Yes, and Brazil too. Perversely it will at least make us equal with the rest of the world for the first time for centuries. But you have to look beyond that.'

'Aren't you underestimating potential allies?' responded Anna. 'I know you will – we will – have the heavyweights against us.' She ran through them in her mind, listing them to Roberto as she did so. 'America, Japan, Germany, Britain, France; actually they'll probably rope in the European block, Holland, Italy, Spain, Denmark, Sweden, Norway.'

'Plus Greece, Portugal, Turkey, Austria, Switzerland,' added Roberto, casting a slight smile at her. 'And in my corner I'll have Zaire, Indonesia, Peru, Guyana and the Congo,' he laughed lightly. 'Nothing to worry about then.'

She raised her glass to him and finished her wine, pleased that Manuel's death had not cast so large a shadow that the only emotion he could portray was sorrow.

'Is Angela's report still the blueprint?' she enquired.

'Well it will do for starters. There's a lot of detail missing though, which, until we get our climatologists on board, we can't really put in. We're going to have to slash and burn hundreds of thousands of square kilometres of forest, we know that much. Anyway, you tell me what you believed to be Angela's blueprint.'

'You mean the worst-case version?'

'Yes. The world's bottom line. What is it?'

Anna thought back to the article, running through the key points quickly in her mind.

'You cut down all your trees, oxygen levels fall and the world can't breathe so well. Carbon-dioxide levels also soar, the world heats up, the ice caps melt, sea levels rise a hundred and fifty feet. New York, London, Tokyo all disappear. World financial markets are thrown into pandemonium, shares plummet, banks collapse because their collateral has either disappeared

164

with the stockmarket or is at the bottom of the sea.'

'Not bad. Actually very good. But it doesn't work quite like that. The world won't get hotter overnight from increased levels of carbon dioxide. It takes decades apparently. We'll need a much quicker fix. I think it will hang on the oxygen thing. That's far more immediate. Anyway we'll have to be careful about the sea level rising. We do want to threaten rising sea levels but we don't actually want sea levels rising a hundred and fifty feet. It would be a disaster. Never mind New York, London, Tokyo. Think about São Paulo, Rio – our entire west coast. They would go as well. Then what?'

She couldn't argue against that, and he continued.

'As I said, we have to get our climatologists on board and then we'll have a much better idea of what we have to do.'

'Haven't you talked to them yet?'

'No. Not until after the election. I daren't approach them until then.'

They talked on for a further half-hour. Roberto gave her details of where their headquarters would be after the election. Anna noticed that even he now spoke about it as a foregone conclusion, and it was more than hard to disagree. She was to meet him on the first morning of his presidency at a military base in Brasilia. An apartment would be provided for her there by General Valto, whose acquaintance she still had the pleasure of making.

○

Roberto arose early the next morning. Manuel's funeral was

to take place that afternoon. He had been forced to agree to a meeting with General Valto at eight-thirty. The sun was already up, the sky a cloudless blue. He read through some of the papers and took coffee and toast for a makeshift breakfast.

'General Valto,' a guard announced. He was a bit late with the introduction – Valto was already through the door.

'Senhor Justi, how are you? How are things these last few days?' enquired Valto, offering a brief salute.

'Difficult, General. I'm sure you can imagine.'

The General waved some papers in the air and moved to the window.

'Well, I am sorry to intrude but I thought I ought to detail the report on the issue of the tapping of your phone lines.'

Roberto opted to sit out in the garden and trusted Valto would not consider it an undue security risk.

'Nonsense – you are the safest man in Brazil,' responded Valto. 'They are the finest snipers we have,' he continued, waving towards the roof. Roberto looked up – he was sure one of them was asleep. The two men sat down on a couple of faded striped deckchairs, Valto finding the manoeuvre rather exacting, his legs appearing to give way under his own weight causing him to half collapse into the chair from about a foot above. Roberto tried not to smile; he was, however, looking forward to Valto getting up again.

'Now to business,' said Valto, passing Roberto the papers. 'You were right. All your lines were tapped.'

'Do we know by who?'

'No.'

'No idea at all, General?'

'No. It is a big world, Senhor.'

'Can't we trace them though?'

'This is not possible. Anyway, they are not tapped now. This is the main point.'

Roberto gave up and changed the subject.

'And the papers I asked you to look at?'

'Ah yes. They were genuine and we believe that Sir Anthony Duce was a key figure in British Intelligence.'

'Any more on how he died, General?'

'No. A most strange affair if I am not mistaken.'

'Indeed, General. Is everything else running smoothly?'

The General ran through security measures for polling, detailing the route for Roberto to cast his own vote and then plans for the remainder of the day when, at late evening, possibly even in the small hours of the morning after, he would be officially declared president and he would have to make some sort of public appearance to the crowds that would throng São Paulo's streets and squares. Roberto proposed the balcony of the new São Paulo museum, an imposing building built in ancient Portuguese style facing a vast plaza that had been reclaimed from run-down industrial land in the north of the city for the millennium celebrations. Their meeting concluded, the General tried to stand up, reluctantly accepting Roberto's hand in assistance.

'Everything is running perfectly,' concluded Valto, patting Roberto on the back. 'Tomorrow you will be president.'

CHAPTER ELEVEN

The room was some sixty feet below ground level of the army's headquarters in Brasilia, and despite its depth it was far from small – about ninety feet square, with a high ceiling. In the centre of the room was a large round table. The wall to the right of the room's entrance had five clocks hanging on it in a neat row; they were identical, with white circular faces, roman numerals, hands of black wrought iron, glass fronts and dark wood casings. Each clock showed a different time and beneath each was a brass plate giving the location of the time shown: Brasilia, New York, London, Berlin, Tokyo. A large white marker board covered the opposite wall. A member of the military staff had scrawled over it in bright red marker pen, JUSTI PRESIDENTE!!!! But the room's dominant feature was on the wall that faced the entrance – a huge map of the Brazilian rainforest; a vast mass of green with the occasional streak of blue denoting the many waterways draining into the Orinoco and Amazon rivers.

This was Justi's war room. It contained emergency living quarters for both himself and his staff if needed, although they also had separate apartments in the grounds of the headquarters. As to how long the room would be needed, no one really knew, but it would be the nerve centre from which events would unfold on the world stage.

Anna sat alone at the round table, surrounded by masses of papers: deforestation reports, meteorological models, global-warming projections from the greenhouse effect, macro slash-and-burn techniques. It was late evening on the day after Roberto's landslide victory. He had polled an incredible ninety-one per cent of the vote on a huge turnout for Brazil of eighty-eight per cent. He was supposed to have met with Anna earlier but the vote had taken longer than anticipated to declare above the fifty per cent mark, and it had been four in the morning when he had finally strolled into the cool night air on the São Paulo Museum balcony, to wave for the first time as president to the crowd estimated at half a million partying in the plaza below. He had, however, gained full clearance for her to enter his headquarters and start preparing whatever she felt necessary for their first meeting the next day.

Anna looked up from a deforestation report to study again the map in front of her, the size of it helping her grasp just how naturally vast it really was. Two million square kilometres of forest cover, larger than the whole of Western Europe. It was hard to take in its enormity. Its importance to the world was clear, producing one-fifth of the world's fresh water and, crucial to their plans, one-third of the Earth's oxygen. Surely the world must see that Brazil was exporting a commodity that no one could do without, she thought to herself. The fact that its oxygen production was not put in little canisters and shipped all over the world was only an argument about sales distribution – it was academic. Her mind ran forward to the political battles they were about to face. She could almost hear US President Hall facing the world press from the White House lawn.

'Few things in life are free, but the air that we breathe is one of them. The United States has protected the rights and freedoms of peoples the world over for countless decades, we do not intend to turn our back on them now. We have to stop this crazed administration in Brazil destroying the planet, and whatever it takes to do that, well we've got to do it.'

Anna looked back at the mountain of papers she still hadn't even glimpsed at. She had hoped to consolidate all the reports that Roberto had collated over the last decade in time for their meeting the next morning, but it was a hopeless task. She stood up, stretched and retired to her apartment.

●

At ten o'clock the following morning Roberto introduced Anna to General Valto. Anna struck by the excellence of Valto's English; Valto was struck by her elegance and poise. 'An English rose if ever I have seen one,' he had said to her as they shook hands, a warm smile lighting up a broad and genial face. The three of them sat round the table to discuss strategy.

They agreed that there was no real likelihood of the world paying them billions of dollars just because they threatened to cut down their trees; the world would say they were bluffing, the threat therefore had to be backed up. They had to prove that Brazil really meant business.

'Have we had anything through from the climatology office?' Roberto asked.

'Yes, they've sent this brief report on the edited version of Angela's article. Obviously it's limited – they haven't had much time,' replied Anna, passing round a copy to each of them. Roberto read it and then walked over to the map.

'The problem is more complex then,' he said, as much to himself as the others. 'You can what they are talking about. This line is the Equator. The majority of our forest is south of the line.'

He looked up at Anna and Valto. Valto's face was blank, but Anna was nodding. Roberto continued.

'If there's no movement of air systems across the Equator we can only play the oxygen card against the West by cutting down forest north of the line.'

Anna completed his point for him. 'And because we haven't much forest north of the line we would have to fell the lot to see any real impact on oxygen levels in the US, Europe or Japan, and any potential thaw of the Arctic ice cap.'

Roberto nodded, Valto still looked confused.

'We could get more forest north of the Equator if Guyana would join us. Columbia too.'

'Presidente, really!' Valto understood that suggestion perfectly well. He shook his head. 'There is no prospect of us ever asking Colombia to join us. And we have an ongoing dispute with Guyana over boundaries.'

'But they might bury the hatchet, General.'

'Guyana might. But Colombia is a no.'

'Okay. Could you sound out the Guyanese over a deal?' he enquired of Valto.

'They'll want to know terms. What are we to offer them?'

'Tell them that whatever we benefit we'll give them a share based on their forest size as a percentage of ours. If they don't like that then try a deal on mineral-reserve mining rights for them in some of our adjoining forest,' Roberto suggested.

'I'll pick it up with them this afternoon,' mumbled Valto, making a note of the offer.

Roberto continued. 'In any event what I think it amounts to is that we can only play the oxygen card against the US, in particular, just once.'

'Play it straight away then,' interjected Valto. 'Think about it – if the Americans are finding it hard to breathe they'll be at the negotiating table in an instant.'

Silence fell on their deliberations. What would be the response of the Western alliance if Brazil did manage to engineer a serious reduction in their oxygen levels? It required a great deal of thought. Anna spoke first.

'I see difficulties with that, General. For one, if oxygen levels are down and we have already destroyed all the forest north of the Equator, how will negotiating raise them again? It's not as if we can replant the trees, no treaty will give them back their air, and they might treat our actions as a declaration of war.'

'Which we don't want,' Roberto added hastily, before continuing. 'In addition to the military intervention, we have the issue of the ice cap. It's winter north of the Equator, so starting temperatures are minus fifty degrees, possibly as low as minus sixty. No sun's rays are getting through either, it's the land of permanent darkness through their winter. So how can we raise temperatures anywhere near to zero degrees for a thaw from such a low base?'

Anna agreed. 'Whereas it's summer in Antarctica, if we could push temperatures there up above freezing then they'd understand that this was no idle threat. Even if we didn't quite make it, as long as we achieved a rise of at least ten degrees in Antarctica we'd still have proved we were capable of doing very real damage.'

'Just as long as we achieved it with no more substantial area of forest than we have north of the Equator,' added Roberto.

'South of the Equator then.' Anna nodded.

'General?' enquired Roberto, awaiting his acceptance of their decision. Other than the suggestion of doing a deal with Guyana and Colombia, Valto had found the debate a bit beyond him. His whole military life had revolved around tank divisions, air power, naval strength – not tree felling and ice caps.

'I think I'll leave it for you both to decide,' he replied. He sat quietly and listened with interest as Anna and Roberto discussed suitable areas of forest to target. From there on, their discussions became frustrated by a lack of knowledge in key areas such as high-altitude airflow patterns, which would carry the Earth's warmer temperatures to the South Pole, and surface airflows that would carry reduced oxygen levels. But to where? Roberto jotted down a brief for Brazil's climatologists, giving a provisional figure for how much of the forest they would need to fell to make the rest of the world sit up and take notice. A quarter was discussed at the outset, an area of some half a million square kilometres, but it would all have to be felled in a matter of days and then burnt a few days later. Anna questioned why it had to be burned at all, and Roberto replied, to her satisfaction, that to sell the idea innocently to the world, they could not simply cut down trees for the sake of it; the felling would have be portrayed as a means to an end and that the easiest thing to hang it on was an expansion of agriculture and mineral exploration and extraction. Valto was unequivocal on the need to burn it swiftly after felling.

'We must afford no opportunity to the West to take military action to prevent our plans. If we move quickly enough they will be unable to stop us,' he stated.

It was, however, an undoubted logistical Everest; a suggestion that a quarter of the existing rainforest was to disappear from the map in four days was hard to imagine, yet that was likely to be the requirement.

'It's an area twice the size of Great Britain, Senhora,' explained Valto. 'But that's why I'm here, that's why the military are involved. Don't think it's impossible – we've worked on this for months now. It'll burn, don't worry. Burn like nothing the world has ever seen. We've developed incendiary and high-explosive warheads that will take out a square kilometre of forest with one bomb.'

Anna looked back up at the map.

'But we'll need five hundred thousand such warheads.'

'Only for the highly inaccessible areas, that's all we need the bombs for. We can deliver payloads of some forty warheads per plane. One hundred and fifty planes and we can take out six thousand square miles in one hit. Average turnaround of five hours and we'll be taking out thirty thousand square miles a day. We should be able to eliminate the worst areas in three days. With the big blaze already lined up ready to blow in the rest of the forest, it will be quite something.'

'So what's happening to fell the majority of the area?'

'Ah. Foot soldiers. Tens of thousands of them. In addition to the bombs for our planes we have smaller versions for the soldiers to detonate remotely from a half mile distant. These smaller devices will be placed in the centre of an area of one hundred square metres, hundreds of them placed at a time and then simultaneously detonated. But they are not just high explosives, they are also incendiaries. It will all burn, believe me. I've seen a test, it was awesome – the forest burnt, no problem.'

Anna listened to Valto intently. He may well have appeared out of his depth on climate issues but he was undeniably sounding confident about the logistical issues surrounding slash-and-burn on this vast area of rainforest.

'Good,' she replied. 'So we know we can do it. I just feel we could do with something we can hang all this on for the world press. For better or worse, the world will want something to centre the whole debate on, some sort of name. A reference point.'

'I agree. In fact I have suggested to the presidente on a

number of occasions to call this project the Justi Plan, but you were against it,' replied Valto, turning to Roberto.

'I am concerned that if I sanction the use of my own name it will appear as some kind of ego trip.'

'Perhaps you would prefer something along the lines of the Rainforest Reclamation Scheme?' suggested Anna.

Roberto shrugged his shoulders. Anna thought quickly about Valto's viewpoint. 'But the good thing about the Justi Plan is that the name can mean anything. No matter how the issues work out it will still remain valid. After all, what does it mean? Anything? Something? This thing? That thing? We could do what we liked with a name like that and never be stuck in a corner, but it would obviously always belong to us.'

'Presidente?' enquired Valto.

'Well, if you are agreed, I will go with it,' replied Roberto. He had no better name for it; he had tried thinking of one for months now.

They talked on, agreeing to reconvene in two days. Roberto, in the meantime, was to brief more fully their leading climatologist, Professor Carlos Fernento, and invite to the next meeting both him and Georges Santez, chairman of Brazil's central bank. The Justi Plan was taking shape.

●

Theirs was not the only meeting taking place that morning to discuss future Brazilian policy. The Federal Reserve in New York, the Bank of England in London, the European Central

Bank in Frankfurt, the Bundesbank in Bonn, the Bank of Japan in Tokyo – all found themselves round the table. Instructions had been received from their respective governments to prepare an immediate strategy to handle any Brazilian loan-interest payment difficulties, although they thought it unlikely that Brazil would default. Of greater importance was the need to agree an approach to any demands from Brazil for rental of its rainforest, with all the attendant risks to the global economy. These issues were to be discussed later that day at an emergency meeting, requested by the Americans, of all the leading G7 economies: America, Canada, Britain, Germany, France, Italy and Japan. It was to be a highly confidential meeting held at the World Bank's offices in Washington.

The meeting proved conclusive on the potential problems and, surprisingly, equally conclusive about what to do about them. A complete devaluation to zero of the Brazilian government debt was considered, with an assessment of the damage to the balance sheets of the world's major banking and investment institutions. Across the entire world-banking sector the prognosis was that the potential fallout was manageable. The difficulty lay with a number of leading US and Japanese banks, which were significantly exposed to Brazilian national debt. Their asset position would suffer dramatically, perhaps even to the extent that liabilities would exceed them; they would be insolvent. Emergency capital was agreed by the G7, such that any bank or investment institution finding itself in trouble, either temporarily or permanently, as a result of the Brazilian situation, would be provided with capital from the World Bank. As for repayment of any such funding, that would be determined after the event. This decision caused some concern from Germany, France, Britain, Italy and Canada. It seemed an open-ended commitment to bad banking and investment.

The second issue, regarding rental demands for the rainforest, created a unanimous view. Under no circumstances would they enter into discussions with Brazil. Any approach would be rebuffed. Provided everyone held the line, then what could Brazil do about it? If Brazil started felling on a grand scale, or made any move to suspend or cancel the outstanding debt, then the West would invoke punitive economic sanctions; there would be a complete ban on the purchase of Brazilian exports and the same on exports to Brazil, including essential items such as grain and other foodstuffs. Never mind the current terms being forced on Brazil by the World Bank, which had removed government subsidies on bread, milk and fuel, while at the same time insisting on the raising of taxes. These were nothing compared to what would follow if Brazil wanted trouble, with empty food shelves undermining Justi to his own people.

Brazil versus the world? If it was to be that way, then the world was ready. The economic battle lines were drawn.

CHAPTER TWELVE

The meeting organised by Roberto with Brazil's
chairman of the central bank, Georges Santez, and
their leading climatology professor, Carlos Pernento,
had gone well. Santez was relieved to be told to maintain
interest payments on their foreign debt – he had enough
problems with the World Bank as it was, without needlessly
adding to them. He was fascinated by the Justi Plan, realising
that if it was successful the cruzado-real, their domestic
currency, would become a hard currency on the foreign-
exchange markets. That had been the elusive dream of every
former Brazilian central bank chairman.

Fernento could hardly contain himself. Here lay the
chance of a lifetime. Climatology would go centre stage to the
whole world. This, then, was the potential making of his
profession in general, and hopefully of him in particular. Of
course, he and a few of his junior colleagues had been talking
about the Justi Plan, or something similar, for decades now. At
last, the world would listen – at long last.

He had been unable to offer any idea as to how much
forest would need to be destroyed in order to make an impact

on Antarctic temperatures, but he was helpful on the greenhouse issue. Despite plenty of publicity stating that carbon-dioxide emissions caused global warming, the question was still not proved conclusively. True, the rainforest was responsible for helping absorb the world's carbon dioxide. The greenhouse argument stated that carbon dioxide allowed the sun's rays in, but the heat rays reflected back from the Earth's surface were trapped by it, and so the world heated up. However, opinion was divided on this.

A less vociferous view expounded that as the world heated up there would be more evaporation of oceans, which would lead to more cloud cover; these clouds would reflect the incoming rays back into space, resulting in the world actually cooling down. No one could prove it either way. Even if carbon-dioxide levels could produce global warming, the biggest followers of the greenhouse theory agreed it would take many years before global temperatures showed any increase from deforestation, even on the scale that Roberto was planning. It would be several decades before the ice caps were threatened by a thaw, by which time Roberto would be out of office. The Brazilian people could not and would not wait thirty years for a solution to their current economic plight. Roberto knew that their patience would be stretched even after a year.

Fernento picked up on one issue that the others had overlooked, though. The fact was that if the whole area was burnt simultaneously it could result in a furnace on the face of the globe that would push up global temperatures immediately; this was not a certainty but it seemed probable. Fernento stated that he would have to consider average flame and soil temperatures, together with the temperature of the burning forest. From there it could only be calculated guesswork. What would become of the air temperature thirty or forty thousand feet above the burning forest? For there in the troposphere was the crucial airflow that carried the Earth's heat polewards. Since the beginning of time, this airflow had moved the heat from the Equator and transferred it to the freezing Antarctic to ensure that the Equator did not burn itself up. How long would the hotter-than-usual air generated by the burning forest take to reach the Antarctic? How much heat loss would it suffer in getting there? And how much of this hot air would never survive the journey, sucked down instead into the surface air systems over the high southern latitudes across an almost unbroken belt of ocean encircling the globe, to reinforce the wind systems dreaded by all mariners. Fernento suggested a fortnight for preliminary estimates.

'Regrettably, at this time of year I have rather a lot on at the university,' he told them.

'Pass all other work to your junior colleagues,' ordered Roberto. 'And report back here a week today.' He rose to his feet to indicate the matter was closed. 'Work through your figures based on a million square kilometres.'

Anna interrupted him.

'I thought we agreed on half a million.'

'I know,' replied Roberto, 'but if we have to really put the frighteners on, we might need a million. It's our bottom-line position I think.'

'Without anything like that north of the line?' she asked.

'I know, but Professor Fernento is already telling us that the heat from the burning forest might be capable of melting the ice caps in the timescale to which we must operate politically. We can't hold off for twenty or thirty years, waiting for the greenhouse effect to bite. Is that so Professor?'

'Yes, I don't think the carbon-dioxide levels are going to be that relevant early on.'

Justi pressed home his point. 'Whereas, water does not respect the Equator. If sea levels rise south of the line they'll be rising north of it, too. It's not quite as we thought, Anna. I agree that reduced oxygen levels will feed through quickly but it might not just be about oxygen levels. We can affect them by what we do to the south.'

Roberto turned back to Fernento.

'Do your work on a million. See what it brings us.'

Fernento shook hands with Roberto, Anna and Valto and left with Santez. Anna asked to talk with Roberto privately.

'You said the other evening that you didn't want sea levels rising. São Paulo, Rio, remember?' she stressed, disappointed that without any consultation he seemed to have changed tack.

'I know, and I still mean that, but when Fernento said the actual burning could do damage to the ice caps, I thought we ought to at least see what he was talking about.'

'But once we go live to the world we can't make policy

decisions on the hoof. It can't be half a million one day and a million the next. There will always be a discussion.'

Roberto felt caught slightly offside. He had not anticipated having to discuss things; he had always listened to all the arguments and then simply made his decisions. That was it. Manuel had never had a problem with operating in this way.

'What do you mean by discussion?' he asked defensively. 'I am the president.'

'Just don't leave me high and dry to be made a fool of by the world's press, that's all I'm saying. I need to know what you're planning. Do you not want advice?'

'There's a difference between giving advice, though, Anna and actually taking it,' he countered. He was getting uptight about what she was driving at; she was his press officer, not head of policy. That was a matter for his judgement alone.

'I mean, say you give me some advice and I completely disagree and do the opposite. What would you do?' he continued.

'Just as long as you'd actually told me before you made any general announcement it would be okay. Then at least we are all on message,' she replied guardedly.

'But you wouldn't agree. That would be okay? Sure?'

'Sure,' she replied. 'If I really disagree, I just leave.'

He stared at her; there was a simmering look in her eyes.

'We understand each other then I think.'

'I hope so,' replied Anna, returning his gaze. 'Now shall we make a start on the draft plan?'

He hadn't expected her to change the subject so soon.

'The daft plan – sorry draft. Did I say daft?'

'Well only if you thought about writing it all on your own, advice-free, so to speak,' she countered.

For the first time Roberto saw her differently. Senhora Hughes was a sharp operator.

'I'll just get some of the extra files we need,' he said retreating, relieved to have a few moments to himself.

●

Roberto and Anna spent the next few days working on a document that would detail the Justi Plan both to Brazil itself and to the rest of the world. Much of their time was spent finding different ways of saying what they really were doing.

'Deforestation to hold the Western World to ransom' became 'a new agricultural and mining initiative to open up the untapped resources of Amazonia'. Anna had wanted there to be a reference to the global environmental issues that would be a natural consequence of this 'agricultural and mining initiative'. In the end they agreed to play to the strong green lobby, particularly in Germany and America, by offering rainforest protection from the Justi Plan for an annual rate of thirty thousand dollars per square kilometre. At such a rate the interest payments on foreign debt would be covered and the entire debt repaid within five years. Valto felt the rate was too low, but when he multiplied this amount by Brazil's two million square kilometres of forest, arriving at sixty billion dollars per annum, he conceded that 'it would do for starters.'

With Roberto tied down by key official duties, much of the drafting of the Justi Plan document was left to Anna. She found it more difficult than she had imagined. She realised how little she really knew about Brazil – nothing was familiar to her. The place names, the government agencies, the rivers, the people, the crop names; at times it was taking her over an hour's background reading to hesitantly pen a single paragraph. She still found time to flick through the international papers. She noted with interest that Roberto's election to president made page two in *The Washington Post*, page four in *The New York Times* but in London it actually made front-page news in *The Daily Telegraph* as well as a paragraph in the editorial. The papers all took a similar line; pre-election promises were one thing, translating them into successful post-election action was another.

●

Carlos Fernento's colour monitor showed a map of the southern hemisphere in crisis. He sat alone in his small private office in the Brazil Meteorology Centre. It was late evening, four days after the meeting in which he had been given his brief to construct a model for the likely impact of the Justi Plan on polar temperatures. His small research team had all returned to their homes – they had not been there to witness the completion of the Justi Plan model, the awesome results of which were now showing on his screen.

The map charted atmospheric pressures; half of Brazil had levels below 950 millibars, a figure equal to the extreme low pressure witnessed in the eye of a hurricane. The burning forest established a warm front thirty thousand feet above Brazil, which then started its journey southward. It was attracted, as if magnetically, to the high pressure of Antarctica. The warm front moved down to latitude thirty degrees and hit the subtropical high-pressure belt. Some of the warm front dropped down into the belt and strengthened the two dominant surface winds: the southeast trades, which returned the air back towards the Equator, and the westerlies that continued underneath the warm front and still headed polewards. But it was the estimate of the size of the warm front that passed unscathed through latitude thirty degrees which gripped Fernento. Before it lay the polar front, beneath it lay the westerlies in a supporting role. The warm front began to distort, jet streams appearing across its air waves and causing them to undulate. He watched as air from deep inside the polar front flooded northwards, deepening the troughs of the warm front, forcing parts of it to rush deep into Antarctica to fill the gap. He sat spellbound by the picture in front of him. The warm front created by the furnace of simultaneously burning a million square kilometres of forest resulted in the model predicting air temperatures way above freezing, invading the polar ice cap.

He opened the bottom drawer of his desk and removed a bottle of Johnnie Walker Black Label, from which he took two mouthfuls, coughing as the whisky hit his throat. His eyes did not move from the monitor; he was trying to imagine what it would be like on the actual surface of Antarctica if this prediction happened. The desolate frozen wastelands stretching over fifteen million square kilometres, would have finally met their match; a warm cloak of destruction would have finally arrived, casting a shadow over the last great, impenetrable wilderness. A mass of brilliant white would turn grey and then literally melt into oblivion.

He took another swig of whisky and ran the sequence through again. He thought about what would be happening on the Earth's surface all the way down from Brazil to Antarctica. He had only looked at air movements high above it, but what would be happening to surface weather systems? He knew it would be devastation in many areas. Hurricanes, flooding, tornadoes ... they would all feature strongly. Millions of homes would be lost, most likely labelling it as the worst natural disaster ever. 'Natural' – the word sat uncomfortably in his mind. He could not advise Justi to burn so much forest, the human consequences were almost certainly cataclysmic.

He paged back through the model to the data-input screen. It gave a menu of variable parameters. Next to sea levels he typed '50 metres'; this was the amount sea levels would rise if the polar ice caps melted. He went to his 'View' options and selected 'All'. The world map flashed up on screen but it was hardly recognisable. Every continent was a casualty. Asia lost China, India, Japan and the Middle East, retaining just northern Russia and the Thai Burmese peninsular. Europe was all but wiped out, only Finland appeared preserved relatively intact. Africa was split in two, forming separate continents. The north lost Egypt, Ethiopia, Sudan, Morocco and Algeria. The seas would sweep over its south Atlantic coastline to engulf Angola, Namibia and South Africa. He looked at Australia and allowed himself a wry smile. It was just their luck that while their continent was the best preserved, the land they would lose was what they would most want to keep. The deserts would be spared but their cities – Perth, Fremantle, Adelaide, Sydney, Melbourne – all gone. America's west coast remained but the east coast would lose Maine, New Hampshire, Massachusetts and Connecticut. The Appalachian mountains would protect much of Pennsylvania, Ohio, Missouri, Kentucky, Virginia and New Jersey but the eastern states coastal cities of New York and Washington would be lost. Fernento looked at South America. Brazil's coastal cities were all in trouble, but the real casualty was her existing rainforests. Well, that should at least put Justi's fire out, he smiled to himself, taking another mouthful of scotch. He ran hard copies of his findings and phoned Roberto's office to advise that he could return earlier if necessary. Their meeting was rearranged for the following morning.

●

Fernento stood in front of the rainforest map in Roberto's war room and began detailing his model's findings. Roberto, Anna and Valto listened intently as he talked, turning the pages of their copies as he ran through each image, explaining pressure levels, wind speeds, air waves.

'My conclusion is that if you felled one million square kilometres of forest and then, a short time later, burned it, you would create a surface temperature of three hundred and fifty degrees Celsius over such a large area of the Earth it would create a warm front big enough to start a thaw in Antarctica. But I have to warn you that the human cost of this would be very large indeed. Not just from the potential flooding if the ice caps melted, as predicted, but also from the surface weather systems that would certainly be running throughout South America; hurricanes, tornadoes, flooding. Widespread loss of homes, and with landslips, many lives too. In the aftermath, disease would spread quickly – with no fresh water and no sanitation conditions would be appalling. Cholera and the like rampant. Hundreds of thousands, millions even, might perish. I must impress on you that Brazil itself will suffer. The heat will create an atmospheric depression, with pressure lower, probably, than in the very eye of a hurricane. I do not need to say what will be happening around it then.'

His presentation over, the room fell silent. Roberto spoke first.

'These findings are based on slash-and-burn of a million square kilometres of forest?'

Fernento nodded in agreement.

Valto spoke. 'At least we now know we can really make an impact on the world. None of us wishes disaster on any peoples, let alone our own, but this is war, albeit of a different type. We have to break the stranglehold of the World Bank. If we lose a few million in doing so I still believe it is a price worth paying.'

Roberto sat back in his chair and opened his arms wide.

'This is dynamite,' he said slowly, emphasising each word. 'No global-warming theory, no global-cooling theory; just one great fire that starts to cook the planet.'

Anna found his reaction strange. They had just been told that the ice caps would thaw, creating terrible damage to Brazil's west coast, and yet here was Roberto almost glorying in it. She tried to ignore him, turning the subject back on to the problems Brazil itself would face.

'You say that we could be in big trouble with our weather systems though, Professor,' she enquired. 'Is there anything you would advise?'

'Well it's a matter of judgement. I need to know what it is you're trying to achieve, as specifically as you feel able to tell me. I can then put it through the model and see what results.'

Roberto was still thinking about Fernento's findings.

'Can you imagine what the West would do if we melted the poles? My God, they'd know who really was running the show.'

'You do understand we don't want to actually raise sea levels Professor,' Anna continued, now looking at Roberto instead of Fernento. 'We don't want São Paulo, Rio and the other coastal towns and cities to be lost. We only want to frighten the world, not flood it.'

Fernento realised that there was a disagreement building round the table and decided not to reply. Sensing his hesitancy Anna continued.

'Perhaps instead of turning the Justi Plan into some sort of Noah revisited, your model could instead tell us what area we'd need to burn to, say, raise the temperature in Antarctica now, in summer, to one degree Celsius?'

Her eyes were still fixed on Roberto. Fernento looked at him; the president was looking everywhere except at Anna.

'Presidente?' pressed Fernento. There was an awkward pause before Roberto spoke.

'That's quite right, Professor,' he stated, turning now to finally look at Anna. 'Yes – one degree above freezing.'

Fernento was beginning to find the tone of the conversation a little uncomfortable, but it wasn't his business how they talked to each other – or to him. Valto, on the other hand, was finding it difficult not to grin. Fernento waited for everyone to look at him, but eventually gave up.

'The model should be able to make such a prediction. Within certain tolerances you understand.'

'Is it on your notebook – the model?' enquired Roberto, pointing to the laptop case by the professor's seat.

'You want to look now? No problem,' replied Fernento, grateful that things seemed to be moving on. He unzipped the case and removed the computer as they gathered round to look on. He entered his security code and selected the file named 'Justi'. The data-input screen appeared. He scrolled down to 'Temperature'.

'We enter the temperature here,' Fernento explained as he keyed '+1'. 'Then we find area code.' He moved the cursor bar down and entered '9'. 'Then we enter....' He hit the return key and shifted up to look at area size. 'And look to see the new variables. Here we are. Area size needed, four hundred thousand square kilometres is your answer, Senhora,' he said turning to Anna. Roberto patted him on the back.

'Thank you Professor. Now what sort of hurricanes will rage through Brazil with a fire that size?'

'Obviously not so widespread, Presidente, but still very damaging to some areas.'

'It's inevitable though. We can't do what we're proposing and think that we can ring-fence Brazil. It's the price we'll have to pay,' Valto repeated.

'Worth paying?' asked Anna of no one in particular.

'Of course,' replied Valto. 'What is our option? We either live and do as we're told by the world, or we turn the tables. If we lose a million homes,' he shrugged his shoulders, 'then we lose them. At least we can build them again if we finally get what we want. If we lose a hundred of our people, or a thousand, or ten thousand, sad, but think of the next generation and the one after that. This is a war, we all know that, but these days they're played with money and we don't have the arsenals to take them on. This is why the presidente is right. We have to change the world, it is Brazil's only way forward.'

Roberto felt slightly pensive. Some of what Fernento had said was beginning to sink in. Anna was right to have checked him. He did not want to start something that would end in countless dead, young and old alike at the mercy of the elements, but Valto was also right. This was the reality of it; it was no longer a theory to be dreamed about or academically discussed and debated. This was now – this was going to happen, and he was to be held accountable for it. He wished Angela was with him to support him. He longed to hear Manuel's voice again. 'Go on Roberto. Don't worry yourself. Here, have a drink.'

The room fell quiet, waiting for Roberto to make a decision.

'We'll take out four hundred thousand square kilometres then General. Try and minimise the forest tribes thinking we're putting them out of their land. Pay them good wages to help cut down the trees. Promise them they can have the land again once we've burnt it.' He turned again to face the map. 'Professor, if we try to choose an area with a clear passage to the south, would that be best for minimising casualties and damage?'

'I don't think one can really tell. It's the airflows around the whole area that will be the big problem and it's impossible to predict them. I guess the only thing would be to keep it as far from the major cities as possible, because you won't want to panic the public into thinking the fire will run out of control and engulf them.'

Roberto took a red marker pen and slowly drew an area to the north-west of the country, with the Equator at the top. Anna noted he became subdued as he drew it.

'General. You have your target area.'

'Thank you, Presidente,' replied Valto.

'Thank you, everyone.' Roberto sat down facing the map, turning away from them all. They left him in silence.

When he heard the door close behind them, Roberto held his head in his hands. The hopes of millions were pinned on him. Who had voted for this? 'New factors' – it suddenly felt a ridiculously lightweight statement. If it resulted in a mother or father holding up the limp body of their child, crushed beneath the collapsed roof of their villa, what 'new factors' were they then? Fine to think of the big picture, but could you really ignore the plight of the innocent? Wasn't that why he had set himself the task of turning Brazil around, to help the innocent victims of appalling poverty, the children living in the streets and sewers of Rio and São Paulo and all the main cities? He prayed for mercy.

He was still sitting there when Anna returned to the room an hour later.

'Roberto. Is everything all right?'

He turned with searching eyes.

'Is it Manuel?' she enquired gently.

'It is many things, Anna. Many things,' he said, getting to his feet. 'I am a little weary. All the electioneering.'

'And a few very late nights.'

He feigned a smile.

'Yes. Brazil was happy on election night. Do you think we can pull this off? Sitting here it is easy to get carried away with what we are doing, but when we go live, what then?'

'Roberto, you are planning an assault on the world's finances. They will resist in every way possible. But think of it another way, if you do nothing, what then? It is worth one almighty try to change things, surely?'

He sighed. 'I agree with you Anna. One big try.'

'Anyway, I must to bed.' He turned away and walked slowly

from the room, touching her lightly on the shoulder as he passed.

Anna stared again at the map. She walked over to it and ran her hand along its length. For the world to breathe, to drink, the map had to stay green, she thought to herself. Time for the world to really wake up to that.

CHAPTER THIRTEEN

'Any questions?' Anna asked.

Not one journalist stirred; they were still all poring over their copy of the Justi Plan. Anna had never witnessed a press briefing like it. The press corps was stunned.

'We might as well have announced that the plague was back,' she whispered to Roberto. He smiled. The Justi Plan was almost too clear; the journalists were all searching for the paragraph in it stating that none of what they had just heard would happen. The document they had been given and the briefing given by Roberto stuck rigidly to a new industrial and agricultural policy for Amazonia. Phase I of the Justi Plan involved the clearing of four hundred thousand square kilometres of primary forest. Phase II would depend on the success and experience gained from Phase I, but a further five hundred thousand square kilometres had been earmarked.

The Justi Plan proposed that much of the reclaimed forest was to be used for subsistence agriculture, to be able to direct food to relieve the millions of Brazilians suffering from malnutrition, instead of having to export the majority of it to help fund her debt-interest payments. The nation simply had to expand its food production and, given the current constraints forced upon it by the World Bank, it was not possible to establish any government-sponsored welfare programme. Aware of worldwide environmental concerns regarding the rainforest, Brazil would be prepared to consider an alternative, whereby the rest of the world paid an annual amount of thirty thousand dollars per square kilometre for Brazil to leave it standing. Money received under this option would go to fund a welfare programme to replace the additional food that would have been provided under the clearance programme.

'I think they've all died,' whispered Roberto in reply.

They looked out from their table on a small raised platform at the army of news media in front of them. Anna caught the eye of Danielle Hart of *The New York Times*; they had last met covering the British general election of 2005, in which a slightly rejuvenated Tory party forced Labour into a minority administration. Danielle looked back briefly before returning her attention to her copy of the Justi Plan. Someone ask something, Anna thought to herself. There was a cough from the audience and Anna turned, hoping that at long last someone would say something, but it was just a cough. Eventually, Stephen D'Arcy from *The Washington Post* spoke, his glasses hanging limply from the corner of his mouth.

'I don't wish to wake anybody,' he began, looking round at the other journalists. A quiet ripple of laughter moved across the conference room. He announced himself.

'President, Stephen D'Arcy of *The Washington Post*.' He held up the Justi Plan document in his right hand and continued.

'I guess most of us here are grappling with the real impact of this plan on the environment – global warming in particular. And also where it fits in with your policy on the foreign debt, which you promised to resolve in your election campaign.'

Roberto, very relaxed and feeling comfortably in control of the press conference – having run through it some five times beforehand, with Anna in the role of hostile journalist – replied.

'I understand the environmental concerns, but we must be permitted to pursue our own future and to use all the resources we have at our disposal to compete in the world economy. To me, the rainforest must start to work to the benefit of my country. It has to start to pay its way for us like everything else. And we are only talking at this stage, in Phase I, of about a quarter of our primary forest.'

'And your debt policy?' D'Arcy repeated.

'My debt policy is to honour our obligations under the existing loan structures. I have, therefore, instructed the chairman of our central bank to make all payments on their due date.'

Danielle Hart rose.

'President. Danielle Hart, *New York Times*.' She looked across to D'Arcy. 'I believe that Mr D'Arcy is getting to the heart of it.'

D'Arcy glared at her, irritated at the interruption.

'My question is that this new policy of yours invites the world to rent your forest for an annual payment of twelve billion dollars; do you agree that figure?'

'It is an option. No one is saying you have to rent. Our main policy is to clear Amazonia for agriculture, mineral exploration and extraction, and industrial use. If all four hundred thousand square kilometres is felt by the world to be something they would rather keep then the figure you gave would be correct.'

'Which, if you applied it to the whole of your rainforest, could end with the world paying sixty billion dollars a year just to keep the forest standing.'

Roberto smiled at her and gave a slight nod of his head.

'Isn't this document really about holding the world to environmental ransom, with the elimination of your foreign debt the ransom demand?'

Roberto replied without emotion.

'It has nothing to do with ransom demands or anything of the sort. The document is explicit – the rainforest must go in order for Brazil to realise her full economic potential in global markets.' He did not even look at Hart as he spoke, focusing instead on the growing number of raised hands from other journalists. He pointed at an elderly journalist, who had sat patiently for the last few minutes with his hand in the air.

'Your question, Senhor.'

'Thank you. Pierre Trente, *Le Monde*. Your document does not point out that Brazil's rainforest supplies the world with significant amounts of water and oxygen. I can't recall the precise numbers.'

Another journalist in the hall shouted them out.

'Thirty per cent of the oxygen and twenty per cent of the fresh water.'

'Merci. Well if you cut down all your trees where is the world supposed to get its air and water from? You can't just do things like this without thinking of the consequences for the rest of the world. This I see as the main problem with your proposals.'

Roberto paused before replying.

'Can I ask you what you propose then?'

Trente shuffled awkwardly.

'I'm a journalist, paid to report not propose,' he replied. 'You see there is no way the world is likely to pay twelve billion dollars, or sixty billion, at the end of the day.'

'Why not?' interjected Roberto. 'A minute ago you were telling me how important my rainforest was to you. And the irony is that the countries most of you represent had your own forests, which you have felled into oblivion over the centuries. So perhaps you need to get some kind of historical perspective on this. You've all done it. Now we will.'

He picked up his papers from the table.

'Thank you all for attending,' he stated. He strolled out of the room. Anna gave Danielle Hart an especially broad smile, and then followed Roberto.

The media's response to the press conference was immediate. A number of networks interrupted their programme schedules to announce the Justi Plan as an emergency news bulletin. Anna and Roberto headed back across Brasilia to the war room, the police escort allowing them to speed across the city. They were back inside ten minutes, a team of media analysts studying all the key Western broadcast channels, waiting for the news to break. Anna sat down at the desk dedicated to BBC World Service transmission. She did not have to wait long. Five minutes later, just as lunch was being brought in, the BBC made an announcement.

'This is the BBC World Service.'

Anna felt a pang of homesickness as she heard English spoken without an accent, the quiet, slightly officious tone that so typified what the rest of the world thought about Britain.

'We interrupt this broadcast for an emergency news bulletin.'

Anna beckoned to Roberto and Valto.

'Within the last hour, Senhor Roberto Justi, the newly elected president of Brazil, announced at a press conference in Brasilia that his administration intended to clear some four hundred thousand square kilometres of primary rainforest, an area substantially larger than the whole of the United Kingdom and approaching a quarter of all Brazil's primary rainforest. Brazil is responsible for producing one-third of the world's oxygen and a fifth of its fresh water. An offer has been made to the rest of the world to establish a rental system that would protect the forest. A figure of thirty thousand dollars per square kilometre has been proposed, amounting to a potential twelve billion dollars annual rental figure. If applied to Brazil's entire rainforest, this rental figure would rise to an estimated sixty billion dollars. There is likely to be widespread concern in the West about the impact of deforestation on this scale on the global climate, and over the financial implications to the global economy if Brazil's rental plans are adopted. More details, including the world's political reaction, will follow in the next scheduled news bulletin. We apologise for interrupting the programme.'

Valto was ecstatic.

'We've done it!' he boomed.

'Well we have at least made a reasonable start,' replied Roberto, playing down the moment, aware that news bulletins meant little to the response of the key world players, the governments of the world's leading nations. But Anna saw a slight glint in his eye, and a smile played around his lips. Her thoughts went to Angela, to Manuel, to Sofia.

●

The switchboard at the White House press office was jammed – television networks, radio stations, newspapers from all over the world were pressing for a response to the Justi Plan. Wayne Ashcroft, President Pat Hall's chief of staff was called to the press office to try and calm things down.

'Just tell them we're considering a response, and then ask one of the friendly ones, NBC or someone, to fax me a copy.' Ashcroft walked out of the press room, wondering how anyone could be expected to respond to a document they hadn't yet seen. He returned to his office and phoned President Hall.

'Mr President. Justi seems to have finally made a move and the world's in a tailspin over it. He's going to cut down his trees or something. No mention of ducking debt interest though from what I can gather, but the environmentalists are having a coronary. Justi issued some sort of paper at his press conference this morning, I'm trying to get hold of it.' He paused as his secretary walked in clutching an NBC fax.

Ashcroft took it from her and glanced briefly at it.

'I think it's just arrived. I'd better come over with it because we're going to have to say something – the press lines are already jammed.'

'Wayne, try and get Gerard to make it too if he can.'

Ashcroft phoned Gerard O'Prey, Hall's chief economic adviser. Fifteen minutes later the three men were sitting in the Oval Office studying the Justi Plan. O'Prey skipped through the document and then casually dropped it on to Hall's desk. He looked at the president and Ashcroft, who were both studying it carefully. He felt contemptuous of environmental issues. For the last decade he had been forced to recommend more and more regulation of US industry over issues such as energy consumption, toxic wastes, industrial pollution and greenhouse-gas emissions. Where would it end? The increased environmental regulations were costing US industry at least an extra forty billion dollars each year. How many lost exports because of that? Now some lunatic in Brazil wanted to cut down all his trees – so what?

Hall and Ashcroft finally finished reading. Hall sat forward, still pondering its contents. He looked up at his chief of staff.

'And?'

Ashcroft glanced at O'Prey, who shrugged his shoulders.

'Justi's not saying just how much environmental damage he's going to do if he slashes four hundred thousand square kilometres of rainforest. I guess that's deliberate, but it's obviously the crunch issue here,' said Ashcroft.

Hall nodded in agreement.

'Wayne, see who you can get on conference from NCGef. If Peterson is available then grab him. He's probably already seen the report.'

'And inflated his lifeboat,' added O'Prey with undisguised sarcasm.

Ashcroft shook his head. O'Prey infuriated him, the foul-mouthed head of US economic policy, the epitome of narrow-mindedness. A man who espoused a nauseatingly casual and highly dismissive approach to almost all key issues, except for the dollar, interest rates and tax revenues.

Ashcroft left the office to phone Peter Peterson at the National Centre for Global Environmental Forecasting, in Boulder, Colorado. NCGef was one of the world's leading researchers on the greenhouse theory and, as advisers to the White House, they had been able to utilise state funding to construct unique computer models forecasting the global climatic conditions well into the next century. These models were the envy of climatologists the world over and, unlike Fernento's, which were operated on a four-year-old laptop with a two-gigabyte hard drive and a 180 MHz processor, the US equivalent required enormous mainframes to run them, such was their complexity. Of course no one knew if they were accurate – that would take at least another fifty years to establish, in the opinion of NCGef's finance director at each year's funding review at the White House.

Ashcroft reappeared.

'Any minute now,' he said as he pulled the phone screen down from its storage position in the ceiling. It flashed into life and a very perplexed Peterson – slightly flushed in the brow, his brown check suit as usual hanging off him as if off a peg – came into view.

'Hello Peter,' greeted Hall. 'Have you read the Justi Plan document yet?'

'Thank you, Mr President. I have seen it and I think it is one of the most potentially cataclysmic proposals that man has come up with since nuclear weapons.'

O'Prey shook his head. This was just the sort of nonsense reaction he was fearing.

'Isn't this what NCGef have been praying for,' he retorted angrily, turning to Hall. God – imagine the damage that someone like Peterson could do to markets, to the economy, if he went live to the world on the back of White House funding with irresponsible, ill-thought-out statements like that. Cataclysmic? What an ass.

O'Prey turned back to the screen, his voice strained.

'You've now got the whole world media beating your door down and just listen to the sort of nonsense you've just given us. How objective do you think you can be Peterson?'

He did not wait for a reply, addressing the president instead.

'Mr President. We can't let people like him come out with scaremongering trash. Think of the damage out there if he only repeats what he just told us.'

Peterson pointed into the camera.

'Listen to me, Gerard. I'm telling you, this is a threat to the ice caps, and if they go then you'll have to climb on to the White House roof to keep your socks dry. Why do people like you only take things seriously when it's too late to do anything about them?'

Hall stepped in.

'Gentlemen, please.' They fell quiet. 'Now let's just try and get a fix on this can we? Rationally get a fix, okay?' He did not wait for their agreement before continuing.

'Now Peter. What's the bottom line here as you see it? Facts, as many as you have. What are we up for?'

'Well we're talking about hundreds of millions of tonnes of carbon dioxide being pumped into the atmosphere, which would normally be absorbed by this area of forest. There's no sink to cope with that, global warming becomes absolutely inevitable then,' replied Peterson, in a blunt but nervous tone.

'Sorry Peter, what's a sink?' asked Ashcroft.

'A carbon-dioxide sink. The natural resources that absorb carbon dioxide from the atmosphere. Oceans and forests, they're the main two.'

Ashcroft raised his eyebrows; he was learning something new every day.

'You say global warming becomes inevitable. What are your temperature estimates then?' enquired Hall.

'At least one degree to our existing estimates of a three- to four-degree rise by the middle of the century.'

'But that's just it, Mr President,' interjected O'Prey. 'These people are always talking fifty years down the line. Your average American won't understand that bit, they'll just hear temperatures rising by five degrees and then we'll have national bloody hysteria to deal with. Ask him what the difference on the climate will be in a year's time, when you have to run for office again.'

'That's not the point Gerard, and you know it,' Peterson went on the attack. 'You cannot ignore a build-up of carbon-dioxide levels on this scale. That fact has been recognised by intergovernmental conferences now for more than thirty years, and all leading governments in the world have embarked on policies to limit their emissions of carbon dioxide. We can't let Justi push the clock back thirty years. And no matter what you say about the American people, the vast majority of them are already concerned about global warming so they'll take Justi seriously, even if you don't.'

Ashcroft recognised the truth in Peterson's last statement. Whether temperatures rose or not over the next fifty-odd years was academic. The immediate problem was political. How should they cope with the sentiment of the electorate, which would inevitably have some thoughts towards fifty years hence for the sake of their children, or their children's children? Successfully handling the Justi issue was going to be far from easy. He put forward his view.

'We have to sort out some kind of statement within the next few hours. Even if it's just that we're concerned and considering options. We're under a lot of pressure to speak. Have you made any statement to the press yet, Peter?'

Peterson looked awkward.

'I've had to say something, obviously – that's what people

expect from us.' He looked uncomfortably into the camera.

'A press release or what?' pushed Ashcroft irritably.

'No. No press release. Just verbal.'

'On or off the record, and if on, was it recorded?'

'Wait a minute Wayne. What is this? Some kind of inquisition? It was a small piece for NBC, that's all.'

O'Prey laughed.

'Hey Wayne. Sounds like it was on the record to me.'

Ashcroft ignored him. Peterson continued.

'All I did was to comment that if Justi put his Phase I into motion then global warming was inevitable. Anyway, you'll see it for yourselves on the news.'

Hall was looking less than happy. He knew that Ashcroft shared his concern that their response was going to be restricted by NCGef. It would be difficult, if not impossible, to argue a different line from that being promoted by Peterson. He was, after all, chief climatology adviser to the White House, and both Hall and Ashcroft had made strong supportive statements of NCGef's programmes as recently as last fall. If they decided to ignore Peterson now, their political opponents would have a field day and there was no doubt that the average American would believe Peterson.

'Anything else you think we ought to be aware of Peter?' Hall asked, a touch despondently.

'I don't think so. I take it you'll want our detailed report on the Justi Plan, with implications on the global climate.'

'Sure,' replied Ashcroft. 'Fax it as soon as you can, but don't – and I mean *don't* – release it to the press. In fact, don't say anything more to the press until we've sorted out a workable strategy this end. Okay?'

'No problem,' replied Peterson. 'Thanks for the call.'

Ashcroft cancelled the call and the screen went blank.

'Might as well see what NBC are going to run, Mr President,' said O'Prey. 'I don't trust Peterson. I bet he said more than he's letting on.'

He pressed the TV button on the control panel and it flashed back into life. He flicked it on to NBC, then looked at his watch. The news wasn't for a few minutes yet so he hit the mute button.

'Someone ought to teach the CIA to shoot straight,' Hall muttered. 'Wayne, fix some drinks will you?'

Ashcroft walked over to the drinks cabinet.

'Scotch and American, Mr President?' he enquired.

Hall nodded.

'On the rocks,' said O'Prey.

Ashcroft poured the drinks.

Hall took a long sip of his scotch, then sat back in his chair.

'Gentlemen, remind me next time we really need to do something, not to involve the Germans and Japanese. The Brits are all right but the other two....' He took another long sip. 'Yes, those two are delay this, hold off that, wait and see here. You can't maintain the status quo if the people making the decisions keep running scared.'

'Actually we didn't involve the Germans and the Japanese – it was the British who did that,' commented Ashcroft for the sake of historical accuracy.

'Well, why did we let them do a stupid things like that?' asked Hall.

'You've got it the wrong way round Mr President,' replied Ashcroft. 'It was the British running this from the start. It was their thing. Not ours.'

Hall shrugged his shoulders and sighed. Almost lamentably he added, 'Basically if we'd hit Justi a lot, lot earlier we wouldn't be having this meeting, we wouldn't be having this media aggravation and we wouldn't be facing a banking crisis.'

'No, no, no!' responded O'Prey. 'There's going to be no banking crisis over Justi. We've already ring-fenced any problems over Brazilian debt with the World Bank. Plus, who the hell does he think we are? He hasn't a prayer. No one's going to offer him a dime to save his trees – certainly not us. I mean look at this Mickey Mouse figure Justi's dreamt up.' He turned to his copy of the Justi Plan fax and found the 'rental' option. 'Thirty thousand dollars a year per square kilometre. And what's he thinking of chopping down? Here it is. Four hundred thousand square kilometres. He's asking for twelve billion bucks. He's a headcase.' O'Prey laughed.

Ashcroft pointed to the screen; the news was starting. He pressed the volume-control button and dimmed the office lights. The Justi Plan was the lead NBC news item. There were pictures of the rainforest, film footage of spider monkeys playing in the treetops, commentary on the myriad rare animal, insect and plant life that was being threatened, charts of carbon-dioxide levels and estimates of possible global temperatures. Film footage of the ice caps followed. O'Prey fetched himself another scotch when film of polar-bear cubs playing on the ice came on, muttering about why the White House didn't force Congress to withdraw their broadcasting licence. A clip from Justi's news conference was shown. Ashcroft pointed at the screen.

'There's that Hughes woman!' exclaimed Hall.

'Who?' enquired O'Prey.

Ashcroft sat back in his chair while O'Prey waited for a reply. When he realised that Ashcroft was not saying anything further, he looked back at the screen. Finally Peterson appeared. He was introduced as the White House adviser on the greenhouse issue.

'No way,' commented Ashcroft. 'We don't want him sounding like our mouthpiece.'

Peterson was asked for his opinion on the impact of the Justi Plan on global warming. Ashcroft and Hall braced themselves for his response. Peterson bowed his head slightly and with his right hand resting on top of an illuminated globe he talked gravely into the camera.

'I am afraid that the impact will be disastrous.'

O'Prey shook his head in disbelief – what a way to put it, he thought to himself. Peterson continued.

'If Justi carries out this threat, and I am deliberately calling it a threat not a plan, then global warming is past the debating stage. It will be a matter of fact. What we need is a positive response to either stop Justi or, if he is allowed to continue, to quickly forge international agreements on carbon-dioxide emission reductions by limiting, for instance, the burning of fossil fuels. If we don't do anything we are going to witness an environmental disaster that will threaten our entire existence.'

The footage switched from Peterson to comment from leading environmentalists. Hall motioned to Ashcroft to turn off the broadcast. It was pointless saying anything. Peterson had put them well and truly in a corner, that was all there was to it. Hall picked up his phone and called his London ambassador, who reported that the British government was saying little and was calling for a discussion of the Justi Plan by the United Nations. Good idea, Hall thought. He turned back to Ashcroft and O'Prey.

'The British are boxing clever,' he said, trying to sound upbeat, forcing half a smile in an attempt to raise morale. Ashcroft in particular was looking very flat indeed.

'They're saying it's a global issue, best left with the UN.'

Ashcroft thought for a few moments.

'That at least takes the heat off us for a few days.'

'Yeah. And all we have to keep on saying is we'll make our position clear in the UN when the response of all the leading nations is heard,' continued Hall. 'Agreed?'

They nodded.

'Right,' said Ashcroft as he finished his drink and rose to his feet. 'I'll get over to the press office and sort out a statement.' He turned to Hall. 'Do you want to see it first?'

Hall shook his head.

'Just a copy by tomorrow morning Wayne.'

O'Prey jumped in.

'Well do me a favour then and stick something in it that

raises some concerns about NCGef. I mean, Peterson needs a smack.'

Ashcroft blanked him.

Hall finished his scotch.

'Tomorrow morning then Wayne?'

'Certainly Mr President.' He turned sharply away and strode out of the office to avoid leaving with O'Prey.

'Can I go?' enquired O'Prey.

Hall nodded. Once O'Prey had left he walked slowly across his office and looked out across the White House lawn. His instinct told him to keep out of the limelight on the Justi issue. After all, there wasn't likely to be an upside to it. The US election was only twelve months away. He'd see how things developed before making any personal public statement.

CHAPTER FOURTEEN

N ews that the United Nations secretary general, Helena De'Boer, had called an emergency meeting to discuss the Justi Plan reached Anna just before she met with Roberto the next morning. They had intended to spend a few hours reviewing international coverage, but there was little time for this now. They looked through the headlines while waiting for Valto, who Roberto had asked to join them the moment Anna told him that a UN meeting was imminent. The headlines summarised most of the coverage in any event.

> *'Brazil takes world to the brink.'*
> *'Global warming imminent as Brazil to cull forest.'*
> *'Ice caps to melt as Brazil fells forest.'*
> *'Brazil threatens global climate.'*

Anna could not help smiling at the front page of *The Sun*, the leading British tabloid. It had Roberto's picture with the simple headline, 'MAD!'

Valto entered the room.

'Presidente Justi. Senhora Hughes,' he said, bowing slightly.

214

'This is a real turn up. The United Nations, no less. Can you feel it, Senhora? Brazil has become centre stage. Centre stage now and to stay. This is the way for us.'

'Well the UN's called an emergency meeting to discuss it, so we've certainly raised the political temperature,' replied Anna cautiously.

'Who called it?' asked Roberto.

'I hear unofficially it was Britain and that there's a resolution likely to be submitted as well. The UN have promised to fax the resolution as soon as they get it themselves. Looking at these headlines, I think we'll find we're up against it quite quickly. It could be a fairly damning resolution.'

Valto shrugged his shoulders.

'Mere words, that's all. Just rhetoric.'

Roberto picked up the phone to his office. The fax had just been received; it was brought straight down. Roberto read it out loud.

'*UN Resolution, sponsored by Her Majesty's Government of the United Kingdom:*
To condemn the promotion by Brazil of the Justi Plan, a plan designed to threaten the global climate balance to the obvious danger of all United Nations members, and to secure from the Secretariat a mandate to prevent Brazil from enacting the said Plan, by the application of comprehensive economic sanctions and if necessary by military force.'

'Military force? Military force did they say?' asked Valto.

Justi nodded.

'They're coming on very strong very quickly,' Anna commented, 'and knowing how these things tend to work, they wouldn't have put it down as strongly as that without first getting at least the US to agree to it.'

'Has a date been set?' replied Roberto.

Anna scanned the document.

'It doesn't say but it will be at least a week away. These things take a bit of organising.'

'So we will have some time to gain support?'

'Yes. A little time, but equally the Western nations will be on a charm offensive over the same period, and they have a lot more resources than we do.'

'Forgive me Presidente, but isn't the real concern about military intervention? And if so, isn't it just the permanent members of the security council that are key?' interjected Valto.

'That is correct General. And?' replied Roberto.

'If this is the case, all we really need to think about is how we get either Russia or China to vote against the resolution, then we'll always have the veto in the security council. There'll never be UN backing for military action.'

'The General is right, Roberto. We only need Russia or China to veto the resolution and the UN can't act.' Anna noticed Roberto looked a little edgy, as if doubts were creeping in.

'General, what are our relationships like with Russia and China?' he asked.

'We don't even talk to the Chinese,' Valto replied.

'Has there been a fall-out?' Anna asked.

'No. We're just not close. But that's mainly because we are very close to the Russians. I could talk to Melintikov, their ambassador.'

'Could you phone him now, General?' Roberto asked.

'How important is it to get them on our side?' Valto replied.

'Extremely.' Anna nodded in agreement.

'Well, the Russians will need a deal. If they support us in the UN we'll have to buy them off. Some MIG fighters, high-level reconnaissance planes, armoured personnel carriers, their new ZF9 tanks.'

Roberto stared at him.

'How much might we need to spend?'

'About four hundred million dollars.'

'But General we don't have that kind of money. The World Bank has us in a vice at the moment. I don't know if we could raise four hundred million.'

Valto looked surprisingly relaxed.

'Tell me, Presidente, how much do you think defending a military strike from the West would cost us?'

Roberto went quiet.

'Four hundred million. You think that is a lot of money. If they strike against us we won't have a single plane, or airfield, or military base, or frigate. They'll destroy the lot. We have over twenty-six billion dollars of hardware that they'd go for. Four hundred million seems a modest sum, and our armed forces are strengthened for free.'

Roberto stayed silent. Valto was probably right. If Russia had to be bought off then it was a lot cheaper than trying to defend military action. But finding that kind of money was still a major problem.

He stretched across the table, took the phone from beside Valto and called Santez at the central bank.

'Yes. I know it's a very large sum, but we need it.... I realise it is strange to buy lots of military hardware at the moment, yes.... Yes. I realise that we have chronic social and welfare problems at the moment.... No, there will be no publicity.... You will have to trust me. We need the money.'

He replaced the receiver and turned to Valto.

'Okay General. Santez can find your four hundred million.' The concern showed in his face and his voice was uncertain. 'But we don't sign anything or pay anything until we see their support in the UN.'

'Understood, Presidente.'

They sat quietly as Valto phoned the Russian embassy. The conversation was held in Russian. You really are a dark horse, Anna thought to herself. The call over, Roberto asked Valto where he had learnt Russian.

'I spent four years on attachment to the Russian air force. They've always been close to us – just take a look at all the MIG fighters on our airfields,' he replied.

'What are they saying then?' Roberto asked.

'He's going to phone Moscow.'

'And what is he likely to be telling Moscow?'

'Four hundred million dollars probably. You must

understand that even for Russia it is tricky for them to back us. It would mean Russia siding against the world's other leading nations. Oh, and Melintikov will need personal terms.'

'What? On top of the money?' exclaimed Roberto.

Valto held up his hands.

'It is nothing like that scale. It's just that he likes it here in Brazil. He has many friends; and he and his wife, well they would like to stay when he retires in three years' time. Of course when he retires he will no longer have an official residence to live in and....'

Roberto interrupted.

'Whatever. You sort out Melintikov as you see fit.'

'Thank you, Presidente.'

'When do you hope to hear back from him?' asked Anna.

'I'm sure if I phone him this afternoon the deal will have been agreed.'

'That soon?' she said, surprised by Valto's confidence in the speed of any government decision-making.

'Yes. I would have thought so. They're not worried about our trees, Senhora. They are not interested in the environment; you only have to see the poisoning of their own lakes and rivers to understand that Russia cares only for money.'

'Say we know Russia will back us. Should we even attend?' Roberto asked.

Good question, Anna thought. If they attended they would have to speak. Was a war of words across a debating chamber worth it? Especially if they knew that the debate was academic, that, when it came to the vote, Russia would at the very least abstain and the resolution be automatically defeated.

'Only to up the political temperature. These emergency meetings are relayed around the world,' she replied. 'If you were to address the UN as you did at Copacabana I think it could be highly beneficial for us.'

'I agree Senhora. Presidente is a fine orator. I also think the Russians would be a little offended if we weren't there.'

'Anna, can you organise things and let me know? I do not want to stay in New York, though. Straight in and back out.'

She understood. As the meeting broke up, Valto disappearing in his usual whirlwind manner, Anna collected her papers to retire to work in her own apartment.

'Can you spare me any time?' Roberto asked as she was about to leave. Anna was surprised – there was nothing obviously pressing.

'Just for a chat, unless of course you're too busy,' he continued hastily.

'No, it's no trouble. I'll just drop off these papers.'

Anna wondered what Roberto wanted to chat about. It wasn't really his style. He had always been very matter of fact, showing little desire to extend work into anything remotely conversational, let alone social. She resisted the temptation to check on her appearance and rejoined him.

'Anything in particular?' she enquired.

'I just thought I'd check that you were happy here, not missing London or friends and family or anything?' he enquired, as they took the lift together to the ground floor.

'No time to even think about home,' she replied, laughing lightly.

'And your accommodation, everything there okay?'

'Yes. It's just fine,' she replied as the lift doors opened. Justi led her through the guard room on to the small plaza that formed the square connecting various military departments and his new presidential quarters.

The presidential guard opened doors for them as they approached. Anna followed Roberto through a grand entrance hall, with ceramic tiled floor on which stood a collection of antique high-backed chairs and half-tables. The walls were decked with large gilt-edged mirrors and fine-art paintings. A private garden was accessed through an ornate wrought-iron gate at the far end of the hall. Roberto stopped briefly to instruct his housekeeper that lunch would be for two, then sauntered across a small lawn to sit in the shade on a large white marble plinth supported by two carved stone columns. They sat quietly for half a minute, Anna enjoying the songs of the small colourful birds that flitted around the surrounding roof and the branches of the bougainvillea in full flower.

'It does beat São Paulo. Rio too,' sighed Anna as she watched the light breeze catch the blossom, making it fall like confetti to the grass below.

'And London? Cold, grey London?'

'Anything beats London in November.'

'I remember the shivering. I was always shivering in London. Sometimes even in the height of summer I used to shiver and Angela would say how could I, when passers-by had t-shirts removed and hanging from the pockets of their shorts. In the end she used to say it was nerves!'

'Ah, but Angela was used to it, yes?'

'Yes. That's what I used to tell her. She'd had twenty-three years to get used to it. I used to say it was only a matter of time. But we liked London. The theatres, the restaurants ... it had a buzz to it.'

'How did you meet Angela?' she asked, surprised to hear him talk so openly about his past, and wanting to take advantage of it.

'She was an economist working for a British merchant bank, Coptham & Co. She was just a junior and they packed her off to Brazil to consider their options on a syndicated Brazilian corporate loan package that was turning sour on them. I was a journalist doing an article on Brazilian corporate debt problems. Our paths met.'

'And?'

'Well, that's it.'

'And you said "Shame about the syndicated loan package but let's get married".'

Roberto laughed. 'Ah. Nearly. No, it wasn't love at first sight. I remember thinking that she was too small! But we thought it would be interesting to compare notes and then she asked if I could give her any background on the socio-economic issues, so I took her to downtown São Paulo.'

Lunch arrived and they moved to sit at a dark wood table with matching chairs. After tasting the wine he talked on.

'You've seen the deprivation. In those days the children

were not in fear of living above ground and there were children as young as two begging. So we were downtown when this S-Class Mercedes swung into the street and we watched as a brightly coloured box was thrown from its passenger window. Of course the children ran to pick it up. A boy of about six got there first and held it proudly in front of his friends. I can still see him grinning with delight as he stood in the middle of the road. He was so excited that he didn't hear the truck behind him. He had no chance. Bang!' He smacked his hands together; the birds fell quiet. He looked away from Anna for a few moments before continuing.

'Angela was distraught. Beside herself. The police came, ambulances too, but it was no use. The boy was killed instantly. We gave witness statements and then I got a cab to take Angela back to her hotel. I saw she was holding on to the box the boy had picked up. I went to take it from her but she held it away from me. I remember her words as if it were yesterday. "It's empty," she said. Then she just sat there, staring impassively out of the window, tears streaming down her cheeks.'

He paused, sat up straight and turned to face Anna, as if coming out of a trance.

'That's how we met.'

'And she became converted to Brazil's poor?' Anna asked.

'Yes. We both did. Angela started thinking about how Brazil could get its dues from banks rather than the other way round. Of course it went down like a lead balloon back at Coptham & Co. Hell of a bust-up, I can tell you.' His eyes now reflected fonder memories.

'And you returned to London with her?' asked Anna, playing with her minute steak and salad.

'No. She left her bank and we married out here. We went back to London the following year. She wanted to write her thesis on contemporary economics – as she called it – for an MA. Which she did.'

'And the rest is history?'

'Yes,' said Roberto wistfully. 'Very, very unfinished history,' he stated purposefully. He pushed his steak, untouched, to one side. 'And now we have a chance to finish things.'

He reverted again to small talk, remaining at the table after Anna had left, gathering his thoughts. He was advised in the early evening that the Russians had agreed to back him in the UN. He tried to resist entertaining dreams of a new era, mindful that the odds were still very much against success. Later, in his apartment, he moved to the window, watching as the sun fell beneath the horizon and the moon retraced its path across a partly starlit sky. He clung to the hope of destiny that felt more fragile than the moonlight itself.

CHAPTER FIFTEEN

From the moment the presidential jet touched down at JFK airport, Roberto was mobbed by reporters. He was concerned about the lack of any meaningful security, as cameras were thrust into his face and reporters pushed and shoved to get microphones or lenses closer to him. He had not spoken to the media since the press conference at which they had announced the Justi Plan, but that had not stopped him becoming the centre of global attention – the man responsible for the Justi Plan itself. His progress to the car frequently slowed to a standstill. Questions rained down on him.

Was he going to withdraw Phase I?

Did he accept he was holding the world to ransom?

Had any government shown an interest in renting forest?

Would Brazil defend itself if the UN sanctioned military intervention?

Had anyone else indicated they'd support Brazil in the UN?

Was he actually going to speak against the British resolution?

In the end he had made a brief statement, hoping this would satisfy them enough to allow him to reach his car. Yes, he was here to speak. No, he did not intend to withdraw Phase I.

He was hopeful that the resolution would fail. He finally made it to his car as the main television network reporters handed back live to their studios, CNN calling his brief statement 'defiant'. When he arrived at the UN, under a notably light police escort, he was relieved to see far tighter security, with the press held back behind temporary railings. His security concerns receding, he gave them a little smile and a half-wave as he strolled into the building.

The UN had received so many requests for press passes they had denied many, causing uproar and claims of favouritism among the numerous disappointed reporters. They would instead have to watch the debate via relay in three further conference rooms adjoining the main chamber.

A hush went round the room as Roberto entered, flanked by his permanent delegate Dominic Durest. They ignored the stares of over five hundred delegates and walked calmly to their seats, halfway up the lower tier on the far side of the chamber. After about five minutes, which Roberto spent discussing with Durest the location of leading delegations, particularly the whereabouts of the Russians, the UN secretary general rose and called the chamber to order. The customary details were run through, explaining who had called and seconded the meeting and who had submitted and seconded the resolution; in both cases Britain with support from Germany. Britain was then called to speak.

Britain likened the Justi Plan to quasi-chemical warfare, expounding that Brazil was intent on suffocating the world and that no matter how they tried to disguise it, they were holding the world to ransom. The Germans then spoke to support the resolution. They agreed entirely with Britain that Justi was an international outlaw, threatening the world with global warming if it didn't pay up. It was quite clear that the Justi Plan had absolutely nothing to do with agricultural expansion or mineral exploration, and everything to do with exploitation and extortion. The world could not and must not sit back and allow nations like Brazil to endanger the world's ecosystem. Justi, for all his mild manners, was trying to become a dictator, using the things that belonged to the world, not to him, to do this. It was the world's air, the world's water; the world was well within its rights to defend itself. Japan then spoke for the resolution, as did the Americans. Roberto listened impassively to the speeches. There were no surprises – he felt he could have written better ones for them himself.

'Justi listens defiantly,' commented CNN.

An hour and a half of repetitive, virulent speeches were heard, all solidly in favour of the resolution. Eventually the secretary general turned to the Brazilian delegation.

'The president of Brazil, Mr Justi,' she announced. 'To speak against the resolution?'

Laughter broke out across the chamber. Roberto smiled back at her, nodded and rose to walk down the steps and across the floor to the rostrum.

'Justi smiled defiantly before speaking,' noted CNN.

Unlike the other speakers, he carried nothing – no script, no dossier from which to recite extracts, not even a scribbled note to remind him of the points he had to cover. For the last two decades the issues had preoccupied him. He thought briefly of Angela as he turned to face the delegates. This should have been her moment. He took a sip of water, gripped the rostrum with both hands and began Brazil's defence.

'Secretary general. Ladies and gentlemen. We have heard some stirring speeches. I intend to be brief, to the point. I wonder if I could ask you to turn your thoughts back to your homelands. What does "home" mean to the people you represent? We have heard from Britain, Germany, America, Japan, France, Canada. They are agreed on the Justi Plan. They also represent people to whom "home" means at the very least a roof over their heads and bread on their table. Is that what you understand it to mean in your country? In Brazil, for fifteen million of our children, the roof over their heads is that of a shop doorway, a cardboard box, even a sewer. Bread is what they have to beg for. The children of my country want shelter, they want bread, but they cannot have it. And I know that they are in the same desperate situation as the children in some of your countries. So what am I to do for them?'

He paused and looked around the hushed chamber.

'Should I not offer them a home for shelter, warmth, security? Aren't they the rights of all peoples? Shouldn't they have bread? Little ones – one year, two years old. Boys, girls aged three, four, five. Young mothers aged twelve and thirteen, babes-in-arms born into the only home they'll ever know, the streets and sewage systems of our cities. Shouldn't all of them have hope? This then is my starting point this afternoon. I know that many of the so-called "developing" countries here today will start from a similar position. I wonder how I can change things. So I look at Brazil today and discover that I can't change it; I can't influence the affairs of my own nation because I find I am not actually president of Brazil, rather I am a puppet of the World Bank. It is the World Bank that tells me what I can or cannot do because it holds our purse strings. But the Brazilian people have given me a mandate to change that, to seek economic freedom and prosperity that will bring dignity to all Brazilians, hope to all our children.'

Roberto took another sip of water.

'Amazonia.' He paused, and again looked round at all the delegates. 'Brazil's vast, untapped resource. Who knows the riches she holds? We decide to tap them, to release her potential wealth for the good of the nation. To plant crops for our nation's hungry; to develop our infrastructure further throughout Brazil and so strengthen our industrial base; to explore for minerals which, if discovered, will provide more foreign exchange. But suddenly we are told that this is not permitted, that the forest supplies the world with life-giving oxygen and removes the harmful carbon dioxide. Therefore, Brazil must not tamper with her forests. Strange, then, that if I were to ask you all to buy from us a tree in our forests, a tree that gives you the air that you breathe, you all say no. But if I cut it down, strip it of its leaves and branches, cut it into table tops or doors or skirting boards, ah, then you'll pay.

'The truth is that, in the market economy in which we all

operate, there is a value placed on Amazonia being left untouched; there has to be a value because that, after all, is why we're here today. You all value our forest, you just don't want to pay for it. Its products are the air you breathe and the water you drink – the essentials of life itself. Since the dawn of time, Brazil has exported these free to the world. But now we take a leaf out of the book of the industrialised world. Supply and demand, natural-resource capacity, commodity exchanges; we have placed Amazonia's products into the world market. You need our air, fine. Pay for it. You want to drink our water, fine. Pay for it. After all, if we want your oil, your gold, your televisions, your cars, your whisky, what do you say to us? "Fine. Pay for it." This then is the principle of free trade, where commodities are valued in an open market. The question is, what are you prepared to pay?

'Brazil is not saying you *have* to pay. We don't mind if you decide not to. We will then get on with the job of clearing the forest to regenerate our economy. It is not us holding the world to ransom, it is only the world finally realising at last that nothing in life is free and that the things it values have to be paid for.

'Finally, the resolution carries the threat of military action against us. Isn't that rather rich, coming from two countries, Britain and Germany, that were themselves once completely covered by forest and woodlands but which have cleared vast tracts to make way for agriculture. Why don't they replant forests across their fields? Why is it always one rule for them and one rule for the rest of us – poor countries beholden to *their* money, *their* banks?

'I am not a military person. I care deeply for my country, for its people, for its children. I come here in peace. But I come here determined for the Justi Plan to succeed.' His speech over he stood back from the rostrum.

There was a profound silence. In the packed bars of the villages, towns and cities of Brazil, men and women of all ages greeted his speech with loud cheering, many on their feet, some punching the air. From around the chamber some delegates removed their headsets, which had provided them with an interpreter for the speeches, and stood to applaud. The Congo, Namibia, Sudan, Venezuela, Pakistan, Malaysia. They were joined by other poorer nations – Ethiopia, Poland, Hungary. What had begun as isolated applause was spreading across the chamber. Zaire, Gabon, Nepal. But the Western European nations sat firm. Roberto glanced across to the Russian delegation. They too remained seated, as did China. He left the rostrum and returned to his seat, the applause only abating as he sat down again.

'The Russians aren't looking terribly supportive,' he whispered to Durest.

'They never give much away. It was a tremendous speech, Presidente,' he replied.

The secretary general asked if any other delegation wished to speak against the resolution. Slowly, representatives of several developing nations, who rarely spoke, came to the rostrum to support Brazil and to express their hope that a new world economic order might result, in which wealth was more evenly distributed. The array of clothes and languages brought colour to the usually staid proceedings. An hour later, having heard from all nations wishing to speak, the secretary general called for a recorded vote by show of hands. She re-read the resolution.

'Those in favour,' she called.

Roberto looked at the Russian and Chinese delegates and was relieved to see that their hands were not raised. He watched as American and British delegates turned round to see if the same two countries had supported it, intense discussions breaking out when they realised that they had not.

'Presidente. See – Russia and China have not supported it,' said Durest reassuringly.

'But Dominic,' said Roberto, 'we need them to actually vote against it. Otherwise the security council could still take military action.'

'I know they could, but if there's a strong vote against here, it would be tricky. They wouldn't have much of a mandate.'

'There are thirty-two recorded votes in favour,' announced the secretary general.

'We should win this now then?' queried Roberto.

'Not necessarily, Presidente. Many nations abstain to avoid causing offence, particularly when the Western nations have voted for it. It might be tighter than you think.'

'Those against,' called the secretary general.

Durest turned to see both the Russians and the Chinese had their hands raised. Roberto hugged him, the chamber succumbed to uproar as he stood up, smiling broadly, hands raised high. They watched the consternation of the American, British and German delegates, who were already clearing their tables for a speedy exit and private conference.

'There are forty-four recorded votes against,' the secretary general announced over the commotion.

Roberto and Durest were swamped by the congratulations of countless delegates. Roberto felt elated. In the battle for the hearts and minds of the world, Brazil was coming out on top. They walked in triumph from the chamber, flashbulbs blazing as they left the building into a cold, overcast New York.

Roberto strolled over to the massed ranks of the world press. Questions were shouted at him, but as he came nearer and motioned to the journalists for silence they quietened into the murmur of lens shutters.

'I would like to say that for the people of my country this is a victory to cherish. It means that the Justi Plan will commence unhindered. We will lose no time now in setting Phase I in motion. If the world decides to take up the option of renting forest from us then they have to move speedily. In respect of the leading Western nations, they need to be far more conciliatory than they were in their speeches this afternoon.'

'Will you stay on in New York?' asked one journalist.

'No. I am returning immediately to Brazil.'

'Should be quite a party,' noted another.

Roberto smiled at him.

'Well, we're very good at parties.'

He turned and with questions again flying through the air,

he gave a small wave before getting back into his car for the return journey.

●

President Hall watched the scenes of jubilation on television from the comfort of his private lounge. He had been impressed with Justi, but the outcome was nothing short of a disaster. He ran his fingers through his hair. Where on Earth did they go from here? Russia and China had voted against, despite the British assuring him that China would abstain and Russia would actually support the resolution. How had they got that one so wrong?

Not only was it the worst outcome conceivable, but the West had been humiliated in front of billions of viewers the world over. A military response to Justi was now out of the question. Should they start to negotiate over renting forest? No, he said to himself, shaking his head. He stood up and walked across his lounge to look out across the White House gardens. Of all the things he had ever thought he might have to face as president of the United States, this was not one of them.

He thought of the oil embargo operated by the Arab states in the early 1970s. What was the way out of that one? Like Justi, the Arab leaders had come from nowhere to pre-eminence on a global stage. Sheikh Zaki Yamani; Prince Fayed. He returned to his desk. They had ended up paying the Arabs. Should they pay Justi? What for? Who was to say that Peterson was right? The greenhouse stuff could be a lot of hot air. He laughed at the irony of it. If Justi did fell a quarter of his forest, who was to say the world would start to heat up? What would change? The day after they had done the deed would there be any noticeable difference in the world? Probably not. Hall knew, though, that it was not that simple. Not all Americans would agree. As for their allies – well, they were in an even more difficult situation than he was. The Germans really believed that this was a pending disaster. Britain, too, was firmly in the greenhouse camp. That was how they had justified the UN resolution, but this had failed and now they were cornered. At least he had yet to say anything on the subject, he mused. How could they play down the greenhouse issue?

He phoned Ashcroft.

'Wayne?'

'Mr President. What a shambles at the UN.'

'Yes I agree. I watched it from my office.'

'He's a smug sod that Justi.'

'Actually I thought he came across very well.'

Ashcroft felt rebuffed.

'Anyway,' continued Hall. 'I want you to try and find some academic who can actually take issue with this greenhouse stuff. We have to start playing things down a lot – and quick. Otherwise we'll have no option but to pay Justi.'

'I can't think of anyone, Sir,' replied Ashcroft, alarmed at the way events were unfolding, particularly the mention of actually paying Justi.

Hall was starting to get irritated by the whole thing.

'Just find me one and get him to the White House as soon as possible. And if the press gets wind of it there'll be hell to pay.' He hung up.

Ashcroft stared at the phone. He had never heard Hall talk like that before. O'Prey, yes, and very regularly, but not Hall. He picked up his jacket and walked over to the press office, thinking as hard as he could for the name of a scientist or college or institute that was anti-greenhouse, but it was difficult to think of anyone. They had spent the last decade ignoring all other views; the greenhouse theory was official policy. Perhaps someone in the press office would know someone.

He walked in and immediately wished he hadn't. The staff were besieged by journalists.

'What's the line on the UN decision Mr Ashcroft?' asked a harassed Carol Whyte, one of his senior press officers, a woman in her mid-forties, with yellowed teeth from smoking since her teens. Ashcroft shrugged his shoulders, to the disappointment of all the staff.

She sighed. I need a fag, she thought, and left the office for the glorified closet that was technically the smoking room.

Ashcroft began poring over the editorials of the world's leading English-speaking broadsheets, hoping to find a comment that might raise doubts over the greenhouse effect. There was none. He turned to his staff.

'Hey, everyone. Just leave the phones for a minute please.'

Callers were placed on hold; everyone turned to face him. Perhaps he was going to give them a statement after all – it would make life an awful lot easier if they could at least give some official line.

'Does anyone here know of a scientist or institute, college

or whatever, which believes that cutting down the rainforests *won't* result in global warming? You know, someone who thinks the greenhouse thing's wrong.'

He met with blank stares. They were disappointed that Ashcroft seemed not to want to issue a statement. He looked round the room, fifteen heads shaking one by one.

'Think, will you. Are you all sure?'

The room was silent. No one could recall anything other than support for the greenhouse theory. Ashcroft bit his bottom lip, a habit he'd had for as long as he could remember when things were going wrong for him.

One of the press officers asked him what the official line was over the UN decision to turn down the resolution.

'The official line is we don't have an official line, okay?' He was half shouting. He left the room in a growing temper, where in heaven's name was he supposed to find a credible anti-greenhouse theory? He almost walked into Whyte as she returned from her smoke.

'You don't know of anyone anti-greenhouse, do you?' he snapped.

She thought for a moment. She had read something earlier.

'I think so,' she replied. 'I think I came across something like that this morning.' She moved past him. 'I'll just fetch it.'

She returned with a paper tucked under her arm and handed it to him.

'Thanks,' he said dismissively, already studying the article in *The Washington Post*, which quoted a Professor John Thorne of the Massachusetts Environmental Institute. It was only a few lines but there was a glimmer of hope in it.

'The greenhouse theory carries too much weight in academia, the media and government. It's not proven. This growing hysteria over the Justi Plan and global warming is unnecessary.'

Excellent! Ashcroft thought. He looked up at Whyte, who had remained by his side while he scanned the piece.

'Brilliant. You're an absolute darling,' he said to her, squeezing her arm gently. He returned to his office and phoned the Institute straight away. Yes. Thorne was available. Sure, just putting you through. Were there any flaws in the greenhouse theory? Good. Could he come to Washington? No, the White House would not pay the airfare; they would send a private jet. Yes, he would be met at the airport. No, he was not to mention the meeting to anybody, everything, including this phone call, was classified.

Meanwhile Whyte had returned to her desk and phoned her lawyers. Yes, squeezing her arm was sexual harassment. Yes, they'd be delighted to file against the chief of staff, who should be setting a far higher example. She could expect damages of over ten thousand dollars.

●

Ashcroft met Thorne off the plane. They talked in the limousine as it sped back to the White House, Ashcroft informing Thorne that the meeting would be with the President, but, worried about how to establish Hall's interest in anti-greenhouse theories, he avoided saying too much.

'We just want a second opinion on NCGef, that's about the long and short of it,' he explained as they walked through the White House to Hall's office. Thorne wondered why this entailed fetching him at the drop of a hat in a private jet for an emergency meeting with the president himself, but thought it wise not to express this.

'Mr President, Professor Thorne from the Massachusetts Environmental Institute,' Ashcroft announced.

'Professor Thorne, very pleased to meet you,' greeted Hall, shaking him warmly by the hand. 'Do sit down.'

'Well this is an honour, Mr President.'

Hall smiled at him.

'I wish it was under less pressing circumstances Professor, but here we are. Brazil wants to suffocate us or flood us – or both – and it's getting a little difficult. Wayne, perhaps some drinks?'

'Certainly. Professor?'

'Just a mineral water. Still.'

'I'll have my usual thanks.'

'I was just saying to Professor Thorne on the way over here that we need a second opinion on NCGef,' said Ashcroft as he fixed the drinks. 'We've never really had to question it before, but then, it has never been quite the issue it is now either. Isn't that so Professor?' He handed round the drinks.

'I can understand your predicament,' replied Thorne.

'Oh, I wouldn't say predicament, Professor,' Hall interjected. 'But we have to get a more detailed understanding of this issue. We want to try and calm things down generally.'

'But the UN has strengthened Justi's hand, Mr President. Don't you agree?'

'Well let's stick to the subject in hand shall we,' said Hall coolly, reluctant to allow Thorne to enter a discussion on US policy against Brazil. 'Now, does the greenhouse theory hold water or not?'

'Not entirely,' responded Thorne. Hall and Ashcroft waited for him to expand on this reply but he didn't. He took his glass and sipped his water before looking back at them both.

'Not entirely what?' prompted Ashcroft. He noticed that Thorne suddenly looked rather strained – intimidated even.

'The big picture is that the White House cut our funding six years ago because it had budget problems. As I said a few minutes ago, I do understand your predicament. I was wondering if, before we go any further, you could understand my own.' His voice was shaking and a few drops of sweat had appeared on his forehead.

Ashcroft flashed a menacing glance at him. Was he stark raving mad? This was the president of the United States! Hall smiled at Thorne.

'Let's say then that you have fifteen minutes to convince me to recommence funding. How does that sound, Professor?'

'I'm not sure I can.'

'Fifteen minutes,' Hall reiterated.

Thorne shuffled on his chair. He had done his best, he supposed. He could look the Institute board in the eyes and say he had tried.

'Okay. NCGef turn a blind eye to certain data. Firstly, they say that global temperatures have already increased. That's based on temperatures reported from thousands of weather stations throughout the world.'

Ashcroft interrupted.

'Twenty-two million of them a year.'

'That's right,' Thorne continued. 'Twenty-two million a year – but they're all land based. The problem is that land makes up just thirty-two per cent of the Earth's surface, so when you just use land data and try to apply it on a global basis, you're making enormous assumptions that sea air temperatures are behaving in the same way as land ones.'

'But that doesn't mean the NCGef research is wrong, does it?' asked Hall.

'There's more. There's the problem of heat islands in respect of the land data.'

Ashcroft raised his eyebrows. A few days ago it was carbon-dioxide sinks, now it was urban heat islands.

'Urban what?'

'Urban heat islands. Many of these measurements are taken from the middle of towns and cities. Basically, when you replace vegetation with concrete buildings you distort the temperature patterns, the buildings heat up during the day and then they release their stored heat at night. And don't think that it's insignificant. It's not at all. It can add up to two to three degrees.'

'Whereas the greenhouse theory is only basing itself on a one-degree rise this century, right?' asked Ashcroft.

'That's right. Their data may just be about towns and cities warming, not global warming. I mean, NASA has analysed data from satellites that monitor global rather than just land-based temperatures. They do this monthly and to within one hundredth of a degree. They eliminate the urban heat islands from their research and this shows that the Earth was warmer in the first half of the nineteen-eighties, but has been cooler ever since then.'

'And what does NCGef say about temperatures over the same period?' asked Hall.

'They have temperatures now two-tenths of a degree higher since the nineteen-eighties, whereas NASA is saying there's been no rise in temperatures globally at all.'

Hall smiled at Ashcroft. Things were looking up. Here was a story the American people would buy, no problem at all. So would the world. Satellites didn't lie; NASA was the undisputed authority on global and space-data measurement. Perhaps all those trillions of dollars funding NASA was worth it after all. The White House could do a U-turn on the greenhouse theory, saying there was no conclusive evidence that the increased levels of carbon dioxide witnessed throughout the world since the 1980s had raised global temperatures, and that this was supported by NASA research. Hall laughed to himself. They'd be home and dry.

'NASA will verify this?' asked Ashcroft

'Of course. Shall I continue?' replied Thorne.

They nodded their enthusiastic support.

'This is first-rate material, Professor,' replied Hall.

Thorne felt a warm glow, which grew over the next twenty minutes as he explained his analysis of available data on the greenhouse effect. He pointed to a growing list of flaws in the NCGef model. Not all of these were understood by Hall and Ashcroft, but that did not prevent Thorne from talking about them at great length. Feeling tired, Hall finally stopped Thorne from going into any more detail about rumours that NCGef had been supplied defective microchips for their computer systems, thereby rendering questionable all their data.

'We'll just stick to the NASA stuff I think, Professor.' He turned to Ashcroft. 'I think this NASA issue needs to be given to the country at large. Do you agree?'

'Most definitely,' replied Ashcroft, banging his fist down gently on to Hall's desk.

'Well Professor, I'd like to make you our new adviser on climatology.' He stood up, reached across his desk and shook Thorne by the hand. 'I think NCGef had better go back and do some more homework.'

'Very much so, Mr President,' agreed Ashcroft.

Thorne was clearly delighted.

'Can I thank you both for giving my Institute the privilege of this meeting and you have my word that we will at all times do everything....'

'Very nice to have met you, Professor,' Hall interrupted, walking towards the door.

Thorne looked a little taken aback. Ashcroft came to his aid.

'If you come with me Professor, we can sort out the funding arrangements. We also need to draft a press statement.'

Thorne shook Hall by the hand again as he left the office with Ashcroft.

'Thank you,' Hall said to him, before turning to Ashcroft. 'Make sure you speak with NASA and get them to agree any press statement before we make this official.'

'Naturally,' replied Ashcroft, patting Thorne on the back as they walked passed O'Prey, who had been pacing up and down outside, anxious to talk with Hall about the first bout of downward movement in world stockmarkets that had followed the UN defeat that afternoon, and the growing sales of the dollar in Far East markets since Wall Street had closed.

CHAPTER SIXTEEN

The first of the sun's rays clipped the top of the forest canopy, a diffuse yellow tint edged the rising mist. Anna found the view mystical as she looked through the small cabin window of a Brazilian army helicopter, flying low across the top of the forest. Such a vast area, she thought to herself; mile after mile, and then mile again of forest, as far as the eye could see. A cloak of gentle green covering the surface of the Earth. Every now and then they passed across rivers, appearing as dark lines between the forest, the sun still low in the sky, yet to cast its rays upon the face of these deep meandering waterways. It was innocent, its almost naive vulnerability impressed itself upon her. Virgin forest she thought – it was aptly named.

Anna looked to the horizon and tried to imagine what the scene would look like once Phase I was over; it didn't bear thinking about. She felt saddened – it was different now she could see it for herself. The whole area of forest she was looking at through the window would not even cover her thumbnail on the map. She turned to look at Roberto and Valto, who were deep in conversation about that morning's mission. Valto was to demonstrate 'in the field' how mass destruction of the forest could be achieved. She noticed their indifference to the view. She had already realised that few Brazilians cared much for the forest. The Justi Plan had been reported with enthusiasm in Brazil, with some papers calling for Roberto to fell it all. Other countries spoke of the forest as a unique ecosystem on which the world depended and, as such, it must be preserved at all costs, but not Brazil. The people there believed it was hiding things from them: oil, iron, bauxite, gold. Itinerant farmers wanted rights to clear more of it, to make way for subsistence crops and perhaps to herd cattle.

She turned again to peer across the forest, seeing it now as a primaeval portrait, unchanged since the beginning of time, but the thought was held only fleetingly before succumbing to the sound of Roberto and Valto's loud discussion above the din from the engine and the rotor blades.

After a flight of about two hours, and with the sun now high in the sky, the helicopter set down at the edge of a clearing. Once the blades had stopped, Roberto alighted. A line of soldiers stood to attention about twenty yards away, and he inspected them quickly before walking with Valto and Anna to a small timber hut in the far corner of the clearing. The deafening noise of the helicopter ride finally cleared from Anna's ears. She listened to the noises of the forest, completely foreign to her.

'General, what are the sounds?' she asked.

He looked at her strangely, finding it hard to understand why she should be bothered at all about forest noises.

'Monkeys,' he replied. 'And some birds I guess.'

Anna looked up into the canopy but she could see nothing other than branches and leaves.

They entered the hut; it was empty except for a few small drums that stood neatly in the centre.

'Now, here we are,' said Valto, bending down to lift the lid off one of them.

'Goop, Presidente. This is goop.' The smell of petrol was unmistakable as Valto replaced the lid.

'It smells just like petrol, General,' she said.

'It is, Senhora,' he replied, smiling broadly. 'But if you add a little extra something it becomes goop. So a little magnesium powder in with the petrol, forty litres of petrol in each drum, and you have a one-hundred square yard fireball, burning at up to one thousand degrees Celsius for a period of ten minutes. More than enough at those temperatures to set a felled forest ablaze.'

Anna looked at the drum again; it was hard to imagine such destruction contained within it.

'How many drums, General?' asked Roberto.

'The drums we will use are ten times the size of this. We have three million of them. That we believe will be sufficient.'

'Three million? What, the equivalent of thirty million of these?' Anna exclaimed, pointing at the drums in front of them. Valto nodded.

'What do we need them all for?' she asked incredulously.

'The rainforest is well named,' replied Roberto.

'Indeed so,' said Valto. 'It's one of the wettest places

247

on Earth, Senhora. And if you want to burn it you need something to help you. A firelighter for your barbecue, yes? Remember the incendiary aspect we talked about?'

He spread a map out on the wall of the hut.

'This is the area we are in, here,' he said pointing to a small cross on the map. 'And this is Phase I area.'

Anna looked at it.

'What are those lines, General?' she asked.

'Goop lines, one hundred goop lines; each one seven hundred kilometres long and containing one hundred and forty thousand drums; each line seven kilometres apart,' he explained, pointing to the relevant lines on the map. He turned to Roberto and Anna, holding his hands in front of him as if they were supporting a book.

'One thousand two hundred million litres of petroleum simultaneously ignited across four hundred thousand square kilometres of Amazonia, creating a wall of fire sweeping all before it. Imagine?'

There was a moment's silence.

'Shall we see it in operation then?' said Roberto, putting his arm gently round Valto's shoulders and leading him outside.

'I must say, Presidente, I have been looking forward to this for some time now. It is quite a sight, I can tell you.'

Valto called over the captain of the small detachment and gave him instructions regarding the demonstration. They were provided with three folding chairs, a small table and coffee, which was poured for them from a flask by a tall, powerful-looking soldier with a large scar down the side of his face. Anna noticed his wild eyes.

'One of our finest soldiers,' Valto whispered to her, as he finished pouring the coffee and fetched the goop drum from the shed. 'Elite Forces. He's been on many missions for us in the neighbouring states. Top of most drug barons' hit list.'

She watched him carry the goop drum to the centre of the clearing. The captain issued further orders to the remaining soldiers, who turned and walked swiftly across the clearing to a small stack of tree trunks, already stripped of branches and cut into lengths of about twenty metres. Ropes were passed around each trunk and, with muscles straining to breaking point, the soldiers dragged each trunk to the goop drum.

Valto removed a detonator from a crate by the hut and walked over to the drum. He taped the detonator to the drum, fixed the timing device and retreated to Roberto and Anna.

'Two minutes,' Valto told them.

'Aren't we too close?' enquired Roberto.

'No. We should be okay here. The drum is only half full. It might get a bit warm, but we will be fine.'

'Perhaps the helicopter should be moved off the clearing,' said Roberto, not entirely at ease with Valto's response. It was not as if they could walk home.

Valto signalled to the pilot to take off. The noise of the forest was again drowned out by the sound of the engines starting up, blades turning. The helicopter generated a welcome breeze, particularly for the soldiers, whose exertions had left their green shirts with large damp sweat patches down their backs and under the arms. As the noise of the helicopter finally drifted out of range Valto raised his hand, looking at his watch.

'Three ... two ... one ...' They all braced themselves for the detonation.

Nothing.

Anna smiled to herself, remembering childhood days of hide and seek with her father, who, to give her more time to hide, would count down from ten, ending with 'one-and-a-half, one-and-a-quarter, one-and-a-little-bit, one-and-a-tiny-bit, one. Coming!'

'Quite a blaze indeed, General,' muttered Roberto.

Valto looked momentarily embarrassed, but almost immediately they were rocked back on their chairs and the air filled with the short crack of the explosive charge. A split second later the goop ignited with a deep roar, creating a fireball that enveloped the stack and the floor of the forest. The heat from the flames reached them – a dry hot wall of air. They stared at the flames, which showed no signs of dying down; it was as though there was a pump beneath the stack, feeding the fire. Sweat began streaming down their foreheads, irritating their eyes. They watched in silence, wiping the sweat away with first this hand, then that forearm, then the other hand. Anna felt as though she was melting.

Valto looked at his watch.

'Eleven minutes,' he said triumphantly. 'See, the flames are dying down now, but it was eleven minutes.'

They watched with a sense of relief as the flames died and the oppressive heat abated.

'Come, see,' Valto invited, standing up and walking towards

the stack. He turned to them.

'See them burning, They're white hot. Felled only yesterday, Presidente, and now well and truly alight, yes?'

Roberto and Anna stared at the stack, which crackled and spat as it burned, red and white embers falling to the floor and glowing, a mirage above the fire distorting the view of the forest behind it. All the trunks were ablaze; it was still not possible to get anywhere near them, the heat was so intense.

'General. I think you have cracked it,' said Roberto, withdrawing to the cool of the hut. Two of the soldiers brought them bottles of water. They drank some, but tipped most of it over their sweat-covered faces and necks. Half an hour later, when the helicopter returned, the stacks were still blazing.

'You will see a bomber very shortly,' shouted Valto as they took off. 'We will follow at a distance of about fifteen kilometres to watch the drop.'

A few minutes later, Valto pointed out of his window at a grey jet bomber. They hovered and watched the bomber gain height, getting smaller and smaller as it flew towards the horizon.

'There it goes!' exclaimed Valto, pointing to a tiny black dot falling from the plane. There was a sudden flash of red and blue across the forest canopy, followed by a deep rumbling and then leaping flames.

Roberto clapped.

'Fantastic!' he shouted to Valto. 'Absolutely fantastic!'

Anna did not know what to think. She had just witnessed a weapon of mass destruction, not pitted against man but against the Earth. It troubled her, bringing to the surface an instinct she had not even known she had – a need to protect the natural world, a custodianship of creation. Was that not the duty of all men?

'Senhora? What a show, eh?' shouted a beaming Valto.

Anna faked a smile.

'Very good, General,' she replied.

They moved to circle the area now burning less vigorously; the incendiary itself was burning out, but flames still leapt as high as the surrounding canopy. As they came closer the damage to the forest became clear. An area of at least two square kilometres of forest had been completely destroyed, splintered trees covering the forest floor and burning strongly. It was a scene of unbelievable devastation, akin to a war zone. They circled it for over twenty minutes, the forest floor ablaze in colours of red, yellow and white.

Valto finally signalled to the pilot to return to Brasilia.

'That's the first demonstration ever of the forest bomb,' he shouted to Roberto and Anna. 'We need to see if the forest keeps burning, particularly when it starts to rain. We'll have the results by tomorrow.'

'Does the goop-drum fire stand up to the rain then?' Anna shouted back at him.

Valto nodded.

'If the results of the bomb are positive then start felling tomorrow,' shouted back Roberto. Anna looked at the smiling Valto. She sat back into her seat and closed her eyes. Start felling tomorrow, Roberto had said. So this was it – and who knew what the outcome would be? She felt a pang of regret that she had been present at the moment the order was given.

●

By the time Anna had returned to her quarters she was feeling distinctly uneasy about her involvement with the Justi Plan. It had all had such a pace to it that she had barely found a moment for any sort of reflection, but now she realised she was party to a policy that could wreak untold damage to the global environment. She was involved in a system trying to bring the global economy to its knees. How had she become part of this? Because of a few thousand children in poverty.

She thought back to Sofia and her friends in the sewers of Rio. Their plight was tragic, but did it justify threatening the entire world balance of nature and the global economy? All the issues were so large they were irreconcilable, that was the problem. And Sir Anthony – what she did to him had become an undercurrent in the river of her mind, exaggerated in significance because of her lack of feeling as she had stood there and watched him die. What had happened to her? Where was Anna Hughes in all this? And who could she turn to now to talk things through? She tried to sleep but could not escape thoughts of forests, sewers and Sir Anthony.

A knock at the door roused her. There had been a major development in Washington; she was needed straight away. Breathing a deep sigh of relief, she dressed and went to the control centre. She was met by a worried-looking Roberto.

'The White House have pulled out of the greenhouse theory. They've got NASA saying that there is no such thing as global warming.'

Anna felt sick in her stomach. So the world was going to call their bluff. A quarter of the rainforest would now be destroyed and, if burning it failed to thaw part of Antarctica, then the Justi Plan was finished and Roberto would be branded a failure in Brazil and a despot all over the world.

'What's happened to NCGef?' she asked.

'They've sacked them,' replied Roberto, handing her a copy of Ashcroft's press release. 'Some new guy called Thorne.'

Anna studied the paper.

'And what's the press response been to this?'

'Well, if you want to meet them they're all at the gates. Wanting to know what's left of the Justi Plan in light of NASA's findings.'

'Do you want me to speak to them?' she asked him.

'You or me. I don't know Anna,' he replied, tapping his foot nervously. 'What do we say to them? I'd hoped after the UN decision they'd be at the negotiating table in a week or so. We'd start felling, they'd really start panicking and then they'd do a deal. But now? Now they're saying we can cut and cut and cut again for all they care.'

'But Fernento's view on the heat transfer from the fire – that hasn't been altered by this NASA research, has it?'

'No, I don't think so. But I never thought we'd have to bank on that one hundred per cent. What if he's got it wrong? What if four hundred thousand kilometres isn't enough?' He was sounding increasingly agitated. Anna held his arm.

'Roberto. Don't worry so much. So they're going to call our bluff. We always thought they would, remember?'

He breathed deeply and she took her hand away.

'I hope we're doing the right thing, Anna,' he said quietly, looking away from her.

She wanted to voice her own fears about the forest, but knew deep down that they were starting to come at the subject from different viewpoints. He from fear of failure – she from fear of success.

CHAPTER SEVENTEEN

The White House was the toast of the Western World. Hall had received phone calls from all the main leaders: Japan, Germany Britain, France, Canada, Italy, Australia. They were delighted with the breakthrough and indebted to the good sense of President Hall himself for resolving what had become potentially the most damaging world issue since the Arab oil embargo and the Cuban missile crisis.

He had enjoyed a champagne breakfast with both Ashcroft and O'Prey. Justi had been seen off, it was business as usual and re-election – hopefully – in a year's time. He had phoned his wife, Anthea, to organise a family long weekend. It was Thursday and he would leave at lunchtime for their villa in Florida. He was looking forward to seeing his children, and especially his four grandchildren. He loved to feel little chubby hands holding his own as they walked around the villa talking about the real issues of the day, like sweets, strawberry shakes and a day-trip to see Mickey.

Even a call from the White House head of legal services advising him of Whyte's sexual harassment charge against him had failed to put a damper on Ashcroft's morning. He was basking in the press coverage; he was worldwide news. Thorne had annihilated the greenhouse theory at the press briefing the previous evening, and even Peterson could not argue against the NASA research. It had been a complete triumph. O'Prey had even patted him on the back. 'Bloody well done. And I thought you were just a wank.' Praise indeed.

Ashcroft was dining that lunchtime with Thorne and Danielle Hart, journalist for *The New York Times*. She wanted a profile of Thorne and Ashcroft, the new eco-policy dream-team, and had promised a full-page article with a colour photograph of them both, along with a very supportive editorial. He had decided, unusually, to have lunch outside the White House, partly because he wanted to be seen in public with Thorne and partly because he wanted to be seen in public with Hart. He had selected the Roof Garden restaurant at the new Hotel Capital – 'Washington's latest place to be seen'. The restaurant manager had promised him the finest table, commanding superb views across the city and prominently sited at the far end of the restaurant, which would obviously maximise the impact of both their arrival and departure. It was going to be a perfect lunch for a perfect day. He hadn't felt so good in ages. His secretary buzzed him.

'Miss Hart and Mr Thorne are in reception for you.'

'I'll be right there.'

He paid a quick visit to the cloakroom to comb his hair and check the alignment of his tie. He grinned at himself. Surely it was Danielle Hart's lucky day.

It was almost a triumph in itself to stroll across the restaurant, smiling at the other diners, some of whom stood up to shake him by the hand, congratulating him 'for showing *that* Brazilian just who does run this planet'. A bottle of Krug Grand Cuvée awaited them at the table.

'With the compliments of the general manager, Sir.'

Conversation flowed with the champagne. Hart listened attentively to Thorne as he spoke of his childhood, his education, his research, his family, his religion.

'Well, Danielle. We'll be finding out what was in his shopping basket last week if we go into any more detail,' Ashcroft finally interjected. Hart smiled warmly at him.

'I'm sure even the professor won't mind me saying I've left the main event till last.' She gave a light laugh. Thorne nodded in agreement.

'If it wasn't for Mr Ashcroft my dear we'd still have NCGef telling us we're all about to cook.'

'Hey, steady on now,' replied Ashcroft, basking in the commendations. 'Waiter, more champagne please. Sure, same again. Why not?'

The fresh bottle arrived and, glasses replenished, Hart and Thorne toasted his health.

'Never felt better in my life,' he replied.

'And here's to John and his team,' Ashcroft continued. They raised their glasses to Thorne, and he downed his in one go.

'Hey, you've earnt it,' said Ashcroft filling it up again. 'And I think we ought to toast quite the most sought-after lady in the country,' he gushed.

'Absolutely,' replied Thorne, raising his glass to Hart and then dispatching it again.

Hart laughed at them both. 'Gentlemen. This is quite a lunch.'

Thorne loosened his collar. So this is real politics, he thought to himself. Never mind a crusty sandwich and a coffee for lunch. This new champagne, Krug something, this was the thing. As for Peterson, Thorne betted himself that he had never lunched with Wayne Ashcroft – he wouldn't know where to start. Thank God he had spent some time socialising during graduation thirty years ago. It lined the stomach. What, more champagne? Of course. This was the life!

Hart began to notice that Thorne was finding even the most straightforward questions amusing, and Ashcroft's replies more amusing still. Not that Ashcroft seemed to mind. Far from it – they were behaving like a couple of 'Nam veterans on a reunion.

'John, as I say, if you want to laugh I want to join you,' Ashcroft had said, putting his arm round Thorne.

'And I'll drink to that,' replied Thorne.

Hart counted back the number of bottles of Krug they had drunk between them. They were almost at the end of the fourth bottle. She knew she had limited herself to three glasses at the most, which meant that the two men had managed to down around three bottles between them, with Thorne probably responsible for a good two of those. She checked her watch; they had only been at the restaurant for a little over an hour.

'You know the thing I don't ... can't get?' stumbled

Thorne, his head rolling slightly as he spoke, his eyes suddenly looking a little glazed. 'Why no one, no one at all, has asked me what will happen instead of global warming. Even Wayne. Wayne, you haven't asked me have you?'

'Well everything just stays the same, John,' replied Ashcroft. Hart sat forward, her interest heightened.

'Well everything jolly well don't,' replied Thorne, laughing again. 'That's the thing that makes laugh me most. And no one's, no one sausage even, ask ... ask ... asked!' he exclaimed.

Ashcroft's euphoria began to fade away. He sensed Hart's anticipation that Thorne was going to reveal something that he himself knew nothing about.

'Well *I'm* asking you,' she said to Thorne. 'I'd love you to tell me.'

'Come on now, Danielle. It's obvious John's feeling a little heady now,' Ashcroft interjected, putting his arm around Thorne again and whispering quietly to him. 'Stay off it John, okay? This is the press, get it?'

Thorne leaned across the table and took Hart's hand.

'You are a truly, truly. Truly, hmm, stunner.' He swayed on his seat. Hart went to reply but Thorne held up his hand.

'And ... and the answer to your question....'

'Shut it,' Ashcroft said suddenly, pointing his finger in Thorne's face. 'Let's just leave things alone shall we? We don't want any idle speculation. We've just sorted out Justi. The country's grateful. The world is, too. So let's just leave it there.'

Thorne turned on him, his eyes flashing.

'Speculation! Did you say speculation? Well, well, well. I get you off the hook and then … then … yes then, you. Well, of all the low tricks.' He took another sip of Krug. 'We haven't con … concluded it all yet, but we're going to, at least we … are sure we get an ice age.'

Thorne stopped talking, noticing that Hart now appeared to be moving round in circles.

'Ice age? Professor, did you say you reckon it's going to end in an ice age?' Hart asked incredulously.

'Of course he didn't,' replied Ashcroft, panicking. The whole lunch was getting out of control and Hart was on to a story that would simply reignite the whole Justi issue.

'He's slurring every word. Look at him. He shouldn't have had so much champagne. I think I ought to get him to a room to rest.'

'Did you say an ice age, Professor?' Hart repeated.

Thorne nodded. 'Yeah. Glaciers,' he slurred, getting to his feet. 'Glaciers half a mile thick,' he continued, stretching towards the ceiling. 'Up the … up the goddamn Hudson River!'

Ashcroft pushed his chair back and tried to get hold of Thorne, who was now drawing the attention of other diners.

'We'll all freeze,' shouted Thorne, turning to face the restaurant. Ashcroft feigned tripping over his chair and collapsed on top of Thorne. Waiters ran to the table to help them to their feet. Ashcroft stood up and brushed himself down, hugely relieved that Thorne remained motionless.

'He just needs to lie down,' he said to the restaurant manager. 'Can you get him to a room?'

'Certainly, Sir. Shall I call the hotel doctor to attend?'

'Oh fine. Sure. Fine, get the doctor to see him in a room.'

'Will you accompany him, Sir?'

Ashcroft looked at Hart, who was making notes. He did not dare leave her.

'No. I'm going to finish my lunch,' he replied and returned to the table as two waiters struggled to get Thorne upright. With an arm placed round each of them, he was dragged through the restaurant to the lifts and then to a bedroom on the floor below.

Hart ignored Ashcroft's reappearance at the table and continued writing.

'Danielle – he was drunk. You could see that. You're not going to listen to any of that stuff about glaciers?' he pleaded.

'Well he did say it, Wayne. He reckons Justi could bring about an ice age.'

'Oh, don't be silly. Hey, he was drunk. These scientist boffins aren't built for drinking. He was talking gibberish. I mean, how much had he had to drink?'

'Two bottles,' replied Hart, reading from her notes.

'Exactly. I mean, talk to him when he sobers up.'

'What, after you've worked him over?' she responded with a hint of sarcasm. 'Come off it, Wayne. Drunk or not, he said it and I believe he meant it, and I think we need to find out why he thinks it.'

Ashcroft went quiet, his mind in turmoil. What if *The New York Times* published? It didn't bear thinking about. She had to be stopped.

'This lunch wasn't on the record, though,' he floundered.

'Nonsense,' Hart replied, getting to her feet. 'You know it was.'

She left the table and strolled out of the restaurant. Ashcroft watched her leave, wondering if he ought to chase after her. But what could he say? He stared out across Washington, sighed heavily and asked for the bill. His only hope was for a retraction from Thorne.

'Where did you put my other guest?' he asked.

'Room two-four-one. Next floor down, Sir.'

Ashcroft arrived at the room to find a doctor already examining Thorne.

'He's just drunk,' advised Ashcroft.

The doctor removed Thorne's tie and undid his remaining shirt buttons. Feeling for his pulse he asked Ashcroft details of how much alcohol had been drunk, in how short a period, and what had been eaten. He opened Thorne's eyes and shone a pencil torch into them.

'I tend to agree,' he stated at the end of the examination. 'He's the worse for wear all right. Best to let him sleep it off, but we need to keep an eye on him just in case he starts vomiting. Can you stay with him?'

Ashcroft recoiled.

'How long before he comes round?'

'Hard to say exactly. Maybe four or five hours.'

Ashcroft panicked. He needed him talking long before then.

'Doctor. I don't have four or five hours.' He passed the doctor his business card.

'Ah, Mr Ashcroft. How nice to meet you,' said the doctor,

offering his hand. 'I thought it might have been you but I didn't like to ask.'

'The thing is, doctor, I need to talk to my colleague here very urgently. This is an issue regarding US security, no small issue either. I have to impress on you that we simply must get this man conscious immediately. He can sleep it off later.'

The doctor looked at Thorne.

'I'm afraid not. He's getting on and you have to be careful. I could inject steroids, but I'm guessing you don't want to run the risk of coronary failure.'

Ashcroft weighed up the alternatives.

'I'll take that risk,' he replied after a moment's hesitation.

The doctor stared at him.

'I don't mean to sound unhelpful, Mr Ashcroft, but it's not your decision, if you understand?'

'Doctor, the country needs me to speak to this man this minute. Now get him talking.'

There was a silent impasse. The doctor closed his bag and looked at Ashcroft.

'All my professional life I have only ever worked for the benefit of my patients. You'll have to find someone else.'

As he left the room Ashcroft called after him, but the doctor paced away down the corridor. Ashcroft gave up and turned instead to look at Thorne, who was now snoring. He bit his lip hard. He had to keep control and wait for Thorne to come round. He tried to run through possible scenarios and timings. Hart would write copy for tomorrow morning so the cut-off time to get Thorne on to either her or her editor was going to be about nine o'clock. It was now only two-thirty so that option was likely to be a runner. Thorne couldn't sleep it off for six hours, surely? If he wasn't awake by eight-thirty then, never mind a doctor, he'd wake him up himself, even if it meant dragging him to the bathroom and sticking his head into a basin of cold water. But even if Thorne agreed to retract – and Ashcroft suspected that he might not – *The New York Times* was still likely to run the story. What then?

He sat down at the foot of Thorne's bed. How could he get out of this one? If they went public with theories about an ice age.... How do you get an ice age by chopping down trees? He shook his head. Nothing seemed to make sense any more. What had happened to the usual knock-around politics of jobs and welfare and foreign policy? Why was he stuck in a hotel room with a drunk professor whose specialist subject was urban heat islands? It beggared belief. It beggars the end, more likely, he said to himself. What would Hall say? He would have to tell the president what had happened, and he knew that there was nothing more disastrous than forcing Hall to cancel a weekend with his family. Perhaps O'Prey could make the call. No – he already knew the answer to that one: 'You ballsed it up, you sort it!' All he could do was to sit and wait for Thorne to regain consciousness and then to find out what on Earth this ice-age stuff was all about.

After four tedious hours spent relentlessly flicking through the fifty-five television channels, he noticed that Thorne was showing signs of life. The snoring stopped and his legs started to move around a bit. Ashcroft got up from his chair and went to stand by the top of the bed.

'Thorne,' he said, slapping him very gently on his cheeks. 'Thorne, wake up. Come on now, wake up. We've got to talk.'

Thorne started to groan.

'That's it. Come on now. Let's come round.'

'Where am I?' asked Thorne, sounding dreadfully groggy and still with his eyes closed.

'You're at the Hotel Capital. Remember – the lunch? You collapsed. All that champagne, remember?'

'Ohh!' Thorne held his head. 'I'm going to be ill.'

'Not here, no, you go through to the bathroom.'

Thorne squinted as he opened his eyes and after struggling to his feet and banging into first the wall and then the bathroom door he was sick seven times in the bath.

'I feel like death!' he moaned, kneeling over the bath.

'Never mind that. You went and told *The New York Times* that we're in for an ice age. Now you've got to pull yourself together fast,' said Ashcroft, remaining well away from the bathroom. 'Now what is all this nonsense? Tell me it was the drink talking.'

Thorne attempted to clean the bath by running the tap but he just ended up blocking the plug hole. He gave up and staggered back into the bedroom, clutching his head.

'My head. Do you have any aspirin?'

'No. Now you can sort yourself out in a few minutes, after you've told me what all this ice-age stuff is about,' Ashcroft told him sharply.

Thorne lay back down on the bed. Staring up at the ceiling he started to explain the ice-age theory.

'First of all the increased carbon dioxide does make the world get warmer, but only for a short while. Because it's warmer the sea evaporates more, creating a lot more cloud; more cloud means less sunshine. The world cools down.'

'And your Institute. They believe that?'

Thorne nodded. Ashcroft could hardly believe it.

'Well why didn't you ever tell me or the president that? Now we've got the whole of America on the brink again. And what are we going to say now, with the mad Brazilian about to chainsaw his forest? Eh? You tell me. What are we to do?'

Thorne tried to lift his head. Ashcroft was shaking with rage and for the first time ever drew blood as he bit his lip.

'Damn it!' he exclaimed, as he walked into the bathroom for a tissue. The smell was awful. He decided to get out of the hotel as quickly as he could. Thorne was no use to him now.

'I must apologise, Wayne,' said Thorne limply. 'I know I've dumped you in it. I'm sorry. I didn't tell you because we hadn't finished all the models, we're ninety per cent there but we had to button down a few things.'

'Like anything that would destroy the theory?' asked Ashcroft in vain hope.

'No. Just data such as how thick the ice was going to be,' replied Thorne.

Ashcroft shook his head slowly and left the room. He had no option but to phone Hall.

'Mr President. We have a problem.'

'Like what, Wayne?' replied Hall, irritated that he had been called away from dinner.

'Thorne's gone and told *The New York Times* that Justi's going to start an ice age.'

'A what?'

'Yes. I know it doesn't make a lot of sense but apparently the extra carbon dioxide makes less sunshine and then we all freeze.'

'Now listen Wayne. I don't find this funny, okay? I'm having dinner and I'm in no mood for practical jokes.' He replaced the receiver.

'Everything all right dear?' enquired Anthea as Hall returned to his seat.

He grunted. 'Ashcroft's flipped, that's all.'

The phone rang again.

'It's for you again, Mr President,' said the housekeeper, popping her head round the door of the dining room. 'It's Mr Ashcroft again I think.'

'Of all the cheek....' fumed Hall, striding back to his study. 'Now look here Ashcroft....'

'I'm not joking, Sir,' interjected Ashcroft. Hall went quiet. 'I'm deadly serious. Thorne and his Institute believe that Justi will bring us into an ice age and *The New York Times* is going to run it tomorrow, almost for sure.'

Hall sat down in his leather captain's chair.

'What does all this mean, then?' he asked, suddenly tired.

'I don't know,' replied Ashcroft, still thinking desperately for any way out.

'Why didn't Thorne tell us earlier?'

'I know. I asked him that. Their ice-age model is not ready to launch yet in detail.'

'Why has he decided to speak now?' pressed Hall.

Ashcroft wondered what to reply, not wishing to admit that he had helped get Thorne drunk in front of *The New York Times*, but it was a better-than-evens chance they would mention the fact that he was there when these facts were revealed.

'I don't think he realised that it would do us any harm. You know what these scientists are like.'

'Well we're in deep trouble now,' said Hall, realising that he would have to return to the White House immediately, and regretting the pressures of office yet again. Maybe he would not run again in a year's time.

'I'm on my way back,' he said. 'Get O'Prey. And start putting out a few hints to the Senate and Congress that things could turn nasty tomorrow on the Justi front.'

He walked slowly back into the dining room, trying hard to find a smile for the grandchildren as he announced his return to Washington.

'Grandpa going? No Mickey?'

'Just Grandpa. Mickey's still going to be around for us tomorrow,' replied Anthea gently. Their youngest grandchild smiled and turned back to the more pressing matter of how to keep jelly on the spoon without using his fingers, as Grandma had insisted he should learn to do.

The White House pessimism over the potential fallout from *The New York Times* article was well-founded. 'It's an ice age claims White House!' screamed the headline.

Hart had managed to find more details from the Massachusetts Institute, which proved that Thorne had not been overstating himself at lunch. The Justi Plan would lead to a mini ice age, burying the northern cities of America and Europe. The editorial finished the job with relish.

'The world has to get to grips with the Justi Plan. First the White House stance was global warming; now we find it's global freezing. Either way, the world is threatened with being flooded by 50 metres of water or being buried in places by up to 800 metres of ice. Meanwhile, the root cause of all the world's current problems, the rainforest, is still basically intact and Justi has an offer on the table. Can we afford to see if he's bluffing? If he's not, and he slashes his rainforest, how does the world find a way back?'

Anna had caught the story from Reuters. Roberto was elated, it was a huge and timely lift, and the editorial hinting at the need to open negotiations was the best news of all.

Not so of course in Washington. The Senate and Congress were in a state of pandemonium, with splits appearing on environmental rather than political lines. The key question to politicians was not about their Democratic or Republican status; were they pro-global warming or pro-ice-age theory? Any decision from the White House was going to find Capitol Hill's support difficult to read.

Ashcroft's soundings suggested that Congress appeared to have a greenhouse-theory majority, but the Senate could go either way. Hall had invited senior Republicans from both the

Senate and Congress to a crisis meeting at the White House; they had to get their act together. Central banks around the world were expressing concern that public opinion may move to support negotiations with Justi. Stockmarkets were falling sharply, so too were bond markets. The Dow Jones was off over 1,800 points to below the 10,000 level; it was a bloodbath in US treasuries with falls of over eighteen per cent at the long end. London had closed with the FTSE 100 index down 966 points at 4,900. Tokyo had yet to open but trading in Japanese stocks quoted in New York were already dramatically lower. It was important to stabilise markets, but that could only happen when the uncertainty about the Justi Plan had been removed.

O'Prey had met with Ronald Deakin of the Federal Reserve for breakfast. The two men agreed that the crisis was potentially far larger than they had made contingencies for, which was the suspension by Brazil of debt interest payments. The trouble now was that if they did negotiate with Brazil, what would they end up paying? Justi had said thirty thousand dollars per square kilometre, but if they agreed to that, who was to say he would not simply raise his price? It could be a blank cheque. On the other hand, if they did nothing, markets might collapse under concerns for the future. What was anything going to be worth if sea levels rose by the projected amount, or if a mini ice age occurred? There was no easy way out. Every solution carried with it huge risks.

Ashcroft convinced Hall to turn his crisis meeting into a working lunch. 'Plenty of good claret – that's the way to get a result,' he had said. The atmosphere was more than a little

271

tense at the lunch table. Ashcroft had chosen the senators and congressmen carefully. Senators Ted Morgan and Sean Tye were both adept politicians. They had been strong backers of Hall since he took office, and both chaired important committees. Congressman Bob Gredansky was probably the press's most quoted Republican. He had a knack – a gift almost – of judging both the mood of the party and the American people.

Waiters busied themselves; one by one each course was completed; the claret went down at an alarming rate. Hall felt like it was the Last Supper. Despite this, the subject matter under discussion gripped the table, creating an electric atmosphere.

'Gentlemen, we have to secure a consensus on all this environmental nonsense and we have to secure it at this table first.' Hall was emphatic.

No one disagreed. Politically the issue was completely out of control. Gredansky was not slow in coming forward.

'Pat, I have to say that, so far, your administration here at the White House hasn't helped. First of all we accepted a UN solution as the way forward, when we ought to by now have learned that you cannot submit American foreign policy to the UN. Justi made us the laughing stock of the world.

'Then we have your sacking of Peterson and NCGef and the appointment of Thorne, who within the space of a day first solves your problem and then completely stitches you up. There's now no rabbit left in the environmental hat. We either cook or freeze. Whatever way it goes it spells big, big trouble.'

'There's a lot of background you don't know about Bob,' replied Ashcroft defensively. 'The fact is that both Congress and the Senate have been preaching the greenhouse effect for over a decade. So it's not just the White House. If we hadn't had the Thorne debacle we'd still be in trouble.'

'And I don't think that finding pigeonholes for blame is going to help any of us,' Hall added. 'We all know the story to date, what we want is the way forward. Now have any of you any good ideas about what we do from here?'

Tye leaned forwards.

'It strikes me that all the avenues open to us from here are painful. I think Ted will agree with me that the Senate is split on this issue, in a way I can't remember for years. It's like Nixon's impeachment, do you agree Ted?'

'If we use the military now to stop Justi we would suffer worldwide condemnation for acting against a decision of the whole UN.' Morgan nodded while he spoke.

'Plus we would have the threat of Russian and Chinese military action against us,' interjected Ashcroft. 'We've spoken to their ambassadors here and they have made it quite clear that they will support Brazil against any military action, including action led by us.'

'Well that's the end of that one,' said Tye. 'I guess the next one is to buy Justi off. Offer him a few million bucks a year if he agrees to drop his plan.'

O'Prey finally spoke.

'But Sean, he's not talking a few million. He's talking sixty billion dollars a year if he pushes for us to rent his entire forest.

And why should this stop at Brazil? I mean, if we pay them won't every other two-bit country with a few hectares of forest come knocking on our door? No way can we pay. I say we just tell him to chop it all down and to hell with it.'

All the senators and congressmen shook their heads. Gredansky intervened.

'The nation won't stomach that, Gerard. We cannot ignore the environmental issues here. We're talking about people out there scared witless for themselves and for what we leave for the next generation, for their kids to inherit. The people will be up in arms if we let Justi attempt Phase I. Calling his bluff is not an option.'

'Well if we can't call his bluff, and we can't blow him to bits, and I won't hear of him being given rent, what else is there?' O'Prey replied.

'Well there is one other option,' said Tye hesitantly. 'I don't much like it, but I think it's the only alternative to negotiating rent. Basically, if we want to stop the panic about the greenhouse thing, with carbon-dioxide levels rising, we'll have to drastically cut our own emissions to a level that the forecast rise from Phase I of the Justi Plan will only return overall global levels to where they are today.'

The room fell silent. It certainly seemed to make sense. O'Prey saw the catch.

'Hang on a minute,' he stated, hands raised slightly above the table. 'Are we talking about reducing the burning of fossil fuels? Shutting down power stations and banning people from driving? Can you imagine what that will do to the economy?'

He looked around at the grim faces.

'I only said it was an option, Gerard. I don't like it any more than you do but the only other alternative is to pay Justi the rent he's asking. Now, how do you like that one? Where are we going to find an extra sixty billion dollars each year to buy off Brazil's forest? Taxes?'

O'Prey clenched his fists. This was driving him nuts; there was no solution that would not seriously damage the economy. It was like fighting against something too big; you could never actually come to grips with it.

'Okay,' he said, taking a deep breath. 'I agree we can't rent.'

'Are you agreeing that we cut our own emissions then?' Hall asked him.

O'Prey looked down at the table and offered half a nod.

Hall turned to Tye. 'Will the Senate buy it?'

'I guess so. There aren't many who reckon we should go and talk to Justi.'

'And Congress?'

'I'm with Sean and Ted,' replied Gredansky.

'Gerard, what will the markets do?'

O'Prey sat still. Exactly the point, he thought to himself. What would happen to the stockmarket if energy was rationed and industry was put on to a shorter working week?

'Profits collapse, markets will read that the moment we make any sort of announcement along these lines. We could see the market halve, which in turn would put our banks' solvency into question. We could see the nineteen-thirties all over again. You can't rule it out. Still, at least it's Friday. If you delay an announcement until tomorrow we'll at least have the weekend to put together measures to stop a complete bloodbath.' He spoke quietly, staring down at the table.

'Well we coped with the nineteen-thirties gentlemen,' said Hall, trying to lift spirits. 'And if we all stick together we'll see this thing through as well.'

Hall shook them each by the hand as they left, aware that the biggest crisis of his presidency was imminent, bracing himself for the dark days ahead. The storm clouds had well and truly gathered.

CHAPTER EIGHTEEN

Roberto, Anna and Valto gathered around the large television that had been brought to the headquarters for President Hall's live press conference from the White House. They watched as the president strolled across the lawn to the rostrum, looking tired and tense. He did not speak for very long.

'Ladies and gentlemen, thank you for attending. I want to spell out the US policy on the Justi Plan. It seems that our scientists are unable to agree on the impact of an increase in carbon dioxide, which will undoubtedly occur if Phase I is initiated in Brazil. However, they do agree that temperature extremes will occur and that these could be of tremendous harm to the environment worldwide. I have considered at length all the options available to us. None of these is attractive, but an ultimatum has been delivered and we must respond.

'I have decided that America will reduce its emissions of carbon dioxide by an amount that will directly counteract the increased levels resulting from Phase I of the Justi Plan. This means that power stations will close for some days during the week, in turn limiting electricity to homes, schools, shops and factories. All essential services will be maintained, including medical and law enforcement. We ask each citizen of this country to reduce the use of their cars.

'My ambassadors are seeking the support of all the world's leading nations by mirroring this action. Once the extent of this support is known, reduction levels can be agreed.

'This is a truly global crisis, in which America has been forced to take the initiative. If we all work together, though – if our allies join us – we can see off the menace of Brazil and its irresponsible conduct towards the basic freedoms of air to breathe, water to drink and a stable global climate.

'I have asked for the Brazilian ambassador and his staff to be expelled from the United States and we are already in the process of withdrawing our ambassador from Brazil. I have also put in place, with immediate effect, a complete trade embargo against Brazil. She has determined to work against the interests of her fellow nations. She will not succeed.'

He stepped back from the rostrum.

'Mr President!'

'Mr President!'

Hall decided to take a few questions.

'Sir. First of all you held a pro-greenhouse position. Then you moved to a position that resulted in a potential ice age. Now you don't seem to know quite what to believe. Isn't this policy on the hoof?' The question rang out from NBC.

'Well, no offence to all you climatologists,' replied Hall, a touch sarcastically, 'but when I took the presidency I never thought I'd be faced with this. It's never easy taking decisions where precedents don't exist, where scientists bamboozle you.' Ashcroft winced – 'bamboozle' would make a great headline and Hall's tone was a cause for concern. The exchange was becoming heated.

'Why don't you go to Justi and talk about renting?'

Hall did not recognise the journalist, a black man.

'Where are you from?' Hall asked.

'Why does that matter?' responded the journalist.

Ashcroft was now extremely agitated. The whole press conference might break down; he could not allow the president to become engaged in slanging matches with journalists. Stepping in at this point could be even more damaging though.

'What I mean is, are you from one of these rainforest nations, looking to screw us and our friends?' retorted Hall.

Ashcroft moved to the lectern and whispered to Hall.

'Mr President. Can I take over now?'

Hall looked him in the eye. 'Take it,' he said, turning away and striding back towards the White House, his blood boiling.

Ashcroft took to the rostrum to handle the barrage of increasingly hostile questions. How had he allowed a racial element to rear its head?

Anna turned from the television and looked at Roberto. He returned her stare apprehensively.

'Quite a show,' he commented.

'Well, aside from the whole race issue, they've just managed to complicate things for themselves. And I think they're in awful trouble now,' she announced. She picked up the phone and spoke to one of Roberto's aides.

'Can you get Senhor Fernento to join us immediately please? Tell him it is of the utmost importance.'

She turned back to Roberto and Valto.

'They're not taking into account that we intend to *burn* the forest, I'm sure of it.'

'What makes you say that?' enquired Valto.

'Only because they've committed themselves to reducing their emissions by the amount we increase ours. They're looking at a rise in carbon-dioxide levels caused by the felling of our trees. We've never said that we intend to burn the forest once felled, and we know how much carbon dioxide that's going to throw out. They haven't enough power stations, I'm certain. And never mind voluntary pressure over car usage – they'd have to ban cars altogether. Can you see that sticking? No, Hall's overplayed his hand.'

Roberto was impressed and Fernento confirmed Anna's view. The US policy could not possibly work if the forest was burned after felling. They simply would not be able to limit carbon-dioxide emissions to the amount caused by Phase I.

They discussed how best to now counter Hall's statement. Santez had asked for a meeting to discuss the implications of the economic sanctions and he joined the debate. He advised that Brazil's own stockmarket would virtually collapse when trading began on Monday because of the US trade embargo. He listened with delight when Roberto explained that by Monday lunchtime the US would, more likely than not, have reversed their sanctions against Brazil and entered into negotiations over the rainforest.

To ensure that the Brazilian stockmarket did not suffer, Santez asked if he could close it until Tuesday, a move that Valto thought a good tactic. Santez also suggested the ideal timing of Brazil's reply to Hall.

'Leave it until mid-morning on Monday. By then his stockmarket should be lurching into oblivion.'

Valto reported that the felling was taking slightly longer than planned, but that these were teething problems that were being resolved day by day. More than fifty thousand square kilometres of forest had now been felled, and this would rise by thirty thousand a day. He had reconnaissance pictures showing progress. They showed a large brown patch appearing in a sea of green.

'Give the picture to the press,' Roberto told him.

Anna studied the picture and moved quietly away.

●

O'Prey spent a frantic weekend organising central bank support around the world for the inevitable problems securities markets would face on opening. It was agreed that markets would close for an hour should they experience falls in excess of twenty per cent – this would prevent pre-programme sell trades forcing markets into an even steeper decline.

Germany, Britain, France and Japan had all agreed to support the US policy of reducing carbon-dioxide emissions. They believed that to balance the damage caused by Phase I of the Justi Plan the US would have to shut down all solid-fuel power stations for half a day a week initially, rising to two days a week once the phase was complete. There would still be no statutory restriction on car usage, but everyone was to be encouraged not to use their cars unless absolutely necessary.

With energy supplies down by ten per cent immediately, and set to rise to forty per cent, profits in the corporate sector would be entirely eliminated that year. Rather than shut all power stations part-time during the week, carbon-dioxide reduction targets would be met by slowly shutting down fossil-fuel power stations and converting several of them to nuclear power. As more nuclear stations became active, life could begin to return to normal. The downward pressure on stockmarkets in particular, whose fortunes relied so heavily on company profits, could be limited and profits would be seen again after the first year. All central banks and G7 finance ministers had agreed that line.

By eleven-thirty on Monday morning, Gerard O'Prey was comforted by the fact that things seemed to be going according to plan. They had announced the extent of the power-station shut-down programme just before European markets had opened; the Dow was off twenty per cent within minutes of its opening and trading had been suspended for the hour as planned. Once open again it had fallen a further fifteen per cent but then it had stabilised. It was now down thirty-three per cent on the day, the largest fall since 1930. All major markets were similarly distressed. Europe had led the way with losses of between thirty and forty per cent. London, Frankfurt, Paris,

Madrid, Rome – all had seen massive falls, but not to the point of collapse. Across the world investors looked ashen as they saw their portfolios reduce by one-third in a single morning. Added to the loss on the previous Friday they had now experienced a staggering two-day collapse that had more than halved their portfolio value.

O'Prey could not face turning on the television. He knew the tragedies – the personal ruin of millions of people – that lay behind these market movements, but at least the markets were still there. Few would congratulate him, but he was pleased that they had actually held off a complete meltdown. If they were queuing outside the banks, he would really have something to worry about, he thought to himself.

He fetched a cup of coffee and returned to his screen to see that another automatic shutdown had been forced on to the stockmarket.

'What?' he exclaimed. This meant another thirty per cent drop in the stockmarket. Prices had collapsed by more than sixty per cent now – in a single day. What was going on?

A newsflash had appeared.

'Justi claims US plan unsustainable.'

O'Prey paged to the Reuters report.

'The Brazilian president, Roberto Justi, announced just minutes ago that the assumption on carbon-dioxide levels used by the Hall Plan to prevent global warming is flawed. Brazil intends to burn its felled

trees releasing vast additional quantities of carbon dioxide. US power stations and those of the other nations supporting the US, would have to be shut down permanently for the policy to work.

President Justi has invited President Hall for talks in Brazil, stating: "We want to help find a solution to the difficulties the West is experiencing because of Phase I of the Justi Plan. We hope that for the sake of their financial markets they will now choose to negotiate over forest rental."'

He read it again, mesmerised, only waking from his trance when the phone rang. Ashcroft struggled to find his words.

'Gerard. Have you heard?' he blurted.

'Yeah, I've heard. Every last word.'

'And?' asked Ashcroft, his voice trembling.

'And Hall's plan is fucking dead. Justi's just fucked him over completely.'

Ashcroft screwed up his face. O'Prey disgusted him.

'So the markets won't cope then?'

O'Prey laughed.

'And you're a fucking tosser. Course they won't cope. They're worthless. Can't you understand – if Hall's great scheme is enforced now, then all power stations will close indefinitely. And guess what happens next? We'll have to shut all our offices, shops, factories ... and then all companies go bust. Get it? Bust!' he screamed.

Ashcroft put the phone down. He'd heard enough. Hall's plan was over, destroyed in five minutes by a few lines from Justi. Who the hell was he anyway? How could anyone fight this thing? How had Justi played his cards so well when they had played theirs so badly? He thought back to the original press conference, when the Justi Plan had been announced, and remembered seeing Anna Hughes. Perhaps she was making the difference. Well if so he was in desperate need of someone like her.

A call came through from the president.

'Wayne, tell me what Gerard's saying,' Hall said. Ashcroft noted how calm he sounded.

'It's the end of it, I'm afraid. The plan is dead.'

Hall went quiet for a few moments.

'Well that only leaves one option, Wayne.'

Ashcroft felt close to tears. 'I'm sorry, Mr President, very sorry. We've been completely outplayed by Justi and I have to take some of the blame. I feel I have to offer my resignation.'

'Nonsense. That's just what he wants.'

Hall could hear the tears in Ashcroft's voice. It was understandable. The pressure on them all now was immense. Americans had, that day, lost literally trillions of dollars, the threat to the global climate remained and their opponent was coolness himself in the warm Brasilia sunshine, his stockmarket cleverly closed for the day while the world was in meltdown.

'Come on Wayne. We can still beat this thing, yes?' Hall encouraged him.

Ashcroft tried to compose himself but he found it difficult. Perhaps he was suffering a breakdown, he thought. He couldn't speak; his throat was tight and he felt paralysed. Hall continued, aware that Ashcroft was still in difficulty.

'Look. I'm going to contact Justi. I'm going to have to deal with him head-on now.'

Ashcroft felt the bitter taste of defeat as he heard Hall's words. It was his worst nightmare.

○

The US ambassador to Brazil clutched the letter tightly in his left hand and paced awkwardly round the reception room outside Roberto's official presidential office. He could hardly contain his embarrassment. Firstly, Hall had recalled him to Washington in some sweeping economic and communication moratorium, then two days later it was apparently time to unpack the suitcase and establish a belated charm offensive.

Finally, Roberto's door opened and the ambassador was beckoned in. Roberto rose from behind his desk.

'Ambassador, welcome. Please, take a seat. Can we get you anything? A coffee, whisky perhaps?' he asked with a knowing smile.

The ambassador shook his head.

'Presidente, I have here a letter from our president, President Hall.' He handed Roberto the letter before continuing.

'President Hall would appreciate an immediate response.'

Roberto opened the envelope, removed the letter and sat back in his chair.

'Well I had better read it first, if that's okay?' The ambassador nodded, while Roberto added with a broad grin, 'Unless of course you've things still to pack?'

The ambassador looked uncomfortably at Roberto, who smiled again before turning to look at the letter.

Hall wished to meet with him at the White House to discuss the forest rental options.

'Well, I am flattered, Ambassador.'

'You are most generous, Presidente. And your reply?'

'Oh, yes,' said Roberto playfully. 'Now that's a little awkward right now.'

'Awkward? I would have thought that this meeting was extremely important to Brazil, if you will forgive me saying so.'

Roberto stood up and walked across the room to the window that looked out across the gardens.

'Important. Now there is a funny word, Ambassador. Don't you think so?'

The ambassador again avoided Roberto's gaze. He had specific instructions direct from Hall to get Justi to the White House at the earliest opportunity, but he knew that this could prove difficult – he had nothing in his arsenal to persuade him.

'It is a very difficult time for us,' the ambassador replied.

Roberto thought of Anna; he felt uncomfortable making a decision of this significance without asking her. He wondered why he felt this need to confide in her. Was it because he wanted to or because she had been upset about him taking decisions without her knowledge. Or was it something else?

'Presidente, I do need an answer.'

'Oh yes. My apologies. Can I come back to you?'

'President Hall was rather hoping that you might have an early answer.'

'Sorry,' Roberto told him, walking back across his office to stand by the door. The ambassador got the message, rose and made to leave. He held out his hand to Roberto.

'President Hall has also asked me to apologise for our stance over economic and embassy withdrawal.'

Roberto almost felt sorry for him.

'Don't worry, Ambassador. Tell President Hall that we thank him for his offer and we will be in touch.'

'And soon?'

'As soon as possible,' Roberto replied.

The ambassador gave a small bow and left Roberto's office. By the time his car was leaving the presidential quarters, Anna was walking over to meet with Roberto. He saw her out of his window and went into the hall to wait for her. As she entered he waved Hall's letter gently in his right hand.

'I'm invited to the White House, no less,' he called out to her, his face beaming.

She smiled back.

'So we are in business then?' she replied, taking the letter from him.

'We certainly are. And I want all of Brazil to know. I want a party. I want our stockmarket to open tomorrow. I want Santez to re-float the cruzado-real. They are breaking Anna, and the World Bank's grip is breaking with them!'

'So we can stop felling?' she asked.

He heard the hope in her voice.

'No. We must keep felling. It's the only way we can keep the pressure on them to do the deal.'

'Thirty thousand dollars per square kilometre though. And you're felling thirty thousand square kilometres a day, Roberto. That's nine hundred million dollars of rental income a year that you're losing every day. I remember four hundred million being a showstopper with the Russians.'

He sat down at his desk and gave a huge sigh. Why could she never live for the moment? She always had something extra to add. Manuel would be dancing on the desk at this moment. Perhaps it was the British reserve.

'Anna – be happy.'

He noted her distant look, and remembered she had been the same when Valto had talked of progress in Phase I.

'Anna, is there something wrong?'

'Yes. I'm struggling with what you're doing to the forest. You and Valto don't seem to care about the destruction.'

She instantly regretted her words. He had looked so happy, so close to victory, she thought to herself.

'Would you prefer that I called off Phase I – just until I've seen Hall and discovered the colour of their money, if there is any? Only a postponement you understand?'

She could not look at him.

'I would be relieved if you would,' she said quietly.

'No, I said happy, not relieved.'

She looked up. He was grinning at her.

'Okay. Happy *and* relieved then.' She feigned a smile.

He rose from his desk and, placing his arm momentarily around her shoulders, walked with her back to the main entrance of his quarters.

'I was thinking I might decline Hall's invitation.'

'To invite him here, yes?'

'Yes. To the middle of the felled forest in Phase I. We could build a little hut for the occasion.'

They both smiled at the thought.

'Can you phone his ambassador and tell him I'll meet with him tomorrow afternoon.'

'So soon?'

'Shouldn't I?'

She thought about it briefly; there was nothing to be lost by keeping up the momentum.

'No, it's fine. And you want me to make a press statement about Hall's letter and your reply?'

They reached the main entrance.

'And the party and the stockmarket. And phone Santez and tell him to re-float the currency.'

'Does he know how to re-float a currency?' she enquired.

'Well I don't,' breezed Roberto. 'One last thing, Senhora. Tonight I would like you to dine with the President of Brazil. Seven-thirty, my car will pick you up from your quarters. Time to party remember?'

She was caught off-guard.

'Oh, it really is a very kind offer but I have a lot to do and it might be a bit tricky getting it all done and....'

'Seven-thirty it is then,' he interjected. He smiled briefly at her, then turned back into the hall. She watched him for a few seconds, then wandered back across the lawns to her apartment. What was she to do about dinner? He had said his car would pick her up. Did that mean that Roberto intended to take her out for dinner, to be seen in public with her on unofficial business? Would that not start rumours that they were an item? Had he even given that a thought? Time to party he had said. But she hated parties, always had done. Perhaps she would cancel, saying that she was feeling unwell....

○

Anna glanced at her watch and was alarmed to see it was just before seven o'clock. She had put off making a decision about dinner, and now it was too late to cancel. She had spent the afternoon sorting out the press releases and speaking with Santez, who, it turned out, did know how to re-float the currency.

'Senhora it will be a proud moment for Brazil,' he had said with great aplomb.

Most channels had interrupted their programming to announce Hall's invitation to Roberto. Anna had chosen not to make public Roberto's comment about partying; she knew the Brazilian people would do so anyway.

A sudden thought caused her to panic. What was she supposed to wear? She had left Britain in such a hurry, bringing very little with her. Now it was seven o'clock. Where was she supposed to get hold of a dinner outfit? She had a few dresses that she had bought in São Paulo, but none was suitable for dinner. She thought about asking one of the girls on the staff if they had an evening dress she could borrow but decided against it, not wanting to explain why she needed it. In any event, she was far taller than most of them.

She went into her bedroom and, with a feeling of both helplessness and growing depression, opened her wardrobe. She was startled to find hanging there a deep-blue silk dress with a pale-blue hip band tied in a delicate bow to the side. Beneath the dress lay a pair of evening shoes – soft blue leather uppers framed with platinum silver ribbing. A card was tied to the hanger. Surely Roberto had not arranged the dress, she thought to herself.

'To Anna,
In case you forgot to pack one when you left England.
Roberto.'

Anna was moved by his gesture. Placing the card by her bed she took the dress from the wardrobe. She held it up to herself and surveyed it in the mirror. It looked like a good fit; it was certainly the right length. How could he have known her size, she wondered as she slipped it on. It was almost a good fit, just slightly loose beneath her arms. She tried on the shoes; they fitted her perfectly.

Sitting on the bed, she picked up the card again. She felt touched by his thoughtfulness yet intimidated by what it might mean. Was he trying to tell her something? That he was thinking of her when she wasn't working with him? Or was it just a kind act from someone who knew she would not have a wardrobe of any consequence with her in Brazil?

Yet again she felt her mind fuse as contradictory thoughts competed against each other. She searched within herself for an understanding of why she always resisted the friendship of men. Why was she such an island? She had tried boyfriends in her late teens and then a serious relationship in her early twenties, but she found the strain of feeling for someone else too much, the demands too great. She would feel trapped and have to leave. Not one of them had understood. They would look at her with disbelieving faces, hurt in their eyes, pleading in their voices. 'Anna. I love you. Don't go.' But she always left and, worse still, she never missed them. It made her feel almost inhuman, to be so devoid of feeling. In the end she had decided not to become involved in the first place.

She looked into her own eyes as she finished her make-up. Did she feel for Roberto? She could not find any emotion of consequence. Perhaps her soul was empty.

She smiled at him warmly as he held the car door open.

'You shouldn't have, Roberto.'

'Well it suits you,' he replied. 'And it fits.'

They sat together in the back of his limousine as it turned to leave for the city centre.

'Should I ask how you knew what size?' Anna asked playfully. 'After all, the last fashion items you provided me with were a terribly couture pair of oversized overalls and some matching wellies.'

'Fashion has moved on again. See the special sensors at the main gates here,' Roberto explained, pointing to the security cameras that covered the entrance to the base. 'They send over a million three dimensional readings back to our main computer centre, which can then reconstruct a model of any subject. A separate clothes programme is run to get the fit exactly right and the dress design and size then sent down the line to the terminal of our country's leading design house.'

He turned to her, his face expressionless.

'It is then simply a matter of breaking into your bedroom and putting it into your wardrobe.'

'I see a problem with your computer, Roberto,' she replied, turning to her side and gently pulling at the dress, showing the small gap beneath her arm.

'On the contrary. That is for additional ventilation I believe.'

She laughed – at times Roberto was fun.

'Where are we going?' she asked

'You wouldn't know it even if I told you,' he replied. 'Very special, believe me.'

'Is it Brazilian cuisine?'

'I hope not.'

They pulled up at the restaurant amid a flurry of security activity and the dazzle of press cameras. Roberto smiled and waved. Anna waited for him patiently, not knowing quite what to do, whether to smile, which may suggest they were an item, or to keep her face expressionless, which may suggest that she had an argument with Roberto. Before her mind could complete another revolution, Roberto had joined her and they were walking up the few steps into the restaurant.

As they walked in the other diners rose and applauded. News that Hall had agreed to come to Brazil the next day had already swept the country. Roberto bowed slightly, Anna blushing as he held out his hand, inviting her to walk slightly in front of him as they were shown to their table. She deliberately avoided looking at any of the other tables and, hugely relieved to be seated at their table and that the applause had died down, she finally eyed her surroundings.

The restaurant had a crescent-shaped interior, with tables lit by twinkling candles arcing round the room on various levels, beneath an imposing glass dome roof. A gold-coloured carpet gave way at the centre of the restaurant to an ornate inlaid wooden floor, used for either cabaret or dancing, as well as for a grand piano, from which a medley of popular tunes was issuing, some of which Anna recognised and a number of Brazilian melodies that were new to her.

Their table was situated on a raised platform at the near end of the crescent, close to the restaurant entrance. Each time she looked across the room she was aware of heads turning. This aggravated her discomfort, but she made sure Roberto did not notice anything wrong.

The food was a joy: grilled lobster, fillet mignons in a whisky and cream sauce, monkfish tails in tomato and red wine, accompanied by a superb bottle each of white Burgundy and Pinot Noir.

As the wine flowed, the conversation turned from stilted small talk to more easygoing discussions about their childhoods. Roberto was full of stories about growing up in a poor part of São Paulo, within a happy family where his parents gave practically all they earnt to ensure an education for their sons. Anna told him about growing up as an only child in the restrained environment of an unhappy middle-class marriage in rural England. All the time, she noticed that Roberto had a new enthusiasm for life, as if a great burden was lifting from him. He talked more freely, his eyes less intense, his conversation more lively.

They both declined a dessert and as the piano was being pushed back to make way for a small band, setting up at a feverish pace, their coffee arrived. Roberto leaned back.

'Now Anna. I recall a week or so ago talking to you about Angela, and yet I know absolutely nothing about your previous loves; perhaps you have one even now.'

'Oh, no,' she replied, immediately feeling defensive. Roberto noticed her eyes looking anywhere but at him.

'Do you mind if I ask about these things?' he enquired, his voice hushed and undemanding.

'There's not a lot to say actually.'

'No husbands, boyfriends?' he continued, shrugging his shoulders slightly.

'No husbands; boyfriends, a few, but a long time ago.'

Her hesitancy was tangible and silence fell over the table. The band struck up and couples started drifting towards the dancefloor. Anna watched them and tried to imagine how it would feel to be like them – comfortable with each other, with themselves, as they began to dance. She was aware to the point of embarrassment that she had been short with Roberto about her past. He deserved better than that, she thought to herself.

'I don't think I'm cut out for relationships,' she said suddenly. 'I tend to feel trapped by them.'

He was surprised she had returned to the subject.

'Why? Because of the expectation of the other party?'

'Yes, I think so. I think I'm very bad news for anyone. I have very few friends, actually no friends at all of any real consequence.'

She saw a look of pain pass across his face.

'You see. Now I've upset you.'

'Nonsense,' he replied. 'But I do see you as a friend Anna, a confidante. And even if you don't feel I am your friend I hope you will take my word for it that I am.'

'I guess if I stopped long enough to confront myself, I probably would see you as a friend, Roberto. But my head goes round in circles.' Her tone was steeped in resignation. 'And I thought you were rather like me.'

'Single-minded?'

'Yes. With a cause to work for.'

'A cause that drew you in, too.'

'Perhaps that's it. I relate to issues not people. Maybe that's why I don't have relationships. What do you think?'

'Since Angela there has been no one in my life either. Anna, you and me, we do hold some things in common. That's what I think.'

She looked across the table at him. He was a handsome man; a kind, generous man. She tried to find a spark within her, but there was nothing. She turned away again, a sense of desperation overwhelming her. It wasn't that she couldn't feel anything for Roberto, it was more that she couldn't feel anything for anyone. At moments such as these she was inert to life itself. What was the point of a life that was so hollow, so empty, punctuated only by the occasional feeling of doing good by helping others? Was this real loneliness? What were the beliefs that drove her?

She thought back to her room at the Hilton, her feelings on reading of Manuel's death. That was real emotion. She thought of Sofia and the children in the sewers of Rio. That too was real emotion. But did anything link them – anything she could discover about herself that might make her feel normal, human, rather than the cold, precise creature she knew she had become. Sir Anthony ... Sofia. Was it a contempt for life that had gripped her? Sir Anthony was contemptuous of the lives of others; Sofia, by her circumstances, a testimony to the contempt he espoused.

'You don't feel like dancing, Anna?' Roberto softly interrupted her thoughts.

She shook her head. 'Do you mind if we leave? I'm feeling rather tired.'

She glanced at him, saw his disappointment and looked away quickly. They drove back in silence, Roberto looking straight in front of him as she stared out of her window at the growing crowds that would celebrate Hall's imminent visit until dawn.

As they pulled up at her apartment, Roberto walked round to open the door for her.

'Roberto, I do thank you for a lovely dinner.'

She tried to find more words, to apologise for being such dreadful company, but she could not find them. Roberto looked at her, his eyes dull.

'Perhaps we can dine again?' he said, kissing her gently on both cheeks. Anna smiled hesitantly, turned and without a further word entered her apartment.

CHAPTER NINETEEN

Hall had called an emergency meeting of the governments of the leading industrial nations, to discuss his visit to Brazil. By the time they had all arrived at the White House it was one o'clock in the morning and, with his meeting with Justi scheduled for three o'clock that afternoon, there was precious little time for talking. They had to make fast decisions on Justi's rental option. The prime ministers of all the G7 nations were in attendance, together with their finance ministers.

Their stockmarkets had been savaged, their people had taken to the streets in a state of shock and retribution over seeing their life savings devastated in just a few days' trading. Some violent clashes had been witnessed in most of their capital cities as hundreds of thousands of demonstrators vented their desperation on the authorities, attacking the police lines that were protecting state buildings.

All Western leaders agreed that there was no option left but to do a deal with Justi, but they had still to establish agreement on the rental figure. O'Prey had argued that taxes were the only way to raise the vast sums needed to meet Justi's demands. Sixty billion dollars, shared out in proportion by economic size, would leave America picking up half the bill, some thirty-five per cent divided fairly evenly among the European countries and Canada, and Japan responsible for the remainder.

'We're going to have to raise taxes by a full two per cent to cope,' he said. 'And so will you all, I guess.'

The British finance minister, Martin Jenkins, replied in a resigned manner.

'Right now, Mr O'Prey, if we could restore some confidence to our economies and stockmarkets, then that strikes me as a small price to pay. We have to turn our markets round; we're already very concerned about one of our big five banks. One more day like yesterday and we could see a real crisis in our domestic banking sector. Frankly, if that happens we could well find world finances in a state of complete collapse.'

No one disagreed with his prognosis. The German chancellor still had reservations.

'We remain concerned about the rest of the rainforest countries. What if they all joined forces? If they demand the same amount we could be facing a bill three times as much. We already have intelligence suggesting that a Forest League of Nations is being proposed to do precisely that. I don't think we can afford one hundred and eighty billion dollars a year. The money just doesn't exist. We can't put up taxes by six per cent, our economy simply wouldn't survive that.'

'But what are our choices, Chancellor?' asked Hall.

'I realise that, Mr President,' he replied. 'We don't have

choices. We have really no cards to play against Justi. I am just voicing my concern that he might push the world past the economic brink. Do not forget that his campaign was to break the World Bank.'

'I think his campaign was not to break the World Bank, just to break its influence over Brazil,' interjected Jenkins. 'It is an important distinction, one that allows for a more positive approach to negotiation, in that Justi is not out to ignore the rule of law.'

The others nodded in agreement.

'What if I started by telling Justi that we can't find the thirty thousand dollars per square kilometre? That a figure like that will destroy the world economy, including that of Brazil, and give him another figure, say ten thousand dollars instead?' stated Hall.

No one dissented. At two o'clock Hall retired for a few hours' sleep.

●

Roberto was up early that morning. A helicopter was already waiting to take him to the place selected by Valto for the meeting with Hall. It was set on a small ridge at the heart of the vast tract of forest cleared for Phase I, from which the surrounding forest was so distant that it could no longer be seen. Valto had called it the Justi Ridge. A small hut had been built from some of the felled timber, with a flight of steps leading up into it. The military had laid on more than thirty helicopters to ferry the mass ranks of the world's press to the meeting point. Hall was expected to arrive by US military helicopter slightly after the agreed time of three o'clock that afternoon.

When Roberto arrived he was surprised to see that the area, although felled, had not been cleared. Apart from a small area around the hut and the landing zone, huge mahogany trees littered the ground.

Valto greeted him enthusiastically.

'Presidente. A proud day for this country.'

Roberto was struck by the sincerity in Valto's voice.

'Indeed, General. Indeed.'

He looked around him, remembering, as if Anna was standing there repeating it, her concern for the destruction that he had been wreaking on the forest. He looked at the spider monkeys playing in the branches of the felled trees, the leaves of which were already turning a mixture of yellow and brown. Birds were still calling and cackling, taking refuge in the depleting cover of leaves in branches now just forty feet from the ground.

A family of native Brazilians looked on – an old woman in the company of a young-looking couple; six children of varying ages, dressed in cheap cuts of cloth held together with thorn pins stood by them. They neither knew nor cared who Roberto was. They cared only that the forest of their forefathers had been razed, and with it their livelihood. Roberto looked briefly at them but dared not meet their eyes. A way of life – an ancient way of life – that knew nothing of the conflict of economies was now caught up in the midst of a battle raging for rights and power.

Anna had arrived some time before Roberto to deal with the press. She saw the native family and sensed their bereavement.

A steady stream of press flights arrived, bemused journalists and film crews picking their way across the branches of the fallen trees to the clearing in front of the hut. They looked around them, pleased to be amongst the first on the scene. The area was nowhere near large enough to accommodate all the world's press. When Roberto mentioned this to Valto, the General smiled and said he was looking forward to CNN, in particular, filming from a perch they would have to select for themselves in one of the trees.

Roberto entered the hut. It was now two o'clock and the noise of the helicopters was unrelenting. Inside was a communications officer, who stood up and saluted. Roberto shook him by the hand and told him to drop formalities.

'This is a great day, Presidente,' he said, proud that his country stood on the threshold of gaining an economic future free from the oppression of the World Bank.

Roberto smiled at him, wondering if Valto had instructed all military staff to recite the same line.

'Indeed it is,' he nodded.

A sergeant from the catering corps stepped forward and offered Roberto coffee. He took it and sat on the edge of a table, on which stood a radio and telephone system.

'Does the telephone actually work?' he asked.

'Certainly. Do you wish to make a call?'

Roberto shook his head, but after a few minutes the phone

rang. He hoped it was Anna.

'Presidente. It is for you. Senhor Santez.'

Roberto took the phone.

'Presidente. I thought you would like to know that this morning our stockmarket has risen by over sixty per cent. International investors are piling into it – it's amazing – and our currency is now fully re-floated on international exchanges, attracting enormous inflows of funds. The cruzado-real's international value has already doubled.'

'I am pleased,' replied Roberto.

Santez thought he sounded anything but – a little depressed even. Perhaps it was understandable, though. The meeting with Hall was make or break.

Roberto went outside and sat on the steps of the hut; the cleared area was now completely full of journalists and there were many more taking up positions in the actual branches of the cut trees, their bright shirts colouring the felled canopy. He caught sight of Anna, talking with Valto and then standing on her own, occasionally speaking with some passing journalist. He hoped she would come over to see him, but she kept her distance from the hut. Perhaps she does not like the limelight, he thought to himself.

Roberto went back inside. He thought of the meeting that was about to take place, and of his life after that, when his work may have been completed. What then? He shook his head. What then indeed. His thoughts returned to Anna.

The communications officer tapped him gently on the shoulder.

'Presidente. I believe President Hall is arriving now.'

Roberto stood up and walked to the entrance. The blue and white helicopter hovered for half a minute over the landing site before touching down. Some of the crew jumped down and helped lower steps from the hold. The door opened; two presidential guards came down first, eyeing the ranks of press but admitting to themselves that they could only trust the Brazilian army to live up to its promise of blanket security.

Hall walked down the steps. He looked straight ahead, stopping at neither the top or the bottom. Valto came forward to greet him, and guided him across the clearing to the hut.

Roberto stood before it. He was dressed in a pair of green shorts and a yellow polo shirt, in complete contrast to Hall, who had left Washington in almost freezing rain and was still wearing a charcoal-grey, single-breasted suit, striped shirt and paisley tie in gold and pink.

Hall picked his way carefully through the debris as the noise of camera shutters drowned out the sounds of what remained of the forest. He did not look up at Roberto until he was within a few metres of him, at the bottom of the steps. They shook hands briefly.

'President Justi, thank you for this meeting.'

'Thank you for coming,' Roberto replied.

'Shall we go in?' Hall asked, peering into the hut.

'I thought we might just sit here,' Roberto said, sitting down on the middle step. Hall looked at him.

'Okay, it's your show,' he shrugged, unbuttoning his suit jacket and lowering himself gingerly on to the step beside

Justi. A whisper of laughter could be heard from the press, to the clear irritation of the US journalists, who found both the venue and the seating arrangements humiliating.

'Would you like a drink Mr President? It's a lot warmer here than in Washington.'

'No. I'd prefer to get on with the agenda and then get out of here,' replied Hall curtly.

'Well, you want to discuss renting forest. You have heard our terms.'

'Where did you get that figure from, President Justi?' Hall asked, brushing a large red ant from his trousers.

'We think it's the market rate,' replied Roberto coyly.

'What market? There's never been a market and, in any event, we *are* the market. Surely it's about what we're prepared to pay, not what you're going to charge?'

Roberto looked over the clearing to the journalists perched in the branches.

'Look for yourself President Hall. Why are CNN propped up in that tree over there in the middle of the Brazilian rainforest? And why are you here? I think it says a lot about the nature of supply, don't you?'

Hall did not respond.

'You are thinking about market forces, but you must concentrate on pricing where a supplier has a monopoly position. If you want what we have on offer, you pay our price. We don't accept your pricing – or anyone else's for that matter.'

Hall thought for a moment as he flicked two more ants off his trousers.

'Perhaps we can cut all this nonsense about "monopoly of supply". I mean, you have to start working out a few facts of economic life here. There is no blank cheque. You have two million square kilometres of forest. It's quite possible for you to price yourself out of the market. What if we simply can't afford to pay. Who wins then? How does Brazil benefit if the West can't pay?'

'Sixty billion dollars? You can pay that.'

Hall hesitated.

'We were thinking of offering you twenty billion.'

'Well think again,' replied Roberto, still relaxed.

Hall took his handkerchief from his trouser pocket and mopped his brow.

'So twenty billion dollars is out of the question, yes?'

Roberto declined to respond.

'You can't hold out for sixty billion. Surely you're a negotiating man?'

'I'm prepared to negotiate with you in the same way that the World Bank has negotiated with us. Is that fair enough Mr President?' Roberto countered.

Hall wondered how much negotiating actually went on between the World Bank and a defaulting nation state. Not much he guessed.

'Oh come on,' he urged. 'We're talking about super-league sums here, not a few billion in late interest. This is a very serious number. And we think that it won't stop with Brazil. We need to get a fix on the potential bill the world over. Germany reckons we could be up for two hundred billion a year.' He opened his hands before continuing. 'At that price, frankly the whole world's bust.'

'Surely not,' replied Roberto. 'Surely you're not telling me that a figure of two hundred billion dollars will break the world financially.'

'No, of course it won't,' interjected Hall. 'But the world as we know it will be a far poorer place. Soon it might appear bust. I mean you're talking about annual payments, not just a one-off,' his voice was raised a little and his face tightened.

'What then is the problem with that, President Hall? So your countries are not so rich any more. So what? My country has lived in poverty for as long as we can all remember – poverty enforced on us in no small way by your country, and others like you.'

Hall changed tack.

'Look. I represent not only the interests of the United States, but of many other leading nations. We're not against Brazil – far from it. Perhaps we have been a little excessive in the past, but look at this. Here I am, in the middle of your rainforest, sitting on the steps of a little wooden hut. Doesn't that say something? The president of the United States, sitting here flicking off inch-long ants. Doesn't that tell you that we are reasonable people, people with whom you should do business?'

'But what has brought you here?' demanded Roberto. 'To this little wooden hut in the middle of Brazil. And why are they all here to witness it?' He waved an arm at the mass of people littering the clearing. 'President Hall, the real reason you are here is because you recognise that we are forcing through a change in the world order. What we have here is precious to you and to your friends. You know that, I know that. You pay the Arabs for oil. You might have resisted it, but in the end you paid.'

'I would also say we shouldn't have. We should have held out, but that's history now.'

'So you won't pay thirty thousand per square kilometre?'

'No. Nothing like it.'

'You have a figure in mind then?' enquired Roberto, with an air of indifference.

'Perhaps. Maybe ten thousand.'

'And what happens if we fail to agree? After all, there is a lot of difference between thirty thousand and ten thousand.'

The two looked at each other intently. Hall mopped his brow. What was he doing here, he thought to himself.

'Perhaps some water now?' enquired Roberto. Hall nodded. Two bottles of still mineral water were passed to Roberto. He undid the lids and handed one to Hall.

Hall took a long drink, listening to the sudden whirring of cameras capturing the moment.

'Maybe we should meet again?' suggested Roberto.

'Oh, no,' interjected Hall. 'No, we must nail a deal today.' He was growing impatient; Roberto's indifference to him personally was beginning to irritate. He was the most powerful man in the world, and this Brazilian upstart was making a fool of him.

'But you won't pay our asking price and we cannot negotiate.'

'Can't? Or won't?'

Roberto remained silent.

'Twenty thousand then. But that's it and no upward reviews either. Take it or leave it.'

Roberto stood up.

'Then I choose to leave it, President Hall,' he said quietly.

'Oh come on. We're both reasonable people. I'm at twenty, you're at thirty. Deal, Mr Justi – deal.'

Roberto remained standing.

'Deal Mr President? Deal indeed. Let me give you the same deal as we get from your bankers. Do you know how much that is? Shall I deal to the point that your people cannot even afford bread? Fifteen million little ones living in my streets and sewers, Mr President. Is that a deal?'

Hall fell silent. He had to reach an agreement – he was finished if he did not. But he knew now that it would have to be on Justi's terms. Would the West back him on that? He sat back against the stair post and looked around him. Fifteen million children, Justi had said. He stared across the strewn forest and shook his head.

'Thirty thousand, then,' he said slowly, his eyes on the ground. 'No increase for ninety-nine years.'

Roberto smiled.

'You really think your bankers would agree a deal like that? Unable to raise their interest rates for nearly a century? I have had to listen to them, in their Armani suits, with their multi-million dollar salaries, telling me why it is an absolute necessity to leave my people in poverty.'

'Listen to me, Justi. I'm going to have to explain why I have just agreed to thirty thousand. If I go back without a ninety-nine year deal ... it doesn't bear thinking about. Now in God's name be reasonable. Give me a break here.'

Roberto paid more attention to the tone of Hall's voice than his words. He knew that Hall had little to bargain with, so he pressed home his advantage.

'Without meaning to cause offence, you sit here believing you are the world's most powerful man. This is the same power that put my wife in an early grave, that took the life of my brother just a few weeks ago. And you want a break Mr Hall? From which moral standpoint did that come from? Anthea — isn't that your wife's name? Shall I name your children and their home addresses? How about your grandchildren too?' He turned square on to Hall, bringing his face right up to him. 'Thirty thousand. Annual upward-only rent reviews. Do you understand?'

Roberto's eyes flashed. Hall turned his head away, struggling to come to terms with the reality of the situation. For Christ's sake, I am a husband and father, he thought. What if his life had been affected like Justi's? He sat there motionless, choked, thinking of his wife and grandchildren.

After a few moments he turned to Roberto with resignation, holding out his hand.

'Deal.'

Roberto looked him in the eye.

'Deal.'

They shook hands.

'Have you any lawyers to draw up the agreement?' Hall asked.

Roberto reached into the pocket of his shorts, removed a piece of paper and unfolded it.

'I think you'll find it all there.'

Hall stared at him, then looked at the paper. The terms were already printed, precisely as they had just agreed.

'Perhaps, President Hall, we can now sign it and have it witnessed by about a thousand journalists, which I guess makes it rather binding.'

Hall knew he had been completely outplayed, but he had come to Brazil to resolve the Justi issue and he was now just minutes away from doing so.

'Do it,' he replied.

'You don't, by any chance, have a pen do you President Hall?'

Hall passed him a gold pen from his jacket pocket and they signed the agreement.

'I take it you can find the money within fourteen days?' enquired Roberto.

'We can,' Hall told him bluntly.

'Thank you President Hall.' Roberto offered his hand again.

Hall took it. 'Whoever would have thought, eh?'

'Indeed.' Roberto smiled back at him.

They walked across the clearing together to announce the agreement to the waiting press. Hall spoke first.

'Ladies and gentlemen. I have here a signed agreement between the United States operating on behalf of the G7 nations, and Brazil. Essentially, for an annual payment of sixty billion dollars, with annual reviews, Brazil has committed to preserving its two million square kilometres of rainforest for all time.'

The press gasped.

'Did you say sixty billion per annum, Sir?' shouted one.

'I did,' replied Hall. 'Perhaps the president of Brazil would like to say a few words.'

Roberto stood quietly in front of the world's press. So this was the moment – this was his life's work. He wondered if he was dreaming. He searched the crowd until he located Valto and beckoned for him to come over. He could not find Anna.

He hugged Valto, who lifted him into the air. Roberto saw tears in his eyes.

'Presidente. This is a great day,' he said quietly.

'Indeed it is General. A great day.'

Roberto turned to the press.

'When I came to power I promised my country that I would deal with our crippling debt. Today this agreement effectively cancels our indebtedness. To have such a yearly income places my country in an enviable position. I would like to say now, categorically, that this money will be used to remove all Brazil's children from poverty, from the streets and sewers of São Paulo, Rio, and so many of our cities, to give them, our next generation, hope, and a future in a new Brazil, strong and confident and free.'

The Brazilian press, of whom there were a few hundred, applauded. Across Brazil, in homes, offices, factories and bars, thousands wept in joy and disbelief.

'As I explained to President Hall, my personal path to this

moment in history has been painful. I have lost the woman I loved and a very special brother. I cannot say that it was worth such a sacrifice, though I suspect that they would say it was. But at this special moment I would like the world to remember them – my wife Angela, my brother Manuel.'

He paused for a few moments.

'Thank you.' He stepped back from the microphone.

The questions started to ring out.

'President Justi. What about the other rainforest nations?'

Roberto spoke over his shoulder as he headed towards the US helicopter with Hall.

'I wish them every good fortune. They know how to do it now. Perhaps the small ones should get together.'

'I'm not unhappy, Mr Justi,' said Hall as they reached the aircraft. 'I have my own children, and grandchildren. I look at what happens around the world – my country too has its poor and I see people and realise they are somebody's father or mother or brother or sister. I hope we meet again under more favourable circumstances.'

They looked each other in the eye. Roberto was moved by the sudden glimpse of Hall's humanity. He watched as the helicopter carrying the US president took off and his own landed. He searched in vain once more for Anna. Even as he waved from the top of the steps he tried to find her. But she was nowhere to be seen.

●

Anna stayed at the Justi Ridge for a while after everyone had departed. Her pilot waited patiently for her, chain smoking and drinking a can of beer left behind by one of the press corps. She strolled slowly round the clearing, finally walking up the steps that had seen such history made just a few hours previously. The hut was similar to the one they had been to for Valto's demonstration.

Here then was victory won. She had moved behind a group of journalists out of sight of Roberto as he made his press statement with Hall, uncertain how she felt as he announced an end to poverty in Brazil. Sofia, if she was still alive, was now facing a new beginning. A home would be provided, education, medical assistance. This was surely what she had fought for with Roberto and Valto these past few weeks. And yet she felt anything but victorious. She was empty, hollow. Why?

The question had become relentless. What was the matter with her? Why did she not want to go back to Brasilia and celebrate as the rest of the nation surely would? Why had she not wanted to congratulate Roberto or Valto, preferring to melt into the background? She stared disinterestedly around the hut, there was nothing in it anyway, except a few cigarette ends and an empty water bottle.

She wandered out into the late-afternoon sun and sat on the step. What awaited her now in Brasilia? She was certain Roberto would insist on her presence at his own celebration. She had felt him looking at her differently again today, noticing him searching for her in the crowd. There was a longing in his eyes. And after a restless night, in which the loneliness of her past revisited her countless times and sleep came but for a few hours, she had finally watched the dawn break over Roberto's presidential quarters, searching in the first rays of light for a sense of feeling for him, but none had come. She looked at her pilot, an attractive young man in his late twenties who winked at her every time she flew with him and who had invited her out for a drink on numerous occasions. 'Just to see the real Brazil,' he had said. 'I didn't know you could squeeze a country this large into your apartment,' she had finally replied with a wry smile, after which he had stopped asking.

●

'General!' exclaimed Roberto, champagne bottle in hand, at the impromptu party now in full swing on the balcony terrace of the Brasilia Museum. Crowds were already pouring into the streets in every town and city in Brazil to celebrate the biggest economic coup in history.

'Ah, Presidente,' replied Valto. 'Here, let me take that. You shouldn't be doing the pouring.'

'Nonsense General. I can't tell you how happy I am.' replied Roberto, topping up Valto's glass.

'Well you have done it. You have broken the stranglehold of the World Bank. This country will never be the same and it owes you a great debt.'

'Stop it,' Roberto almost blushed. 'You are far too kind. Have you seen Anna?'

'No. No, I don't think I have. The last time I saw her was when you addressed the press with Hall. She seemed subdued, but I am not the best reader of women, you understand.'

'Ah well, no doubt she will join us shortly. For now a toast, General. To Brazil, and to her people.'

'To Brazil, and to her people,' Valto echoed.

The balcony was crowded with leaders of industry, public services, finance, education. Santez was there, Fernento too. Roberto tracked them both down.

'Gentlemen – what can I say?'

'What can we say?' replied Santez. 'It is quite unbelievable.'

'Well it was an impressive team effort,' replied Roberto. 'I am indebted to you both. Are you pleased that we will not need to fell the forest?' he enquired of Fernento.

'Of course, but it would have been fascinating from a purely academic point of view. I remember when I first looked at the results of the computer models, just after our meeting. It was quite unbelievable to think what would have happened had you actually completed Phase I.'

'And Carlos. Where did you get that four hundred million for the Russians?' enquired Roberto.

Carlos smiled.

'Presidente. Every central bank keeps a fund for emergencies. The trick is not to let the president know, in case he spends it.'

They laughed. 'Very wise,' replied Roberto, raising his glass to them both.

It was a beautiful gathering, laughter carrying on the gentle breeze to the crowds below to mingle with their joy and celebrations. A band struck up in the plaza and the sound of samba filled the air. With glasses in hand, and arms round anyone close to them, people danced until dawn started breaking.

Roberto glanced around every now and again in search of Anna, but she did not show, despite his personal invitation. Still, more champagne? Yes, today was truly great day.

CHAPTER TWENTY

Roberto awoke just after noon; his head was throbbing. He took some aspirin, showered and with some life returning to him, went through to the lounge to order some food. Nothing too fancy, just something to soak up the alcohol. A plain omelette would be fine. He flicked through the pile of morning papers, laughing again at the sight of Hall sitting with him on the step of the hut. The headlines were wide and various.

> '$60 Billion as Justi Triumphs'
> 'Hall Humiliated in Brazilian Coup'
> 'The West Crumbles at Justi Ridge'
> 'Out-thought. Out-witted. Out-done. Hall OUT!'

After finishing his omelette Roberto retired to his office. His secretary was buried under a deluge of letters, telegrams, faxes and cards congratulating Brazil on its victory.

He made half a dozen phone calls to set up key appointments for his administration, appointments he had put off after winning the election until he had achieved his goal. This accomplished, he was anxious to get state departments functioning again, with individuals he could trust to manage public spending. He retained direct responsibility for child welfare, to ensure he would personally fulfil the dream he had shared with Angela twenty years previously.

He cast his mind back to the day she had sat in the taxi with him, clutching the dead boy's box, her tears flowing. And then he thought of Anna and her emotion in the sewer in Rio. He had felt his feelings towards her grow much stronger these last few weeks. And now with their success what was their future, he wondered? He struggled to understand her. He would write to her, give her time for reflection. Perhaps that was the best thing to do. He took out some sheets of personal writing paper and, having announced he was not to be disturbed, he spent the next few hours crafting his proposal, hoping that she would appreciate its sincerity and genuine affection. After numerous drafts and rewrites he was finally satisfied with it. Sealing it in an envelope he wondered whether to take it to her personally, but in the end decided that perhaps it would be best if he had it delivered.

●

Anna heard the letter drop through her box. She had spent the day deep in thought with the curtains drawn. She had established at last why it was that Roberto caused her to search for her feelings. She knew that he represented for her everything that someone might ever offer her. He was a man of principle, of laughter, of power, a handsome man who had awakened in her a sense of responsibility for the world in which she lived. And her mind's insistence was to court his favour, his attention, his friendship and then his love.

But there was a gulf. Her mind's instructions made no impression on a heart that could not function in that way, could not feel like that – could not love or receive love. That was what Roberto had made her discover, that despite her professional success she had no other life, nor could she ever have one. These thoughts now flooded her mind as a spring tide across the flats of an estuary.

She opened the envelope and removed Roberto's letter.

'My dear Anna,

I thought I ought to write to you and to say firstly I owe you a great debt for all you have done these past weeks. I cannot quite find the words for how I feel now the Justi Plan has succeeded. The enormity of our achievement will no doubt sink in over time. I looked out for you at the party last night but without success. If I missed you I apologise.

I also want to explain how I am feeling towards you. For the last few months I have worked with you, spending much time in your company and I have felt a bond of friendship grow between us. I know you said you feel as though you have no friends but I also hope that, on reflection, you could look upon me as such.

In addition, I often now look at you and know I am feeling more than friendship; a feeling I first had briefly when you left me that day in Rio after seeing the street children. I have done much soul-searching, much thinking about Angela too, and I am now certain of my own mind and heart concerning you.

I would like you to consider a proposal of marriage to me; I feel we could share a life of great happiness and fulfilment together. We have already accomplished so much. I have for so long now pursued a life driven by a cause, I know you have lived similarly. However, I now see that without love there is no life.

If you could consider this and let me have your reply, which I pray deeply will be in the affirmative.

As ever
Roberto.'

She read it again.

'Without love there is no life.'

She looked at the whole letter and felt crushed by it – crushed that all she felt was detachment, provoking in her again the image of Sir Anthony as she walked towards him, tie in hand, to take his life. It was the same feeling.

'Without love there is no life.'

How true, how terribly true she thought, crying desperately for her own plight.

Clutching Roberto's letter she walked slowly to her bedroom.

○

The next morning Roberto was sitting at his desk, working on his plans with a team of advisers to rehabilitate fifteen million children back into society. There was a seemingly endless list of requirements, and it would take time – maybe years – for the problem to be fully solved. At least money was no longer a problem, he reflected.

The intercom disturbed his reflections.

'I am sorry to disturb you Presidente, but the General is here. He says it is urgent,' his secretary told him anxiously.

Roberto opened the door.

'General?' he said.

Valto did not smile as he greeted Roberto.

'General, what is the matter?' he asked, putting his arm gently round Valto's shoulders.

Valto took a deep breath.

'I have come straight over Roberto,' he said. The use of Justi's first name sat uncomfortably between the two men.

'Sit down. Can I get you something? What's happened?' asked Roberto, alarmed by Valto's demeanour.

Valto struggled to find the words, his eyes red and full, his face in anguish. Roberto began to worry for him. Was Valto having some kind of breakdown?

'Shall I call a doctor for you, General?' he enquired, taking Valto by the hand to help steady him.

Valto shook his head.

'It's Anna,' he finally said.

'What about her?' Roberto felt suddenly sick.

Valto leaned against the wall and closed his eyes.

'She's dead,' he whispered, his fists clenched, fighting to remain composed. He could not bear to look at Roberto.

'How?' he heard Roberto ask, the words struggling to break from his lips.

'We believe it was an overdose. A doctor is with her now but he thinks she died yesterday evening.'

'She is in her apartment?'

'Yes,' replied Valto, taking sharp involuntary breaths of air. 'I am so terribly sorry Roberto. I know you loved her.' He looked at Roberto standing quietly, the blood drained from his face, wishing this tragedy of love lost upon himself rather than this man who had suffered so much already.

Roberto left his quarters and walked quickly across to Anna's apartment. A maid was being comforted just outside it. He walked past, unable to look, a fresh wave of grief sweeping over him as he turned into Anna's bedroom. He hardly noticed the doctor and nurse who were talking quietly in the corner.

He looked at Anna and was struck by how at ease she appeared to be. She seemed peaceful, her dressing gown loosely tied, the pained expression that he had seen so frequently, demonstrating the growing torment of her mind, now gone. His letter lay on the floor below her limp, open hand.

He sat beside her.

'Oh Anna,' he whispered, as he kissed her lips gently, willing her back to life, running his fingers through her hair as he grieved her passing, feeling her tide of desperation breaking within him. He lay his head on her shoulder and wept.

●

The rain fell incessantly over the cemetery on a hill above the small village of Georgeham in north Devon. A group of people huddled under umbrellas around a freshly dug grave. Police officers stood discreetly at the cemetery's perimeter, watching as a coffin was lowered. The vicar said a few words and a short prayer, then, after shaking hands with Anna's parents, he returned to his car at the cemetery gates, closely followed by three local women who had come to pay their respects, more for Anna's parents than for Anna. Her parents remained at the graveside, frail and elderly, lost in the pain of memories of their only child, a daughter, their Anna; memories that could never now be added to.

Roberto stood with them.

'I grew to love her deeply,' he said quietly, staring into the grave. A crow flew over, calling plaintively. He watched as it flew across the large field that adjoined the cemetery and disappeared over the roofs of Georgeham.

'But I don't know if she loved me,' he added, his voice trembling slightly.

He turned to the couple, who looked kindly at him. The elderly woman took his hand and, unspeaking, walked with him slowly back down the path.